EXTRAORDINARY PRAISE FOR SARA BLAEDEL AND THE LOUISE RICK SERIES

"Blaedel is one of the best I've come across."

—Michael Connelly

"Crime-writer superstar Sara Blaedel's great skill is in weaving a heartbreaking social history into an edge-of-your-chair thriller while at the same time creating a detective who's as emotionally rich and real as a close friend."

—Oprah.com

"She's a remarkable crime writer who time and again delivers a solid, engaging story that any reader in the world can enjoy."

—Karin Slaughter

"One can count on emotional engagement, spine-tingling suspense, and taut storytelling from Sara Blaedel. Her smart and sensitive character, investigator Louise Rick, will leave readers enthralled and entertained."

—Sandra Brown

"I loved spending time with the tough, smart, and all-too-human heroine Louise Rick—and I can't wait to see her again."

—Lisa Unger

"If you like crime fiction that is genuinely scary, then Sara Blaedel should be the next writer you read."

—Mark Billingham

"Sara Blaedel is at the top of her game. Louise Rick is a character who will have readers coming back for more."

—Camilla Läckberg

THE LOST WOMAN

"Leads to...that gray territory where compassion can become a crime and kindness can lead to coldblooded murder."

—*New York Times Book Review*

"Blaedel solidifies once more why her novels are as much finely drawn character studies as tightly plotted procedurals, always landing with a punch to the gut and the heart."

—*Library Journal* (STARRED REVIEW)

"Long-held secrets and surprising connections rock Inspector Louise Rick's world in Blaedel's latest crime thriller. Confused and hurt, Louise persists in investigating a complex murder despite the mounting personal ramifications. The limits of loyalty and trust, and the complexities of grief, are central to this taut thriller's resolution. A rich cast of supporting characters balances the bleakness of the crimes."

—*RT Book Reviews* (4 STARS)

"Sara Blaedel is a literary force of nature...Blaedel strikes a fine and delicate balance between the personal and the professional in THE LOST WOMAN, as she has done with the other books in this wonderful series...Those who can't get enough of finely tuned mysteries...will find this book and this author particularly riveting." —BookReporter.com

"Blaedel, Denmark's most popular author, is known for her dark mysteries, and she examines the controversial social issue at the heart of this novel, but ends on a surprisingly light note. Another winner from Blaedel."
—*Booklist*

"Engrossing." —*Toronto Star*

THE KILLING FOREST

"Another suspenseful, skillfully wrought entry from Denmark's Queen of Crime."
—*Booklist*

"Engrossing...Blaedel nicely balances the twisted relationships of the cult members with the true friendships of Louise, Camilla, and their circle."
—*Publishers Weekly*

"Blaedel delivers another thrilling novel...Twists and turns will have readers on the edge of their seats waiting to see what happens next."
—*RT Book Reviews*

"Will push you to the edge of your seat [then] knock you right off ... A smashing success."

—BookReporter.com

"Blaedel excels at portraying the darkest side of Denmark."

—*Library Journal*

THE FORGOTTEN GIRLS

WINNER OF THE 2015 RT REVIEWER'S CHOICE AWARD

"Crackling with suspense, atmosphere, and drama, THE FORGOTTEN GIRLS is simply stellar crime fiction."

—Lisa Unger

"Chilling ... [a] swiftly moving plot and engaging core characters."

—*Publishers Weekly*

"This is a standout book that will only solidify the author's well-respected standing in crime fiction. Blaedel drops clues that will leave readers guessing right up to the reveal. Each new lead opens an array of possibilities, and putting the book down became a feat this reviewer was unable to achieve. Based on the history of treating the disabled, the story is both horrifying and all-to-real. Even the villains have nuanced and sympathetic motives."

—*RT Times* Top Pick, Reviewer's Choice Award Winner

will become your favorite crime novel for a long time to come."

"[THE FORGOTTEN GIRLS] is gripping when it depicts some horrific crimes...[An] uncompromising realism...distinguishes this novel at its best."

THE
LOST
WOMAN

THE LOST WOMAN

SARA BLAEDEL

TRANSLATED BY

MARK KLINE

GRAND CENTRAL
PUBLISHING
New York Boston

Copyright © 2017 by Sara Blaedel
Translated by Mark Kline, translation © 2017 by Sara Blaedel
Excerpt from *The Night Women* copyright © 2017 by Sara Blaedel
Excerpt from *The Undertaker's Daughter* copyright © 2017 by Sara Blaedel
Hachette Book Group supports the right to free expression and the value of copyright. The purpose of copyright is to encourage writers and artists to produce the creative works that enrich our culture.

The scanning, uploading, and distribution of this book without permission is a theft of the author's intellectual property. If you would like permission to use material from the book (other than for review purposes), please contact permissions@hbgusa.com. Thank you for your support of the author's rights.

Grand Central Publishing
Hachette Book Group
1290 Avenue of the Americas; New York, NY 10104
Hachettebookgroup.com

First published as a hardcover in February 2017
First mass market edition: May 2018

Grand Central Publishing is a division of Hachette Book Group, Inc.
The Grand Central Publishing name and logo is a trademark of Hachette Book Group, Inc.

The Hachette Speakers Bureau provides a wide range of authors for speaking events. To find out more, go to www.hachettespeakersbureau.com or call (866) 376-6591.

The publisher is not responsible for websites (or their content) that are not owned by the publisher.

ISBNs: 978-1-4555-4107-2 (hardcover); 978-1-4555-4105-8 (ebook); 978-1-4555-4106-5 (trade paperback); 978-1-5387-6025-3 (mass market)

Printed in the United States of America

OPM

10 9 8 7 6 5 4 3 2 1

*To Annegrethe,
with all my love
—your daughter*

THE
LOST
WOMAN

Prologue

Limbs snap under his feet as he wrestles his way deeper into the underbrush. Twilight closes in around him, as water from the drizzling rain runs off his leather jacket. Lights are on in the kitchen and in a few rooms toward the back of the house. He sees her through the window, standing at the sink in the warm light, her hands busy under the running water.

The damp January fog shields him from sight as he leans forward. There is something sensual in the way she dries her hands on her apron—slowly, painstakingly, yet with a certain energy—before grabbing her long hair and putting it up in a bun behind her neck.

He feels his sorrow, his loss.

Her daughter walks into the kitchen. She shrugs out of her short leather jacket and tosses it on the chair by the oval kitchen table. Fifteen, sixteen years old, he guesses. He'd spotted her earlier when she arrived home from school, walking up from the street in her uniform, a bag slung over her shoulder, eyes glued to the ground. Silent, sulky, teenager-ish, he'd thought, as he hid in his car. Yet beautiful in an aloof, introverted way.

Still at the sink, the woman occasionally turns to speak; she laughs at what the teenager says. Through his binoculars, he focuses on her narrow face, studying and committing to memory her feminine features, the way her eyes crinkle when she smiles. He wants to remember every last detail.

One of the girl's shirt straps falls down over her shoulder. He sees her prominent collarbone and the attractive curve below her throat. Taking a few steps closer, he pushes aside a few branches. The mother laughs again and turns. Her back is to him, a silhouette in the window.

Though he's outside, it almost feels as if he's part of what's going on in the kitchen. He imagines the odors from the stove and their lighthearted conversation, how they talk about their days in that uniquely intimate way of a mother and daughter.

He steps out of the brush, closer now. The field is open behind him, as the duplexes stand shoulder to shoulder behind the main road and the half-empty parking lot of the pub. The crowd has thinned out and the rain is keeping people indoors. Lights are now on in the surrounding houses, and once in a while someone drives down the narrow street, but everyone seems focused on getting out of the rain.

A car goes by slowly. Quickly, he steps back into the brush, his heart pounding. He curses under his breath when a branch scratches his cheek and warm blood runs down his chin. The car's headlights narrowly miss exposing him. He closes his eyes and holds his breath a moment. He exhales, heavily. *Easy now*. Suddenly, he feels the cold; he's freezing in spite of his warm coat and gloves, the chill penetrates deep inside his body. Everything about him is wet and cold after waiting first in the car, then in the rain. He should have remembered to wear thermal socks.

He ducks instinctively when the woman's husband walks into the kitchen carrying a bottle of wine. The man says something to his wife and gestures in seeming irritation at the daughter. Then he moves toward her and pushes her shirt strap back onto her shoulder.

Though he can't hear a word of what they're saying, it's easy to read the girl's reaction. Her face darkens, and she screams at her father, turns on her heel, and storms out. He can almost hear the door slam.

The father opens an upper cabinet door and grabs two glasses. Opens the wine. The woman still stands at the sink, pouring boiling water from the pot she took off the stove. Chills run down his spine when she suddenly looks up and out through the steam, as if she has spotted him there in the twilight, or somehow senses his presence. The steam fogs up the window, the grayish film transforming her into a moving outline. It evaporates quickly, however, and once more he sees her clearly.

In the drizzling rain, he lifts the stock of his gun to his shoulder, concentrates on sighting through the scope, takes a deep breath, and pulls the trigger. The bullet rams into the middle of her forehead, just above her eyes.

He watches the man's reactions; it's as if he's in slow motion. The bottle of wine falls from his hand, and he turns to the shattered kitchen window and his wife, her blood gushing out and splattering him before she collapses onto the floor.

Seconds later, just as he is retreating into the underbrush, a door slams. He catches a glimpse of the teenage daughter standing on the step outside the front door. They both freeze for a second in the gray late-afternoon fog, then she sees the window and screams as she runs back into the house.

He backs his way out through the brush and walks rapidly to his car.

1

Louise Rick leaned back in her chair in the Search Department office and eyed her partner, who sat on the floor attending to Charlie. The retired police dog lay on his side, patiently allowing his paws to be cleaned of snow and road salt. Eik Nordstrøm rubbed him with a towel; he clipped the hairs between the pads of his paws and smeared them with Vaseline, praising the dog constantly until Louise at last rolled her eyes and shook her head.

A book about dog care lay on Eik's desk.

Whoa, she thought. She hardly believed that a little snow on the street required this level of grooming. Never had she cleaned Dina's paws of road salt or smeared them with Vaseline. If anyone had, it was Jonas. After all, her foster son was the one who'd loaned the book to Eik.

Watching the tender way the black-haired policeman nursed the big German shepherd, she had the realization that if he moved out of her apartment now, she would miss him terribly.

He scooted over and grabbed Charlie's back paw.

Six months ago, Louise had been anxious about how it would go when her relatively new love—her partner, Eik—moved in with Jonas and her, while Louise's friend Camilla stayed in Eik's studio apartment in South Harbor with her husband, Frederik, and son, Markus. But it had worked out fine. So fine, in fact, that the thought of him moving back to his own apartment now felt all wrong.

Eik had come up with the idea that Camilla and Frederik stay at his place. They'd needed somewhere to live after their manor house near Roskilde had burned down. Markus had left for boarding school along with Jonas, so even though the place was small, it felt crowded only when he was home on weekends.

Louise suspected that Camilla and Frederik had actually grown tired of the manor house, with its high wainscoting and beautiful stucco ceilings, and wanted to move back to the city, though living in a five-hundred-square-foot space when they were used to ten thousand square feet had to be quite an adjustment. When Frederik left the hospital after the fire, he had made it clear that he wasn't going to rebuild his childhood home. Louise understood why. Too much bad karma, too many strange old stories clung to the property, making escaping the past while living there very difficult.

But now they were moving on. They had just taken possession of a roomy penthouse in Frederiksberg, a few blocks from where Camilla and Markus lived before she met Frederik. The past six months had gone by so fast, however, that Louise and Eik hadn't really talked about what they would do once his apartment was free again.

"I wonder what such an uptown dog will think about moving back to South Harbor," she said, teasing him now.

"Yeah, the neighborhood probably isn't his cup of tea." Eik spoke without looking up, while working on the last paw. "You know how Charlie loves sniffing the fancy ladies on Allégade. Plus, there're all his girlfriends in Frederiksberg Gardens."

"Maybe," Louise said. Eik got to his feet and tossed a treat to his now clean dog. "But Frederik and Camilla moved yesterday. And let me see…if I remember correctly, the deal was that you were only going to stay with me until they found another place."

Eik was caught off guard for a moment, but then he smiled. "Oh, didn't I tell you that Olle is coming by with his station wagon this afternoon to pick my things up?" He looked down at the big German shepherd. "And really, a dog needs to learn how to run around all sorts of places."

He said this so offhandedly that Louise had to lower her eyes. Suddenly she went quiet inside. She didn't want him to leave; living with Eik felt so natural, so secure.

"Hey!" He walked over and kissed her on the neck. "I'm not going anywhere. We just need to decide if we should keep the South Harbor apartment. Who knows? Maybe Jonas will want it someday, or maybe we should just get rid of it. But it's so cheap to hang on to."

The knot inside Louise loosened. He swiveled her chair around to him, and she stood and held him tightly. Losing him for a second, only to get him back, made her cling even harder as he pulled her blouse up. She breathed him in, the smell of leather, cigarettes, hair wax, and something indefinable yet unmistakable, an odor that was his and his only. She ran her hands down through his longish black hair, kissing him back.

Neither of them reacted in time when the door behind them opened. Rønholt stood in the doorway, mumbled an embarrassed apology, then stepped back and closed the door. He pounded on the door three times and cleared his throat before walking back in. "Would you be so kind as to step into my office?" As he turned to leave, he added, "Properly clothed, please."

Ragner Rønholt had been the head of the Search Department for more than two decades. A year ago, he had snatched Louise away from Homicide. He was steadily approaching retirement age. No one knew when he planned to step down, but it was becoming clear he was looking forward to the third stage of life, with a lot of cultural travel and bicycle vacations around Europe. Louise had only a sketchy knowledge of his private life. She knew he wasn't married, though he split his time between two steady woman friends. He invited Pytte to concerts in Denmark Radio's new concert hall, and took her on vacations to major cities, while Didder thrived in the kitchen of her home in Skodsborg, where he played the role of handyman. He lived in a large apartment on Østbanegade, a street in an exclusive part of Copenhagen, and grew orchids on his windowsills.

The head of Homicide, Hans Suhr, had once called him a lone wolf and bon vivant, a man who had tailored his life to fit his desires. The Search Department director didn't spend his days making concessions to others. He did the things he wanted to, when he wanted to.

"This can't go on. But then you're both aware of that, aren't you?"

Louise and Eik sat in his office. On the wall behind the door hung three newly pressed white shirts wrapped in plastic from a dry cleaner on Vesterbrogade, and below them lay a pair of bicycle shoes Rønholt changed into before riding home on his new road bike. Standard equipment for a man approaching retirement. Though Louise had never seen him wearing a jersey from one of the teams in the Tour de France. Or cycling tights.

"Everyone knows you're living together. We have to face the fact that one of you is going to have to transfer."

Silence.

"For now, let's just keep our eyes and ears open." He reached for a paper on his desk. "There's a position at the police station in Næstved, for example."

He pushed the paper over to them. "I'm willing to listen to suggestions about how else we can solve this problem. Which one of you is open to trying something new?"

Again, neither of them spoke. Louise stood up and grabbed the paper, promising they would find a solution.

"He's right, you know," she said on the way back to the office. "We can't be partners if we plan to keep living together. But Næstved? No way!"

"You know Rønholt, it'll blow over." Eik put his arm around her. "We're a good team, and if people start talking, I'll just go back to my old office."

Louise raised her hand. "No. It's no different for us than for anybody else here. We can't be out there together."

"All right, I surrender. We'll find a way." He closed the door to their office and patted Charlie. "You looking forward to tonight?"

Louise smiled. "Nick Cave is more your cup of tea, but it's been a long time since I've been to a concert. I can't wait! I talked to Camilla and Frederik. They'll meet us in front of Vega a half hour before it starts, so we can grab a beer. Do you have the tickets?"

Eik lifted an eyebrow and stared at her. She got the drift; she was being too motherly. "Everything's under control" was all he said, and then switched on his computer.

For a moment, she was flustered. They hadn't yet sanded off all their rough edges, and she knew this type of thing would happen now and then as they settled into a life together. It was still mostly one long party for them, and she loved waking up beside him every morning and falling asleep with him every night. But a few times she had caught herself picking his black jeans up off the floor and laying them on a chair, and now she had run into one of his borders. *Got it*, she thought, as she focused again on the job opening.

"One of us will end up working outside of town if we don't start asking around," she said. "And since I'm the last one in, it's only fair that I'm the one who leaves."

Eik was standing now, pulling the dog leash from his coat pocket. "We'll see." It still didn't sound as if he were taking this seriously. "I'm going to run down for a pack of smokes and walk the dog. Come on, Charlie."

She heard him whistling down the hallway. Most likely Nick Cave, though she didn't recognize the song.

2

February 1996

The voices had died down in the confirmation room. The teenagers sat still, listening to the priest talk about death being a natural part of life, about how God didn't always let us know it was coming. Her husband excelled at getting restless adolescents to listen. Sofie had never quite figured out why. Maybe it was because they found what he said interesting. Or maybe the boys respected his success as coach of the sports club's handball team, and they wanted to be on his good side now that it was moving up into a higher league before the tournament.

Stig had been on the junior national team before he became a priest and moved to town, and after he began coaching, she ran a concession stand at the arena. Thinking about it now, she smiled as she grabbed a pencil from the table, lifted her hair up into a bun, and stuck the pencil in. She arranged butter, thin wafers of chocolate, and sliced cheese on a platter, and filled a bread basket with freshly baked rolls.

"Okay, fresh bread right out of the oven," she said, interrupting their confirmation studies as she entered the room. Stig smiled and waved her in. "There's juice, and tea, too. The paper cups are in the cupboard."

Refreshments were always served at the parsonage. She and Stig had discussed whether it might be seen as a type of bribery, but in the end, they'd decided they wanted visitors to feel welcome there, and besides, preparations for confirmation weren't meant to be a punishment. The afternoon class got a sandwich or a dessert, while the early class was served breakfast.

While the teenagers ate, Sofie listened as a girl asked Stig if he believed in life after death. He answered that there was no way to stop life from ending. But no, he found no solace in the belief that a new life awaited on the other side. He took comfort in knowing that when the time came and God called you, it was because you were ready to leave this life. Even when death seemed unmerciful and abrupt. He believed the only thing waiting on the other side was heaven's peace.

"And only God knows when the time is right for each person," he said, when Sofie had emptied the bread basket.

The phone in the kitchen rang. Sofie smiled at Stig, closed the door behind her, and answered.

"Your mother won't drink the protein drink I leave for her," her mother's home care aide jumped right in. "It's not good, not at all. She'll get even weaker and start aspirating again, and she'll end up back in the hospital. You have to talk to her!"

"I'll come over right now," Sofie said. She turned off the oven and wet the dishtowel covering the rolls that were rising.

She was about to dig her boots out from under the mountain of teenage shoes when she noticed the open gun case. Which made her so mad, she could scream! Stig seldom irritated her, but this thoughtlessness, forgetting to lock up his hunting guns when the house was full of kids, was so typical of him.

"Will you please come out here and lock your muskets up," she yelled to him through the door. Several of the boys snickered; she'd done this before, and it was always good for a laugh.

Not much was left of her mother. Less than a week ago, she had been released from the hospital after a serious case of pneumonia. Her white blood cell count had been sky high, and the infection had spread to her blood. Now she sat on the sofa with a blanket over her and a thick book on her lap. Was she reading the book, or did it simply give her a sense of dignity? Sofie had once caught her mother sitting with a book turned upside down.

She was sixty-seven, but after being diagnosed with multiple sclerosis, she had gone downhill fast. Suddenly, she was an old woman. She also had arthritis in her hands, shoulders, and back. Sofie knew the pain was worse than her mother let on, and she couldn't hide her exhaustion. The once-energetic woman had disappeared. She still cleaned her small apartment above the flower shop, but it was a far cry from back when she had kept her large house, mowed the acre of lawn, and washed the windows before driving down to shop—without anyone thinking a thing about it. It was as if the energy had seeped out of her.

"Ohhh, it is so irritating being old; I'm no good at it," she often said. Her mother was now at the point where the day was a success if she had the energy to get out of bed and drink a cup of morning coffee while reading the newspaper.

It was okay to be a slow starter, as Sofie put it. "There's nothing you absolutely have to do. It's okay to slow down," she said, when her mother felt terrible about being old and unable to do anything.

She kissed her mother on the cheek. "Mom, you have to sip on the protein drink, otherwise they'll stick you back in the hospital."

Her mother's steely blue eyes had softened over the past year. "Oh, Sof. I don't want to go on. You have to understand, my time has come, my strength is gone."

"Let's not get into that now, Mom." Sofie walked out into the kitchen for the protein drink. "I don't want to lose you."

Sofie sat down beside her mother on the sofa. "And I'm not leaving before you drink this. Then I'll go down to the pharmacy and pick up your medication. What do you need from the store?"

Her mother laid her hand on Sofie's arm. "Honey... you said it yourself, can't you hear? I can't even walk down the street anymore."

"It's only for the time being. You just got home. Being in the hospital is exhausting."

"No. This is my life now." Her mother let her hand fall. "I'm not myself anymore."

Sofie couldn't hold back her tears. They'd had this talk many times, but it had never felt so serious, so close.

Her mother had made it clear that she wanted an out when she lost the will to live. They'd talked about it even before Sofie's father died. In fact, Sofie had feared her mother would take her own life if her father went first. But it hadn't happened; she hadn't even spoken of it back then, though it was obvious how terribly she missed him.

A year after his death, Sofie had invited her mother out, and for an entire evening they had talked about the right to choose when someone no longer wants to go on.

"Of course it's not something to be taken lightly," her mother had said, to calm her daughter's fears. "But life can take you to a place you don't want to be, and that's when I want to be allowed to end it. I promise you, though, I'll hang on as long as I can."

Now Sofie stroked her mother's hand before walking into the bathroom to get a grip on herself. To stop her tears. She leaned over the sink for a moment, then blew her nose, took a deep breath, and returned to the living room. "But it doesn't have to be now," she said, after sitting back down. "Wouldn't you like to see spring?"

Her mother reached again for Sofie's hand. "My strength is gone."

"But do you even know how much medicine you need to take your own life?" Sofie blurted out. She squeezed her mother's hand. "I will not come here and find you in a pool of blood, and don't try anything with the gas oven in the kitchen. It could be dangerous for everyone else in the building."

They sat for a moment in silence.

"And what am I supposed to do with myself while you're lying here dying? Do you want me to sit here with you? Or should I just pace around at home, knowing what is happening? I just don't know if I can do that."

Her mother shook her head quietly. "Let's not talk

about it anymore." She picked up the carton of protein drink Sofie had placed in front of her.

"I understand you, and I don't want to be egotistical," Sofie said a while later. She held her mother's hand again. "I want to set you free. I just love you so much, and I can't even express how much I'm going to miss you."

"I love you, too." Her mother set down the empty carton.

3

Have you seen Eik?" Louise asked Olle Svensson, when she ran into him in the hallway outside the lounge. The thin-haired investigator had shared an office with Eik before Rønholt moved Eik in with Louise and made them partners.

"No, he didn't come to lunch. He's probably outside sucking on one of his cancer sticks." Olle sipped at his coffee.

Louise shook her head. "It's been over two hours now since he went down to pick up some cigarettes and walk Charlie, and I just think it's strange he isn't back yet."

She didn't like the look on Olle's face. His brown eyes widened, and she really didn't want to hear what he was about to say. Suddenly she wondered if he and Eik had, in fact, talked about moving his things out of her apartment later that day. Or if it actually had been said in jest.

"Is there any more coffee in there?" she asked, nodding at his cup. Before he could answer, she was on her way into the lounge.

Rønholt was right, Louise thought, as she walked back

into the office. Everything was simply too awkward. She couldn't even mention her partner's name to anyone else in the department without it sounding suggestive. But where the hell was he? Surely he wasn't so aggravated by her asking if he had the tickets that he just took off!

Annoyed now, she walked over to the window. This was just pathetic. Had it been anyone else in the department, she would simply have assumed he'd gone for the day and had forgotten to say good-bye. Or else that something had come up.

Or would she?

She leaned forward and stared at the dog leashed to a hook in front of the convenience store. It looked exactly like Charlie. For a long time she waited for Eik to walk out of the store, but when the door finally opened, an older lady pulling her shopping cart emerged. Then the owner of the shop came out and set a plastic bucket of water in the snow by the wall. He petted the dog, then he said something and pointed to the bucket.

Damn, it *was* Charlie! Definitely. But there was no sign of Eik.

It took Louise two minutes to shut everything down in the office and slam the door behind her. She ran down the stairs through the rotunda, and a moment later was outside on the square.

The German shepherd began wagging his tail when she approached. She strode into the store, and after seeing there were no customers around, she asked, "Where's Eik?"

The owner came out from behind the counter and shook his head. "Don't know. He's gone. Bought cigarettes and forgot the dog. I brought him inside, but he started growling every time a customer came in. It's been almost two hours, though, and it's cold out there."

He shrugged his shoulders all the way up to his ears and looked at her as if resigned.

"Charlie's been out on the street all this time?" she asked. "What did Eik say when he left? He couldn't have just forgotten him!"

Once more the shop owner shrugged his shoulders. "He bought a pack of smokes, like always, and a new lighter. He paid and left. Haven't seen him since!"

Louise called Eik's cell phone, but he didn't answer. When she tried her own home phone number, the answering machine switched on. She thought for a moment before calling Rønholt's office. She didn't like the idea of involving him further in their private life, but on the other hand, he must have sent Eik out somewhere and forgotten to tell her about it.

"I haven't seen or heard from him since you left my office," he said. He sounded preoccupied. "But he's a big boy; usually he can take care of himself."

She shouldn't have called. She threw her phone down into her bag and unhooked Charlie's leash. She was so infuriated that she decided to walk all the way home to Frederiksberg. Eik's taking off and abandoning his dog on the street in this cold was one thing; making her look like a complete idiot was even worse.

The sixth-floor apartment was empty. Louise hadn't gotten used to Jonas being at boarding school; the place was very quiet when he wasn't home. She looked through the four rooms and saw that nobody had been there since they'd left that morning. She went downstairs and rang Melvin's doorbell.

"We just got back from Frederiksberg Gardens," her neighbor said. He'd been happy to take on the job of looking after Dina, now that Jonas was home only on weekends. Louise patted her yellow Lab and asked Melvin if he'd seen Eik.

"No, but I don't see him forgetting Charlie." Melvin had offered her a seat on his sofa, and now poured her a cup of coffee. "That dog is his one and only. Almost." He winked at Louise.

She shook her head and stared into the bloodred poinsettia on the coffee table. No, it didn't seem very probable. Unless she had irritated Eik more than he had let on. But she couldn't involve her seventy-eight-year-old neighbor in that.

There was something comforting about sitting on Melvin's plush sofa. The smell of his evening cigars hung in the curtains, reminding Louise of her deceased grandparents.

Melvin had become a part of the family after Jonas moved in with Louise, as a foster child at first, when he was twelve years old. Orphaned during the civil war that ravaged the former Yugoslavia, Jonas had been adopted by a Danish activist minister and his wife, who brought him home and loved him as their own. He was only four when his adoptive mother died, leaving the child to be raised by his devoted single father. Eight years later, Jonas also lost his beloved father, who was murdered by an East European Mafia faction.

Louise had known Melvin for several years, but only slightly, as a neighbor whose life didn't intersect with her own. Jonas and Melvin had recognized each other at once and reconnected when they realized that Jonas's father had presided over the funeral of Melvin's late wife. They'd been living in Australia when she became ill. Her doctors botched her medications so badly that she suffered brain damage and lay in a coma. Thirteen years ago, Melvin had managed to bring her home to Denmark, where her final years were spent at a nursing home five minutes from his apartment. It had been four years since her passing.

"He'll show up," Louise said, after she drank her coffee. "If for no other reason, there's a concert we're going to tonight. Do you have any plans?" She wanted to make it all sound as casual as possible.

"Grete and I are going over to the Storm P. Museum for a lecture. It starts at six thirty, so I'm thinking we'll grab a bite to eat before."

Louise smiled. At first Melvin had called Grete Milling his friend, downplaying the relationship, but gradually it became easier for him to talk about her as a natural part of everything he did. Everyone was thrilled that the two seniors had found each other.

"I'd better get back upstairs," she said. She carried her cup out to the kitchen. "I have to shower before I meet the others at Vega."

The fact was, she didn't at all feel like going to a concert. A prickly unease gnawed at her. Eik wasn't the type to leave his dog out on the street, just because he was angry. Something was wrong. No matter how hard she tried, she couldn't fight off her anxiety. On the contrary, it grew as she changed clothes, fed the dogs, and closed the living room door so they wouldn't jump up on the sofa. Every time she called Eik's phone, it switched to the voice mail.

Louise bicycled to Vega, and while pedaling down

Enghavevej, she went through an entire spectrum of doubt, confusion, anxiety, and fear. She didn't understand what could have happened. It wasn't that they weren't allowed to do anything on their own. As long as they let each other know. If she hadn't looked out the window, she wouldn't have noticed Charlie. And she probably would have taken the stairway past the magistrate court and gone out that exit. The dog would still have been standing in the snow.

Something was very wrong, she was sure of it. More so with every passing second.

4

Camilla waved from a distance. Frederik walked over from the parking ticket machine with his scarf pulled up to his nose. He'd been living in California before he met Camilla, and he never missed an opportunity to say the temperature over there was more his style.

"Do we have time for a beer before going in?" Camilla asked. She looked around. "Where's Eik?"

Frederik held the door open and herded them inside, where it was warm.

"He's coming," Louise said. "He's got the tickets."

She and Camilla sat down at a table. "How's it feel being back at *Morgenavisen*?" Louise asked.

Frederik bought two beers for them and a cola for himself, then he sat down and put his arm around his wife.

"It would be a whole lot better if I weren't on the editorial staff. My most important job is correcting commas and typos in everyone else's articles." Camilla smiled. "But it's good to be back, and Terkel Høyer *says* he missed me."

Several years ago, Camilla had been a crime reporter

at the paper, a job she had resigned from. Louise wasn't sure how big a letdown the editorial position was. Some might call it a promotion, Camilla had explained, when she was offered the job, but it wasn't hard to hear her disappointment. She wanted to write and have her name on the byline.

Frederik laughed. "I'm probably the one who's making the biggest adjustment, now that I have a working wife. I'm home more than she is."

He turned away when his phone rang. Louise and Camilla listened in, curious as to whether it was Eik, but Frederik began speaking in English.

"It's his agent," Camilla said. "HBO wants Frederik to be the head writer for a hot new series. They're negotiating the terms."

"Is he going to move over there again?" Louise asked. "You've just fixed up the apartment."

Her friend shook her head. "He can write from over here, and they can Skype."

Frederik seemed more relaxed now that he had stepped down as director of his family's business, Termo-Lux, and declared that his businessman days were over. From now on, he would stick to screenwriting. While living in Santa Barbara, he had helped write for several major Hollywood productions, but he'd left all that behind when he moved back to Denmark. Which had definitely been the wrong move career-wise, judging from the sparkle in his eye now.

"The concert's about to start," Camilla said. She downed her beer.

Louise walked over to the window to check the line. It was thinning out. Eik had been one of the first to buy tickets online for the small-venue performance. He wouldn't miss it.

Twenty minutes after the concert began, they were still sitting in the bar. Frederik had checked to see if Eik had left the tickets at the gate, but no. And the show was sold out.

"Where the hell is he?" Camilla asked. "Did you two have a fight? What's going on?"

Louise sighed and slumped in her chair. "I haven't heard a word from him since he said he was going to buy cigarettes and walk the dog." Then she explained what had happened.

"So he left Charlie at the convenience market," Frederik said. "That doesn't sound at all like him." He suggested that they drive out to South Harbor to see if he was there.

In the car, Louise felt her anxiety rising again throughout her body. She could barely concentrate on what Frederik and Camilla talked about up front.

When they reached his South Harbor building, Louise looked up. The apartment was dark.

"We still have a key," Frederik said. "Let's go up and see."

The hallway smelled surprisingly clean, considering the condition of the stairway up to the fourth floor. Large splotches of paint had peeled off the walls, revealing various colors from over the decades; lightbulbs hung naked from the ceiling on every floor. The mix of odors—industrial soap, cigarettes, smoke from cooking—wasn't unpleasant. And it not only smelled clean, it looked clean, despite the rundown condition.

"It looks worse than it really is," Camilla said, adding

that it had, in fact, been fun living there. More or less everyone knew everyone else. "It's like they have their own little society here. People stick together and look out for each other, and there aren't many places like that left."

Louise had been there only a few times, while Eik picked up some of his things. She'd been with him to his favorite watering hole, Ulla's Place, farther down the street.

Frederik knocked on the door when they reached the apartment. They waited. The ceiling lightbulb hummed. They heard a loud click when the light shut off automatically; Camilla walked over and pressed the large brown button to turn it back on. Frederik knocked one last time, while Louise stood on the next-to-last step, her hand on the banister.

"We're going in," she said, and she reached for the key in Frederik's hand. She banged on the door and was about to insert the key when the neighbor's door opened. A young man in scruffy jogging pants and a hoodie, with a cigarette in his hand, asked what they were doing. Then he noticed Frederik and Camilla.

"Oh, hi. Did you forget something?"

"Hi, Sylvester," Camilla said. "No, but we can't find Eik. Have you seen him?" She stayed out in the hall while Frederik and Louise walked inside.

It didn't take long to check the studio apartment. There was an alcove for a bed in the kitchen–living room. There was a small balcony and a bathroom. But there was no Eik.

"I don't think he's been here," Frederik said. "It looks exactly how we left it yesterday."

A black two-seat leather sofa hugged the wall; a round

dining table with four chairs stood in front of the long window. There was little indication of anyone living there. But then no one did, for the time being.

Louise looked around one last time before they walked out and locked the door behind them. The neighbor had retreated to his own apartment, and Camilla was waiting for them outside the building.

"Let's try Ulla," she said. She tucked her arm under Louise's. "Did you two have an argument?"

"Not really." Louise shook her head. "This morning we had a talk with Rønholt. One of us has to leave the department, now that we're living together. But that's just the way it is, and anyway, I said I should be the one to find another job. It didn't sound like he was worried about it."

The smoke hit them like a gray brick wall when they opened the door to the little pub. Louise recognized several of the people standing around the billiard table. Ulla stood behind the bar, in front of the wall of liquor bottles, pouring two shots of aquavit. The music was low, possibly Duran Duran; the loudest noise in the pub was the crack of billiard balls ramming each other. Few people were talking. It seemed like some sort of private gathering, almost monotonous, rote, like a theater play that had run too long.

"You two want anything?" Frederik asked.

Louise said she actually could stand another beer.

"I'll have one, too," Camilla said. She gazed around in curiosity.

Small video-game machines lined the wall behind the

billiard table, beyond which hung a jukebox with old hits handwritten on yellowed paper visible through its Plexiglas window. The walls and ceiling were covered with glued-on bottle caps, and tar from years of nonstop smoking. Several of the regulars ogled the three of them.

"Was this where he hung out before you met him?" Camilla asked. Frederik handed her the beers and went back to pay.

Louise nodded. "He's good friends with Ulla." She glanced up at the bar.

"Was he sleeping with her?" Camilla eyed the stocky, middle-aged woman with coal-black dyed hair and arched eyebrows. She wore a midnight-blue satin blouse.

Louise let that hang in the air. She didn't really know. She'd avoided digging into what might have gone on between them beyond their friendship, which Eik had never tried to conceal.

She waited to see if Ulla would come over, but the pub owner held her spot behind the bar, talking to a drunk who almost fell backward every time he downed a shot.

Finally Louise walked up to her. "Hi, Ulla! Have you seen Eik around?"

Ulla had glanced over at them, and though Louise knew she'd recognized her, now she gave no indication that they'd ever met. She merely shook her head.

Louise paused, but the woman said no more. "I'm a bit worried that something might have happened to him," she continued. "No one's seen him since this morning. Do you have any idea where he might be? Have you talked to him today?"

"No!" Ulla shook her head again.

The group at the billiard table stopped shooting, and a

man sitting alone at a table by the door stared at Louise and Ulla while downing his beer.

Louise fought off her irritation with the woman. "Would you tell me if you had seen him?"

Ulla glanced at her before shrugging her shoulders and turning away. Her animosity toward Louise was palpable. Most likely, she believed that Louise had stolen Eik from her and her pub.

Louise walked back to the table. "That was a waste of time." She was about to pull her coat on when Ulla came over. She avoided eye contact with Louise as she began swiping at their table with a red dishrag.

"My advice to you is to leave him be. Don't hang on to him all the time, give him some room. He doesn't like to be controlled."

"We'd better go," Camilla said, when Ulla returned to the high bar.

No one around the billiard table made a sound. All eyes followed them when they left without drinking their beers.

5

Louise's bicycle was still at Vega, but instead of riding back there with Camilla and Frederik, she took a cab to the city center.

The city's lights reflected off the harbor water as the taxi driver sped toward the newly renovated Kalvebod Brygge waterfront, away from South Harbor's unpretentious architectural style. The somewhat dreary buildings gave way to endless facades of glass and steel, a beautiful contrast to the old city's tile and copper roofs. They drove past the Royal Theatre and New Harbor to the King's New Square, which was warmly lit in the winter darkness by restaurants and numerous bars, then through Copenhagen's old red light district. It amazed her that people were hanging out around the enormous sailor's anchor, drinking beer in the bitter cold of January. They took the Esplanade up to Østerport Station, where the driver slowed and began checking street numbers.

Louise had never visited her boss. When she hopped out of the taxi and walked toward his building, she realized that Rønholt must be able to see the apartment on Gefionsgade where her father grew up.

Rønholt opened the door of his fourth-floor apartment wearing slippers and casual clothing. "Something's happened, I'm sure of it," Louise gasped. "You know him! Eik would never leave Charlie out on the street and just disappear, and he wouldn't just not show up for the concert; he'd been looking forward to it for several months. We have to initiate a search for him."

Ragner Rønholt led her into the living room. He picked up his wineglass from next to an open book on a table near the bay window. One of the windows offered a view of the tracks behind Østerport; Langelinje quay was probably visible from there in the daytime. Louise knew he had lived practically forever in this rented apartment, for which he paid very little.

"Eik is a grown man, and he hasn't been gone for twelve hours," he explained patiently. "Can you just see how it would look to initiate a search for one of the Search Department's own people so soon?"

He offered Louise a glass of wine; she shook her head, and began pacing anxiously around the room.

"Louise, please, sit down." He pointed at the sofa, and they both sat. "It's wonderful you two have found each other, even though it's given me problems in the department, of course. Eik is a fine investigator and a good person. I've known him now for many years."

Louise was aware of that, and now she felt embarrassed; apparently Rønholt believed she was there because she and Eik were having problems. "This has nothing to do with our relationship. What's happened...?"

"Nothing has happened to him." His voice was measured, calm. "Eik is able to take care of himself. But it's possible there are sides to him you don't know. Maybe he should have told you, but it looks like he hasn't."

A chill ran through Louise's body, and already she regretted turning down the wine. "I know once in a while Eik hits bottom, and he needs help getting back up." She turned to Rønholt. "You're the one who sent me to pick him up that time he was dead drunk and couldn't get to work. But nothing was wrong today—everything was normal. We were in your office. You saw him!"

"These sprees he goes on, they often come without warning." He seemed to weigh his words as he took a sip of wine. "That side of him can be difficult to deal with, but you'll have to accept it if you want to be a part of Eik Nordstrøm's life."

"So you're thinking he left the office this morning to go get drunk? Then why did he take Charlie with him? He could easily have left the dog at the station." She shook her head, annoyed now that he didn't understand.

"I just came from South Harbor," she continued, realizing it did no good to reproach Rønholt. She needed to convince him. "He wasn't at his pub, Ulla's Place. Ulla hadn't seen him. At least that's what she claimed. I really think you're wrong about this."

Without a word, he stood up and walked out into the hall. He began putting his shoes on and asked Louise to come into the kitchen. "There's something you need to see." He opened the door to the back stairs and turned on the light, then he checked to make sure he had his keys before walking down.

The apartment was in a classic, beautiful Østerbro building, but the back stairs weren't all that different from

Louise's in Frederiksberg. It was where people stored empty bottles, old shoes, sacks of potatoes, and other things they needed out of the way, making it difficult at times to move past.

The light went out, and Louise stopped. In the dark, she heard voices and a television from another apartment. Rønholt reached the next landing and turned the light back on.

"What are we doing?" Louise asked, as she struggled to avoid falling among all the junk on the narrow stairs.

"Patience," he said, as they kept walking down.

His key ring rattled as he leaned over to open the basement lock. A moment later they entered a long passageway. On the left, a few large sheets hung over a clothesline in an open room for drying clothes; it smelled of soap, fabric softener, and dust. He continued down the passageway. The farther they went, the mustier it smelled. Dust was thick on the walls around them. Hot water pipes creaked above their heads, the fluorescents hummed metallically, and the filthy floor crackled under their feet. Their voices seemed enclosed, yet they echoed, as if the two of them were in an endless series of underground passages.

"Okay, what are we doing here?" she asked again, as he disappeared around a corner. When the lights went out again, she pulled her iPhone out of her pocket and switched on the built-in flashlight. "Hello!"

"Over here," he said.

The fluorescents flickered a few times and came back on, their sharp white glare blinding Louise for a moment.

They turned a corner at the end of a hallway. Rønholt stopped in front of the last dark brown wooden door in the long row of basement rooms. A dry heat hung heavily in the air; a furnace rumbled somewhere deeper in the basement.

Farther in, Louise peeked inside the old furnace room, where vents were clicking. Rønholt knocked on the peeling wooden door. "Eik!" he yelled. "Are you in there?"

Louise joined him again, gaping in disbelief. "You think he's hiding in *there*?"

He knocked again. "Come on out now," he said, as if he were waking up a child on a school morning. A moment later, he pushed the door open and stepped aside so Louise could enter the longish, dark basement room. A flashlight and sleeping bag lay on a small rubber mattress on the floor. A full ashtray and an empty glass sat beside the mattress. The space looked like a caricature of a dungeon where a kidnapper would hide a victim.

"What in the world is this?"

"It's your boyfriend's shelter. He stays here when he needs to shut himself off from the world. This has gone on now for several years."

Louise squatted down to check the cigarette butts in the ashtray, but they looked old. Dust and chunks of stucco from the ceiling covered the sleeping bag.

"He has his own key to the basement, and when he's down here, I bring him food and drink. Otherwise, I leave him alone."

"So you let him stay here?" Louise couldn't believe it.

"I leave him in peace," he said, correcting her. "Our agreement is that he can drop out and hide here in my storage room, but if he's here more than three or four days, I head down and get him."

"But why? I thought the black hole he disappeared into was Ulla's Place."

Rønholt nodded and shut the door, now that Louise had seen what she needed to. "Usually that's right. But don't we all sometimes dream about a place where no one can get to us? This is Eik's way of doing that. I suppose it's primitive, but it works for him."

Louise shook her head. "But what about his job?"

"He always has way too much overtime; he takes those extra hours off."

Louise couldn't understand any of this, least of all why her boss covered up for Eik.

Rønholt walked over to the button light switch and punched it a few times. "Eik went through a bad period when his girlfriend disappeared." They began walking back along the passage. "I don't know how familiar you are with that story."

Louise had a sinking feeling in her gut, but she nodded. She knew Eik had been sailing in the Mediterranean when his girlfriend suddenly disappeared. Without going into details, he'd told her they had quarreled, and in the end he had decided to return to Copenhagen. He didn't hear about the tragedy until he was back in South Harbor. The two young guys they had been sailing with, one of whom owned the thirty-four-foot sailboat, were found drowned in the ocean, not far from the boat. There was no sign of Eik's girlfriend, and her belongings weren't on the boat.

"I think not knowing was the hardest part for him," Rønholt continued. "And of course not being there to take care of her."

He slammed the basement door shut behind them.

Suddenly an enormous wave of sadness overcame Louise as they walked up the back steps. Here she thought she was beginning to know Eik, while he might have been deeply unhappy all this time. It hit her hard that she wasn't able to make him happy, to make him forget, if it really was the loss of his girlfriend that haunted him. Exactly like the sorrow she had carried around for years after what happened with her lover, Klaus, a grief she had finally come to terms with just the year before. They had shared so much and forged a life together, but there were secrets. Explosive and dangerous ones she'd uncovered too late.

"It wasn't long after Eik joined the department that he asked for leave to go down there. I admit, I had my doubts about letting him go. He was personally involved in an ongoing investigation his own department was conducting. He wasn't the investigator, of course, and he was kept informed just like anyone else who reports a person missing."

He unlocked the door to his apartment. "I was more afraid he might not be able to handle the situation emotionally. But it was great motivation for him, and he never gives up on a case. And over the years, we've found a way to handle the hard times, when he needs a break. I keep my eye on him, and it's all gone fine up to now."

Louise stood in the hallway, getting ready to leave. "Okay, but right now it's not a pause he needs, it seems. It's been a long time since he's been in your basement room."

Furrows appeared above Rønholt's white eyebrows; he seemed to agree with her. "In fact, he hasn't shown up here since he met you. To me that's a good sign. And no, it doesn't look like that's the case this time."

"Something's happened," Louise said. She was sure of it; her skin prickled again when Rønholt nodded.

"It does seem strange," he admitted. Her boss was beginning to realize the seriousness of the situation. "And Ulla hasn't seen him?"

"She hasn't talked to him, either. At least that's what she said."

That moment, standing there with Rønholt, all remaining doubts disappeared. This wasn't just her being overly concerned.

"We'll put out a search for him tomorrow morning," he said. He asked if she was driving or if he should call a taxi.

"You know what, I'd rather walk." It was very late, but she desperately needed some air.

6

Before rushing down the stairway to leave Dina and Charlie with Melvin, Louise made several calls to Eik's cell phone. His voice mail kicked in every time, asking her to leave a message. She called Rønholt to check if he'd heard anything during the night, but he knew nothing more.

"I'm going to run up to his parents in Hillerød before coming in to work," she said, explaining that she had found their address online. "Have you ever met them?"

"I've only met his sister, but I think Mie is in Africa right now. I'll set everything in motion soon as I get to the station, and I'll see if I can't hurry things up with the tower records on his cell phone."

The red stone house stood at the end of a cul-de-sac on the outskirts of Hillerød. Eik had told her he'd left home at seventeen, and he hadn't had much to do with his parents since then. But she didn't know if the sporadic contact stemmed from some problem, or if he just didn't fit in with suburban conformity.

Louise called his parents from the car, apologizing for

disturbing them so early in the morning. When she said she was with the Copenhagen Police, his father sounded a bit dismissive, but when he heard she was his son's colleague, and that they shared an office, his attitude changed. Suddenly she was more than welcome to come; they would both be at home until eleven, when his wife had a doctor's appointment.

The house stood close to the road, and on her way to the door she noticed what looked like a large lawn on the other side. A classic fifties residential area house. Some lawns had swing sets, others boasted flower gardens in pristine condition. Retirees and families with children, Louise decided. Not very much stuck out. Odd that this seemingly conventional suburban community was where the free-spirited Eik had grown up and played as a child, she thought. She rang the doorbell.

Eik's father was tall and narrow-shouldered, with very dark hair. He had the same high cheekbones as his son, and his hair was combed back flat like Eik's, though there wasn't much left of it. The resemblance made Louise smile wider when she shook his hand and thanked him for allowing her to come.

"Please, come in, come in," he said, and he gestured for her to follow him into the living room. "No need to take your shoes off. We've just brewed our morning coffee. Would you like a cup?"

A worried-sounding voice came from the kitchen. "Hopefully nothing has happened to him." Eik's mother appeared in the doorway. Her right arm was in a cast, but she stuck her left arm out and held Louise's hand as she gazed at her.

"Aren't you the one he's been living with?" She let go

of Louise's hand. "We don't hear much from him, but he did mention you the last time we saw him. He also spoke about your son."

Louise nodded and said that Jonas and Eik got along very well.

The living room looked very different from what she'd expected, judging by the outside of the house. Asian style, lots of pillows, patterns, gold, Buddha figures, and shades of red. There was also a sofa set and coffee table, with everything shrouded in the mild, pleasing scent of incense. Louise felt ashamed of having been so quick to judge this residential area. Given that Eik's name was inspired by the lead singer of a popular sixties Danish band, Steppeulvene, she should have known his parents would have a somewhat alternative lifestyle.

She was offered a mug of coffee and a seat in a comfortable armchair by the window. When had Eik told them he'd moved in with her? she wondered. Recently, or quite a while ago?

His father got straight to the point. "I hope he hasn't gotten himself into any serious trouble. We are well aware of his occasional lapses, when it's hard for him to work."

"Oh, Bent! That was a long time ago; it was back when she disappeared."

"We don't know where he is," Louise said, before they got into their son's ex-girlfriend.

"Well, he does drop out of sight once in a while," his father said. "And Henni is right, it's something that started after the tragedy down there."

A school photo of Eik stood in the windowsill. His hair was longer back then, nearly shoulder length. He wore what looked like a military shirt, and his eyes were a bit sleepy, as if he were bored and had been forced into having his picture taken.

"There are a few special circumstances about Eik's disappearance, and we want to make sure that nothing has happened to him." Louise chose her words carefully, to convey the seriousness of the situation without worrying them too much. "So first I'd like to know, have you spoken with him since noon yesterday?"

They both shook their heads.

"Are you aware of any plans he might have had?"

"No," his mother said. "He usually doesn't let us in on things like that, though."

"But he came by not too long ago," Bent said. "Two, three months ago, wasn't it?" He glanced over at his wife, who was sitting cross-legged on the sofa.

"That sounds about right. It was definitely before your birthday. He brought along that bottle of port."

Louise didn't know he had visited his parents while they had been living together. She would have liked to come along. "So you have no idea where he might be? Is it possible his sister might know something?"

His mother explained that Eik's sister was traveling in Sierra Leone with a female friend who had worked for Save the Children. "Mie won't be home for another month, but, of course, it's possible they've spoken." She promised to ask. "She calls us every two or three days when she's traveling."

"You could also try calling her," his father suggested.

"Her cell phone doesn't work out there," she told her husband.

"Don't worry, just ask her when she calls; that's fine," Louise said.

"How are you two doing, by the way?" Eik's mother asked. "You live in Frederiksberg, I believe?"

Louise nodded. She almost told them they were very welcome to stop by someday, but she stopped herself. That was Eik's decision. She thanked them for their time, then she stood up and promised to contact them as soon as he showed up.

7

"Just short of twenty-one thousand kroner was withdrawn from his account yesterday at Arbejdernes Landsbank on Vesterbrogade," Rønholt said, when Louise showed up just past 10:30 a.m. Her boss sat behind his desk with a bank statement in front of him. "It's one of the branches that still offers counter services."

"That's crazy! Why would he make such a big withdrawal?" Louise was startled. She slapped her cheeks to warm them, blew her nose, unwrapped her scarf, then threw her coat over the chair in front of his desk. Before arriving at the station, she had left her car back in Frederiksberg and rode her bicycle to work to avoid paying for a day's parking.

"The withdrawal took place at eleven fifty-two a.m.," Rønholt continued.

One of the things she respected about him as a leader was that he always involved himself personally in one or two ongoing cases. Naturally, he knew about all the searches his department carried out, and he kept up to date on them. But he'd decided to join Louise in the search for Eik Nordstrøm.

"So someone has stolen his debit card and is emptying out his account," she concluded. She sat down. "Have you blocked his card?"

Rønholt shook his head. "We don't know it's been stolen. We don't know he didn't withdraw the money himself."

"More than twenty thousand kroners? Eik was going out for cigarettes!"

"Fifteen hundred was withdrawn two weeks ago. In general he takes out large amounts. On the other hand, he doesn't seem to use his debit card."

Louise studied Rønholt for a moment; he was pulling out all stops at the very beginning of this search, which meant he was every bit as worried as she was. And that rattled her even more. "We're going to the bank." She grabbed her coat. "I want a look at their surveillance camera."

Rønholt nodded and stood up. He stuck his head into his reception office and asked his secretary, Hanne, to call Arbejdernes Landsbank and tell their security manager to have their surveillance files ready.

"What about his cell phone? Is it being checked?" Louise asked on the way out the door.

"Yes, but there's nothing on it yet."

"Birgitte served Eik Nordstrøm," the bank's branch manager said when they arrived. "We know many of our customers, and, of course, we're concerned when the police show up with a court order." He led them to an office at the back of the bank.

"We'd like to talk to her and look through the surveillance files," Rønholt said, without explaining why they were there.

The branch manager stopped at the open doorway and waved a blond, short-haired woman over.

"I was at the counter when he came in yesterday," Birgitte said. She looked questioningly at them.

They closed the door. "He withdrew a lot of money," Louise said.

Birgitte nodded. "But that wasn't unusual. He always withdraws large amounts to use over a longer period of time. We have several customers who don't like to pay with a debit card."

Louise had never paid much attention to it, but now that the bank employee mentioned Eik's habit, she knew the woman was right. And truthfully, it didn't surprise her that Eik shunned debit cards, just as he hated text messages. If you wanted to get hold of him, you had to call him. When he needed money, he went to the bank.

"So you have no suspicions that his account has been misused?" Rønholt asked.

"No, I've printed out a statement. All the withdrawals have been made here in our branch." She handed them the paper. The first thing that Louise noticed was his account's balance. More than 1.3 million kroner.

Birgitte followed her eyes. "He hasn't spent much, and over the years he's become quite well-off. Eik Nordstrøm has been a customer here since 1989. And he has never been interested in any of our investment proposals."

Being aware of Eik's financial affairs without his

knowledge made Louise uncomfortable. They had never talked about money. They'd never had a reason to.

"Did he seem to be under pressure when he was here yesterday?" Rønholt asked. "Nervous, or in some way not his usual self?"

Birgitte thought for a moment and shook her head, as if she wasn't sure where he was going with this question. "He did seem to be in a hurry. He usually chats a bit when there aren't so many customers, but yesterday he was in and out."

"Was he alone?" Louise asked. She simply couldn't make sense of what she'd heard. She was totally baffled, and her feeling of dread blossomed up again. *What the hell had happened?*

She stepped aside when the branch manager came in and announced that the surveillance files had been sent to his computer. He sat down at his desk and opened the film.

"I think he was, yes," Birgitte said.

"Was it eleven fifty?" the manager said. He made room for the others to crowd around.

"Start running the film at a quarter till," Rønholt said, adjusting his glasses.

Louise leaned forward, convinced that she knew Eik so well that she would notice if he had been feeling pressured or threatened. True, the past twenty-four hours had given her doubts, but right now she just wanted to see him. See that he was alive, and that he had withdrawn the money himself.

The film showed the bank entrance and two cashier counters. Birgitte sat at the counter to the right. One by one, customers approached the counter and took care of their business. Farthest back on the screen, a young woman sat at a desk punching holes in documents and placing them into file folders. Work, routines, nothing unusual. Not even a few moments later when Eik stepped into sight.

A sinking feeling hit Louise when she saw him walk over and take a number. He fingered the small slip of paper as he waited. He seemed impatient, not really there, not present, she thought. But not nervous, not visibly under pressure. When his number was called, he slipped his wallet out of his back pocket and leaned slightly over the counter.

It took hardly any time at all. The teller handed him his money, and he stuck his wallet in his back pocket, ran his hand through his hair, and walked out again. There was no sign of anyone with him—though, of course, Louise couldn't know if someone was waiting outside. All she knew was that it hurt to see him. And it confused her even more. To her it looked like a completely normal trip to the bank; nothing in his behavior indicated that he had plans to go underground.

Up to now, that was the last trace of Eik they had. He left the bank at 11:54 a.m.

Rønholt thanked the bank manager and teller for their help. He and Louise walked out; he buttoned his winter coat and pulled on his gloves. "That didn't help much. What in the world is causing him to do all this?"

Louise didn't answer. Suddenly she felt overwhelmed. She hated that she'd been forced to pry into Eik's private life. First Rønholt's basement storage room, which she hadn't known even existed, and now this! She tried to keep her emotions at arm's length and think rationally. He had invited *her* to the Nick Cave concert. Then suddenly his plans changed, and he abandoned Charlie, her, their date. Instead he went to the bank and withdrew a small fortune. It made no sense. She had to take it from the beginning. Go through everything one more time.

"You have to go out to South Harbor and talk to Ulla," she said. "If she knows something, she's not telling me."

Her boss stuck his hands deep down in the pockets of his duffle coat. He stared at the ground as if he were considering various theories. Then he nodded. "I don't know if it'll be easier for her to talk to me, but you're right. It's worth a try."

Louise assumed they both felt that nothing was making sense. Eik had behaved almost too casually in the bank. She was at the point where she was worrying about him being kidnapped. Knocked down, taken away. She had already contacted every hospital in Copenhagen to see if he had fallen or been hit by a car, but they had no unidentified traffic victims.

Just before disappearing, Eik had been set on their living together. Had she missed some signals? He'd been so affectionate, and she had felt his desire when Rønholt caught them kissing. She just couldn't understand it. His sudden disappearance made no sense. And then, Nick Cave...

On the way back to the station, Rønholt called and informed the garage manager, Svendsen, that they would be needing a car. When they arrived, he had already signed them in and fetched the keys to one of the unmarked police cars. Svendsen led them down to the third level and handed the keys to Rønholt, but Louise grabbed them and got behind the wheel.

A beer truck was parked outside Ulla's pub. Louise found a spot farther down the street.

En route, they had agreed that if they got nothing more out of Ulla, several other officers would be assigned to the case, and Louise would withdraw—her decision. She realized she wouldn't be able to continue. Her emotions would take over and prevent her from maintaining a professional distance from the case. Eik had been gone now for more than twenty-four hours, which wasn't all that long for a forty-two-year-old man. But anxiety was overwhelming her; she was struggling to keep from falling apart.

"You take the lead," she said. She followed Rønholt to the door. A broad-shouldered man with tattoos running up his neck walked backward out the door, pulling a two-wheeled dolly stacked with empty beer cases. "Maybe I should just wait outside?"

Louise very seldom retreated from a situation, but something about Ulla's attitude infuriated her. And it was hard enough right now to control herself.

"No, you'd better come with me," Rønholt said. "Four ears are better than two."

The pub owner stood in the back by the open door leading to the storeroom. It was cool and dark inside. The depressing odor of spilled beer, cigarette butts, and urinal deodorizers hung in the air. Ashtrays were stacked on the bar, waiting to be washed.

Ulla approached them and shook Rønholt's hand. "Is this about Eik?"

They knew each other, Louise could see that. Not that it surprised her, but Rønholt hadn't mentioned it. She walked over and stood by his side.

"We simply can't understand where he's gone," Rønholt said, keeping it friendly to begin with. He turned to Louise. "He left the office around eleven yesterday, right?"

"A little after, I think." Louise nodded. "But like I was trying to say yesterday evening, nothing points to this being one of his disappearing acts."

She noted Ulla's reaction. She was clearly worried, too; she had probably also tried to get hold of Eik as soon as Louise was out the door. Her body language spoke for itself, the way she crossed her arms and rubbed her elbows distractedly.

"I never said it was one of his disappearing acts," Ulla said defensively. She jerked her head, her coal-black hair flying back. She was pretty enough, Louise noted. A little rough around the edges, stocky, but not fat. She also looked younger today, now that she was wearing a pair of loose-fitting army pants and a white blouse instead of her midnight-blue bar outfit. The lack of heavy makeup also helped. "I just said he's a man who doesn't like to be controlled."

"This isn't an inspection, not at all," Louise said, trying to stay composed. "There's a search out for Eik, and shortly after he disappeared he withdrew a large amount of money from the bank. Your cooperation would help."

Rønholt broke in. "Seriously, we're worried about him." He told her they were looking for anything at all that could help explain his behavior. "We're guessing he's alone, but we don't know that. We checked everywhere we thought he might be. Do you have any ideas?"

Ulla's hands slipped through her thick hair as she leaned back, supporting her ample rear end against the table. It seemed as though the seriousness of the situation had finally sunk in. "Usually he does his disappearing act out here." She nodded toward the back of the room. "At least when he doesn't bury himself in that secret place you two have."

Louise tried to hide her reaction to hearing that Ulla knew about the basement room.

"I don't know where the hell else he could be," the pub owner said. She put her hands on her hips. "I haven't heard so much from him since he moved into town. He used to come by and eat a few times a week."

Into town! Louise almost smiled. Was it really so hard for Ulla to accept that she and Eik were living together?

Rønholt excused himself when his phone rang, leaving the two women alone together. Louise stuck her hands in her pockets and was about to move away when Ulla began talking. "He really likes you." Her face was blank; Louise couldn't tell whether she was happy for him or if she was simply stating a fact. "It's good for him—"

"I beg your pardon?" Rønholt spoke loudly in English. He looked at Louise, then pulled a chair out and sat down. He was frowning again. "Damn," he said, after putting his phone down. "He's in England. Apparently he's very drunk and in jail in some little town outside of Bristol!"

"Bristol!" Ulla said, before Louise broke in.

"What in hell is he doing there?"

Rønholt's face was stiff. He spoke sternly. "That I can't tell you, but he's coming home. Apparently the idiot has butted into an English police investigation. He even tried telling them the Search Department sent him over. He attempted to pressure them into giving him access to the victim's files. He claimed she's wanted in connection with a missing persons case he's working on."

"Victim?" Louise said, as he led her over to the door. "What do you mean? I don't know anything about him working on an open case in Bristol."

"Go over and get him, now," he said, ignoring her question. "Go home and get your passport, I'll tell Hanne to book a flight; you can head directly to the airport."

"No, I won't!" She was close to shouting. "It's one thing to send me out here to scrape him up off the floor after a drunken spree, but it's totally something else to fly over to England and clean up the mess he's made."

She felt Ulla's eyes on her from over at the bar. She straightened up. "All right, I'll go get him. But you call his parents and tell them he's been found."

8

The flight was short. The taxi dropped Louise off at a narrow parking lot with a painted board fence in front of the police station in Nailsea. For a moment, she studied the yellow one-story brick building, with a sign announcing the local police station's opening hours. The town looked abandoned, even though there were lights on in the houses clumped together behind the police station.

During the ride from Bristol Airport, Louise had gone through an entire emotional spectrum. She felt completely in the dark, and her initial relief ended up at anger. She had no idea what to expect or what she would say when she walked in. She just wanted to bring Eik home.

Tall mounds of gravel for roadwork stood to the right of the entrance. Louise had to walk over a sheet of plywood to get to the door, only to discover it was locked. She looked around for a buzzer, but then a light went on inside, and a tall man in a uniform came out to let her in.

"Ian Davies," he said. He held the door for her. "I'm glad you arrived so quickly. Normally we don't keep people in jail for more than a few hours. Either we release them or transfer them to one of the larger police stations. But this time we had to make an exception."

The officer was in his mid-forties, Louise guessed. Reddish-blond hair and green eyes, thin and wiry, and she imagined he was one of those obsessive runners constantly training for another marathon. She ran, too, of course, to stay strong and in shape, but marathons and half-marathons had become something that every mid-level manager in the private sphere felt they needed on their CVs. Louise couldn't help smiling when she recalled a question Eik asked her once. Did she know the most important thing about running? She'd said something about breathing. Writing about it on a Facebook profile afterward, he'd said.

She held out her hand, and the sandy-haired man shook it firmly as he spoke. His accent sang at the end of his words. "Because of the case the man under arrest is involved in, we chose to keep him here."

Involved in? Louise tried to hide her confusion. It was her understanding that they had thrown Eik in a cell for making a drunken nuisance of himself. She still had no idea why he had suddenly shown up in southwestern England.

She followed the officer past an empty glassed-in cell to a wide door with barred windows at the end of the hallway. The double doors closed behind them with a loud click that echoed in the closed-in jail.

"Tell me, what's my colleague being held for?" Louise said. She followed Davies into a small room. A room to register arrestees, she guessed, from the equipment for taking mug shots and fingerprints. There was very little space; she had to twist around to get past the camera and the chair resting against the wall. A fingerprint pad and a bottle with a plastic lid containing dark powder stood on the countertop beside the sink. Despite the unimpressive surroundings, she felt a bit out of place in her T-shirt, jeans, and sneakers.

A door opened somewhere in the back, followed by footsteps in the hallway. A uniformed female officer with layered, shoulder-length hair walked around the corner and deposited a bag from a pizzeria on the counter before greeting Louise.

"Sheila Jones. Has anyone offered you a cup of coffee?"

This time Louise raised her voice a bit when she asked what Eik Nordstrøm had been arrested for, and why they were keeping him in Nailsea instead of following their usual procedure.

The woman looked at Davies, who was fishing something up out of the bag. "Is he still asleep?" she said, ignoring Louise's question.

"Could I at least see him?" Louise looked back and forth between the two.

Jones grabbed a set of keys and told Louise to follow her. She unlocked a door that was an extension of the room. The yellow walls of the jail looked sickly and melancholy in the bright fluorescent lights. Two cells with thick, dark blue iron doors stood along one side of the corridor. She motioned Louise to the cell farthest back, pulled aside the slat covering the peephole, and let her take a look.

Eik lay fully dressed on the cot, his hair covering the top half of his face. He was obviously out of it. One arm hung in the air beside the mattress.

What the hell is going on? Louise wondered. She also felt sad, though not so much about his pathetic condition; here he was, in an English jail, and she had no idea what had happened.

"We still need to interrogate him," Jones said. She added that she was the one who had arrested him early that morning. "Your colleague was quite obnoxious, and he was enraged about being brought in, but we had no choice. He refused to tell us what he was doing at the crime scene, and he kept saying that we couldn't deny him access to the house, that the Danish police had sent him, and that it concerned a missing persons case his department was investigating."

She paused shortly, as if she were considering how much she should reveal. "He could barely stand, he was so drunk."

"House?" Louise asked. "Couldn't deny him access to what house?"

At the rear of the jail, a heavy iron-barred door blocked off the rest of the hallway. There was another cell next to the exit, and a pile of bicycles filled a small niche. It looked like a lost-and-found. Jones followed Louise's eyes.

"Mostly we deal with shoplifting, vandalism by minors, and stolen bicycles here in Nailsea. Serious crimes like what happened this weekend are rare."

Louise wasn't interested in the daily routine of the Nailsea Police Station. She wanted to know when Eik would be released so they could return to Copenhagen. And she wanted to know what the hell he was doing at a crime scene in England.

"In fact, there have been only two killings in the

twenty-three years I've lived here," Sheila said, ignoring Louise's question. "One was a mentally disturbed person who killed a neighbor. The other happened after an argument at the pub. A fight started, and one of them fell in an unfortunate way. We've never had a real murder like the one this weekend, so naturally we've accepted assistance from Bristol."

"Murder?" Louise asked. "Eik Nordstrøm is employed by the Danish Search Department. I'm his superior, and I can assure you he would never force his way into a house and disturb a crime scene. There must be some misunderstanding."

Jones didn't answer; she didn't need to. The expression on her face showed there was no misunderstanding. Louise breathed deeply as all her new-found strength evaporated. If Eik had broken into a crime scene still being investigated, either he'd had an incredibly good reason to do so or else he'd totally lost it.

"It's probably best you tell me what went on before the arrest," she said, with all the authority she could muster.

The policewoman peered at her, as if she was just now realizing that her colleague had kept Louise in the dark. "Well, he was contacted yesterday morning when his name came up—"

"Let's take it from the beginning," Louise said, nodding at the door. "Why don't we go in and sit down? I'd like to know about the case, and what your prosecutor believes my colleague is guilty of."

For a moment she considered calling Rønholt, but she decided to wait until she'd heard what had happened.

They walked back to the office. Louise was offered a slice of pizza and a cup of instant coffee. She realized she hadn't eaten since yesterday. While she'd been running around trying to track down Eik, she hadn't thought about food, and then everything had gone so quickly when he'd finally been found. Hanne had booked her on an immediate EasyJet flight to Bristol, and she hadn't had time to eat in the airport. Mostly she needed a cigarette, but she didn't smoke. She thanked the policewoman and accepted the greasy slice of pizza.

Davies sat at a desk, speaking with someone on the phone.

"They're on their way," he told Jones, after joining them a moment later. "We've had a team out looking for the murder weapon, but we still haven't found it."

This he said to Louise, as if she should be able to piece together the fragments of information they had shared with her.

Puzzled, she looked at the policewoman.

"Last Saturday afternoon, Sofie Parker was shot in her home just outside Nailsea. The shot was fired from the garden, but we have no idea who the killer was, or what weapon was used. Bristol police are doing the ballistics. We expect an answer at the end of the week. It's almost certain she was shot with a hunting rifle."

"But what does this have to do with Eik Nordstrøm?" Louise said. She didn't recognize the victim's name, and couldn't recall any department cases that could be connected with this location.

"His name popped up when we learned the woman was Danish. We found her birth certificate, and because we had no motive, we checked her maiden name. A search for her had been conducted quite some time ago, and Eik Nordstrøm was listed as her nearest relation. But there was nothing about him being employed by the Danish National Police, or that he was investigating the case. We contacted him solely because of his private relation to the deceased. Naturally we couldn't allow him access to the crime scene when he arrived yesterday."

She looked pleadingly at Louise, as if she wanted to reassure a fellow police officer that they weren't trying to hinder the Danish police.

"Last night," Davies said, "he tried to break into the house again, and he made a ruckus by standing out on the street and yelling. He believed the husband was inside, and he demanded that he open the door. But the husband and daughter aren't staying at the house. It ended with the neighbors waking up and calling us."

"You mentioned that the victim had a Danish maiden name," Louise said. "How old was she?" Suddenly she had the sinking feeling that she knew where all this was leading.

"Sofie Bygmann was forty-four years old," Davies answered. "Nearly eighteen years ago, she was reported missing during a cruise in the Mediterranean. Does that ring a bell?"

He tossed a case file over to Louise, who slowly began nodding. Eik's missing girlfriend. Her stomach churned; she wanted to stand up and walk out.

She touched the case file without opening it.

"Four years later," Ian said, nodding at the file on the table, "Sofie Bygmann married Nigel Parker."

"You should know that it's easy to disappear here in Great Britain," Jones added. "We don't have civil registration numbers as many European countries do. It's presumed that about a half-million foreigners are living here unregistered. No authorities were aware she had settled here."

Louise was listening with only one ear. She imagined Eik taking the call on his way to buy cigarettes, and how it had made him drop everything.

"There are several years we can't account for," Jones said. "At the moment, her whereabouts during that time are unknown. Her husband says she arrived in England six months before they met. They moved to town after that. He's an optician. He opened a vision center."

"What happened on the afternoon the woman was shot?" Louise still hadn't opened the file on the table.

"It's quite difficult to say," Jones answered. "Her daughter and husband hadn't noticed anything out of the ordinary. They'd all come home, as usual. He says his wife was making dinner in the kitchen, when a shot through the window killed her." She paused a second. "You don't feel threatened while standing in your own kitchen, doing what you do every day."

"He was about to pour a glass of wine," Davies said, "and before he knew it there was blood everywhere. And his wife lay on the floor, shot in the head, and his daughter screamed."

"And nothing had happened earlier?" Louise said.

They shook their heads. "The family says that Sofie Parker occasionally went into London alone," Davies said. "Her husband volunteered that information, and he also said he suspects she might have had a lover there." The policeman's wavy hair was combed back from his forehead, which emphasized his receding temples, but now he seemed younger than Louise had first guessed.

Two boyish dimples appeared when he spoke. "But we have nothing pointing to any suspect."

"Of course, we're also aware it could be a stray bullet," Jones said. "There are fields behind the house; the shot could have come from there."

"But," Davies said, leaning forward, "it looks more like an execution. Our theory is that the killer fired at close range, and we have clear footprints from the garden—they could be his."

"And you've ruled out the husband?" Louise said.

"Yes." They both nodded. "Her blood was splattered all over him. There's no doubt he was standing behind her when she was shot."

No one spoke for a moment. Davies folded up the pizza box and threw it in the trash.

"We have no motive," he admitted. "We've got nothing to go on other than the shot that killed her, the footprints, and several witness accounts among their circle of friends. We still hope to identify the person she went to London to meet."

"If such a person exists," Jones said. "We don't know what she did while in London. That's why we're very interested in knowing everything about her Danish past, and what happened when she disappeared from the boat in Italy. It might lead us to a motive."

"Am I to understand that the search back then was undertaken by your department?" Davies said.

Louise nodded.

"It would be of great help to us if you could gather information about her background. And of course we're going to have a long conversation with Eik Nordstrøm when he's ready to speak with us."

"And you're sure it really *is* the woman reported missing eighteen years ago, that she's not someone who has assumed her Danish identity?" Louise asked.

The two English officers exchanged a quick glance.

"Why would she do that?" Jones said. "But naturally we can ask Eik Nordstrøm to identify her at the morgue." She repeated that no matter what, they were going to interrogate him as soon as he was able.

"May I see the house?" Louise asked.

"We can take you out there right now," Davies said, as if he were about to suggest that very same thing.

"Wouldn't you rather wait, so Nordstrøm can follow along?" Jones said.

Louise shook her head. "No. We're taking a flight back to Copenhagen this evening, so let's just go. In the meantime you can try to rouse him."

9

As soon as they left the Nailsea Police Station in one of the screaming yellow-and-white patrol cars, they were in the countryside. The hilly terrain, dotted with trees and lined with stone walls between fields, stretched out on both sides of the road. Houses appeared at intervals until they reached the Parker family address, located in a cluster of homes.

All the anxiety and worry that had welled up inside Louise during the past twenty-four hours was turning into anger. She couldn't understand how Eik could just take off for England without telling her. If for no other reason than because she was his boss, and he had disappeared in the middle of the workday. But, of course, it was mostly a personal blow. On the other hand, she knew he must have been overwhelmed by shock when he got the call from the English police.

Davies slowed at a pub on the right side of the road. He turned down a narrow driveway leading to three short streets that formed an E. He parked at the last one and shut off the engine.

Louise sat for a moment studying the nearly identical, gray brick houses, two stories, with front lawns and gates out to the streets. Several big cars were parked beside the houses. Everything looked neat and well-kept except for one lawn filled with junk. She could see it wasn't a neighborhood meant for lower incomes. She stepped out of the car.

The Parkers' house was surrounded by tall bushes and trees; the garden was hidden, but the house itself stood on a slight rise. It had an open view of the field behind. A sheet of plywood covered a window facing the street. Davies held the gate open for Louise. Police barrier tape blocked the front door, and a sign forbade anyone to enter. The garden was cordoned off along the sidewalk and farther on to the opposite side, but there were no police officers in sight. Davies lifted the key out of his pocket, but before unlocking the door, he rang the doorbell and waited.

"The cleaners will arrive later today, but we're allowing the husband and daughter to move back in. Our crew of technicians finished up this morning. But I don't know if the two of them *want* to move back. Right now they're staying with his mother in Bath."

Louise nodded. She eyed him for a moment. There was something very civil about the way he and Sheila Jones were treating her. If an Englishman had barged in and tried to contaminate one of her crime scenes, she also would have arrested him immediately, but she wasn't sure if she would have been so accommodating and cooperative before she had finished checking the man's explanation. Apparently they trusted her, and that impressed her.

"Hello," Davies shouted when he opened the door. As

expected, no one answered. He had picked up a newspaper and the day's mail from outside the door. The kitchen/dining room was to the right. The blood had been washed from the room, but the markings around the bloodstains remained for the cleaners to take care of. They stepped inside. It was well lit, with upper cabinets along the entire wall just inside the door. A glass cabinet containing porcelain and wineglasses hung on the opposite wall. The stove stood along the wall bordering the entryway. Davies pointed. "She was standing at the sink when she was shot."

Jones was right, Louise thought. When you're in your kitchen fixing dinner, you're not on alert. You are completely unprotected. You can't see out and you don't know who is looking in.

"I'm reasonably sure he was hiding in the bushes out there." Davies pointed. "That's where we found the footprints. And if he drove here, he could have parked where we did. But no one else living here noticed a strange car, so more likely he parked up behind Battleaxe, the pub we passed on the way. Their restaurant is popular, it's filled almost every evening, and often cars are parked on the road out front. But there are no surveillance cameras, so we haven't been able to track him that way."

Place mats lay on the dining room table, along with a pack of unopened paper napkins. A short black leather jacket hung over one chair. A calendar had been put up on the refrigerator, along with a few shopping lists, and a row of cookbooks filled a shelf on the wall bordering the living room. A metallic odor and a faint hint of chlorine hung in the air.

"Is it possible to borrow a picture of her to show my

colleague, so he can identify her?" Louise asked. She followed him into the living room. She noted a white velour sofa group, a flat-screen TV, and another dining table with high-backed chairs by the covered patio.

"Maybe up in her office," Davies said, on the way to the stairway in the hall. "She kept the books for her husband's business."

Louise glanced around to gain some final impressions. Reproductions of Picassos and small, framed lithographs hung on the walls. The house was decorated in a light style, not particularly Scandinavian. Nor was it particularly English. It was more whitewashed, French, and romantic. A three-arm candlestick holder stood on a buffet, and potted plants stuck in outer pots had been placed on the windowsills. Everything was nice and impersonal, more like a false front. *Though that is probably unfair*, Louise thought. *A home can look nice and tidy if the person taking care of it doesn't have a full-time job.*

She followed Davies up the stairs. There were four doors on the landing, and he opened the one leading into the office. A desk nearly filled one wall. Louise glanced inside a bedroom with a double bed covered by a patterned bedspread. A large wardrobe stood along a wall, opposite a low secretary pushed into the corner, over which hung a teak-framed mirror. Louise then checked the next room: a large bathroom with a bathtub.

The daughter's room was at the end of the landing. Louise opened the door to what resembled a bomb crater. Apparently the daughter wasn't so different from most teenagers. Clothes—black clothes dotted with studs, scarves, and thick-heeled Dr. Martens boots—lay scattered on the bed, the floor, and a dresser beside the desk.

Posters of bands Louise had never heard of hung on the walls.

It reminded her of Jonas. She wondered if his room at boarding school was as chaotic as this one. Most likely. Unless they had rules against such things.

"I think we can use this," Davies said from the office. Louise closed the door to the adolescent cave behind her.

He was holding a photograph of Sofie Parker smiling in a lawn chair, wearing a white summer top. Her hair was pinned up behind her head; her eyes looked directly at the camera.

"Summer, 2013, it says on the back," he said. He waited.

Louise's stomach sank; she felt a sudden and enormous aversion to the smiling woman. Sofie Parker was a few years older than Louise, but even though she looked carefree and happy in the photo, her expression revealed a seriousness seen in women who had grown up early. She was beautiful and at ease with herself, and it wasn't difficult to see that she was a good match for Eik.

"Fine," she said. She handed the photo back. "What else have you found in here?"

The office had obviously been searched. Everything was piled up, systematically checked, in a way a person working there never would arrange things.

Davies stood beside the door, pointing to a wastebasket beside the desk. "The brown wrapping paper from two packages sent from Mexico were found in there. They were postmarked Cozumel. We're examining them now to trace the sender. Apparently the husband knows nothing about this, and it could be anything bought online."

The front door below opened and a man's voice called

out. Davies yelled that they were upstairs, and he started down the steps. Louise stayed behind, studying the desk and the piles made by the English police. Photos of the daughter when she was a young child hung from the bulletin board. She couldn't have been more than two years old in one of them, leaning against a stroller in front of a large lake with mountains in the background. Another photo showed her with a school backpack, smiling toothlessly at the camera.

She took the picture Davies had found. She had no desire whatsoever to be the one who showed it to Eik.

It was like stepping into a paused film when she entered the living room. The husband, a large man with short, blond hair, stood by the kitchen door holding his mail, absorbed in hushed conversation with Davies. His back was to his daughter, who stood by the dining room table with her phone. She looked furious. It was impossible not to sense the tension between father and daughter. Nothing was spoken; it simply filled the room.

Louise walked over to her. "Hello," she said, introducing herself. "I'm from Copenhagen Police. What's your name?"

"Steph." The girl glanced up. Her black hair fell in her eyes. "It's only him over there who still insists on calling me Stephanie. I hate that name."

The girl was pale and dismissive. She wore heavy eyeliner and green fingernail polish, and a small sparkling stone in her nose.

Davies called Louise over. She shook the widower's hand, then offered her condolences and explained that she worked in the Danish Search Department, which had investigated the disappearance of his wife.

"It's news to me that my wife had been missing," he said, as if he weren't convinced it was true. "Of course, I knew she was Danish, but she seldom talked about her past. And I respected her wish to put it behind her."

He looked like a man who hadn't slept much lately. He turned the broad wedding ring on his left ring finger as he spoke.

"This just arrived in the mail," Davies said. He handed Louise a letter from a Swiss bank.

Nigel Parker had tossed the rest of the mail on the kitchen table. A few advertisements, a local paper, a birthday invitation. "I don't understand it. The account is in my wife's name, but there must be some mistake. We have no dealings with a bank in Zurich."

Steph stared at her phone again, as if she weren't listening. Her father took out his reading glasses from his pocket. Confused, he glanced back and forth between Davies and Louise. "There's almost eighty-eight thousand euros in the account."

"The postings have been made over a long period of time; the account can't be new," Davies said. "May I take this with me?"

Suddenly Steph ran out of the room, and shortly after a door upstairs slammed.

Parker seemed to ignore his daughter's behavior and nodded. "Of course." His voice was thick. "But my wife never mentioned a foreign bank account."

He explained that they had banked at Barclays in Bristol since moving to town. "We've always used the same bank."

"We'll look into it," Davies replied.

Parker seemed confused, on the edge of tears. His hands shook as he folded his glasses and hung them in the V-neck of his sweater.

Davies pulled out a chair and guided him into it. Louise gestured that she was going upstairs to talk to the daughter.

"Swiss banks aren't wild about giving access to their accounts," Davies said, as Louise walked up the steps. "But, of course, we'll set the wheels in motion at once."

Louise knocked on the girl's bedroom door before opening it. Steph lay on her bed, face buried in the mattress. "May I come in?"

"Mmmm." Her voice was muffled, but she turned over and sat up.

"It must be difficult, with all these questions being asked." Louise moved the clothes draped over the chair and sat down.

"I can bloody well understand if Mum were seeing someone else," she said, angry now. "That idiot down there was never interested in her. He's always at the store."

The girl stared straight ahead, her expression filled with sorrow and pain. She kicked the boots lying on the bed and sat with her back against the wall.

After a moment, Louise asked, "Do you know what your mother ordered from Mexico?"

Steph shook her head without looking at Louise.

"Does she usually shop online?"

The girl shrugged. "It might be something for the store. Sometimes things get sent here instead. I don't know, I don't have anything to do with it. But Mum always checked the mail. She ran the office."

Another pause. The girl's eyes were blank, her face as closed as a fist.

Louise knew the girl might shut her out completely, but she decided to fish around. "Did your parents quarrel?"

Steph shook her head. "He and I are the only ones that quarrel. He doesn't like me, and I don't care because I don't like him either." Now she looked at Louise. "So you're from Denmark. Like Mum."

Louise nodded and smiled. "Have you been there?"

"No. But Mum had plans for us to visit. That's not going to happen now." She began to cry. She swiped angrily at her tears, leaving black streaks across her face.

"Did you ever go along when your mother went to London?"

The daughter's expression turned defiant as she shook her head again. "She went there when she needed to get away from him. She always said she had to shop there because Nailsea was such a dump. And she had a hairdresser in London; she wanted her hair to look decent, she said. But she never bought anything for herself when she was there, only clothes for me and tea and Stilton cheese from Fortnum and Mason. She would much rather live in London, but he didn't want to."

Louise wanted so much to hug the young girl and take her back to Copenhagen with her.

She hadn't heard Davies come up the stairs, but now he stood at the door. "I'm ready to leave." He stepped inside the room. "I've spoken with your father, and we've agreed that you and I can talk when you come home from school tomorrow. It's important that you think about this. You might have seen something anyway. It's completely normal to not remember much at first, after such a shock, but details often come back after a few days."

The girl turned to the window. Louise sensed that the questioning would be difficult; Davies didn't realize he should have set things up with the girl, not her father. She weighed whether to get involved, but decided against it. She told Steph to call her if she ever wanted to come to Copenhagen. That she would like to show her around.

She laid her card on the desk and smiled at her one last time before following Davies down the stairs.

10

Eik was holding a coffee cup between his hands when they got back to the Nailsea Police Station. Louise noticed that he started to stand up when she came in, but then he thought better of it. His eyes were red and glazed. A thousand thoughts ran through her head, but instead of speaking she laid a hand on his shoulder before leaning over the table for the mug Jones handed her.

"When did you get here?" he asked, when she sat down. The two English officers talked about the bank statement sent to Sofie Parker. As Louise understood it, one of the policemen on the case had been assigned to gather information on the foreign bank account.

"Around three, and we have a ten thirty flight home to catch." That wasn't up for discussion. "We've just been out at the house. The husband and daughter arrived while we were there."

Jones and Davies sat down across from Louise and Eik. "Nordstrøm and I have already gone over the pre-liminaries," the policewoman said. "I have the information, and I've confirmed what Officer Rick explained about Nordstrøm's job situation."

"But before we go further," Davies said, "if you would please have a look at the photo of the deceased. Just so we're sure this *is* the Danish woman reported missing."

Louise sat up and blocked off all the emotions roiling inside her. She pulled out the photo and laid it on the table in front of Eik.

The expression that flashed across his face was almost invisible. He nodded without touching the photo, confirming that this was the Sofie Bygmann he had sailed with in the Mediterranean, the woman he had reported missing after she disappeared from the boat in a harbor town outside Rome.

No one spoke for a moment. Louise was worried about how vulnerable he looked, and she couldn't quite read his expression as he gazed at the photo. It wasn't sorrow, or shock from her suddenly showing up after so many years. Had that been the case, he would have picked the photo up and studied it closely. Held it in his hands. His face showed more distance, or perhaps closure.

"We argued on the boat that morning when she woke me," Eik began. "Sofie had already gathered all her dirty clothes, and she wanted to find a Laundromat at the harbor. But I felt like walking into town to see the old ruins, so I said why not just rinse our clothes out whenever we needed them."

He leaned back into the hard wooden chair, looking like someone who needed a bath and a cigarette. "So things were a bit tense. I got annoyed and I went into town for a cup of coffee. The two others were still asleep."

"Who were the two others?" Davies asked. He sat at a computer, writing down Eik's explanation, which was more a window into what had happened back then than an actual witness statement.

"Two young guys: Christopher and Mark. They owned the boat. Or actually, it was Christopher's father who owned it, but they were sailing around on vacation that summer. We met them on Corsica, we had a fun evening together. They had some weed, we smoked some, and then they let us come along. They were on their way to Italy, then south to Capri, where someone had a house they were going to stay in."

"Were they the ones who drowned?" Louise asked. Eik nodded.

"Did anyone find out exactly what happened?" Jones asked. "There's nothing about it in Sofie Bygmann's search report."

Eik shook his head. "There are lots of theories. The craziest one was that it was a hate crime because they were gay. When the boat was found drifting around outside the harbor, the bodies were only a few meters away. The police found evidence that someone tried to steal the boat, but the ignition had some sort of thief protection and they couldn't start the motor. So maybe they just gave up. Or they were surprised by Christopher and Mark; there could have been a fight. They could have been assaulted while they were asleep; the killers could have stolen stuff from them and tossed them overboard. The police never found out what happened."

He slumped a bit. "When I heard about it, I was thinking mostly that Sofie's things weren't found on the boat, and I was afraid she'd disappeared with the criminals.

Either of her own free will or by force. But she could have drowned and floated away from the others. I never understood why her things were gone."

"Was that the last time you saw her, when you left the boat that morning?" Jones asked.

Eik shook his head. "I went into town and drank a coffee and cooled down. I started talking to some kids sitting at a fountain playing music. One of them had a guitar. It looked like they'd been there all night. We smoked a joint, and then Sofie showed up, and I asked her to join us. But she was still looking for a Laundromat, the one at the harbor was closed. She had a shopping list, too."

It pained Louise to hear that what had happened so many years ago stood so fresh in his memory.

"She kept on about all the practical stuff we had to get done, and that irritated me even more. The weather was fantastic, we were having a great time, and I still wanted to see those ruins. Mark had been there; he said it was something you had to see, and Sofie had agreed right up until then, but suddenly there wasn't enough time, she wanted to wash clothes and do the shopping."

He paused a second as if to calm himself down. "I didn't want to listen to her anymore, so I stuck around there. But when I got back to the harbor a few hours later the boat was gone. With my backpack and all my clothes. I had my wallet and passport on me, but everything else was gone."

He looked over at Jones. "I was so mad that I decided to hitchhike to Rome. I got drunk, then I went back the next day. I thought they'd come back for me."

He stared down at the table. Louise sat bolt upright; he hadn't looked at her once while speaking.

"But they didn't," he said. "Maybe she grabbed her things and left, too. I just don't know! My backpack was still on board when they found the boat. That's why the police contacted me."

"So that's the last time you saw her?" Davies asked from over at the computer.

Eik nodded. "I thought of every possibility. She drowned, she was kidnapped and sold. She was with whoever tried to steal the boat. Or Mark and Christopher tried to defend her from whoever killed them. At one point, I thought I was going crazy from thinking. And now, eighteen years later, out of the blue I get a call from you."

He looked back at the policewoman. "And you tell me she's dead." He ran his hand through his dark, shiny hair. "She's been living here all these years, while I spent so much time thinking about what happened back then."

The silence was heavy. Louise was torn between her role as Eik's boss and colleague, and a chilling fear that this would come between them. That she would lose him. Part of her felt sorry for him, part of her was angry, but also, in a way, she was relieved that he finally had his answer.

"When did you arrive here at Nailsea?" Davies said. The unhappy love story didn't seem to have affected him. "Try to be as accurate as possible with the times."

Eik turned in his chair to face the officer behind the computer screen. "I landed at two ten p.m. and took a taxi from the airport. I have my plane ticket, you can look at it." His fingers still held the coffee cup, even though it was empty. "Maybe your people were home for afternoon tea, I don't know, but no one was at the house when I arrived. It wasn't hard to find, there were barriers everywhere, and I knew the name of the town from when I was called."

"But you haven't been there before?" Davies asked.

Eik shook his head. His eyes cleared a bit. "No. I haven't been there before. I don't know what I expected or hoped for. But I wanted to talk to somebody. To her family. I knew her husband was in the house when she was shot."

"And how did you know she had been shot?" Davies hurried to ask.

"I was told on the phone." His voice was firmer now. "I decided to wait. I walked up to the pub and had a few beers. Well, probably more than a few. Everyone in the bar was talking about what had happened, of course. People seemed to know the optician's wife came from someplace in Scandinavia."

You could have called, damn it, Louise thought. He'd spent all afternoon and evening killing time while she had been worried out of her mind.

"I drank beer and listened to the gossip. And at some point, I walked back to the house and rang the doorbell. Or maybe I knocked on the door."

"The neighbors described it as pounding on the door and shouting," Jones said.

Eik nodded. "That's probably right. I wanted inside. I wanted to know what kind of life she'd been hiding from me!"

Strange, Louise thought. *Why wouldn't you rather know why someone put a bullet through her forehead?*

Louise looked at the clock and apologized, saying they had to leave soon for the airport.

"As we've mentioned," Sheila Jones said, "we are very interested in knowing about Sofie Parker's past in Denmark. Is this something your department can assist us with, or did the investigation take place somewhere else?"

"The search was ours, so the case is in our department." Louise handed Sheila her card. "We want to help, but, of course, I have to talk to my boss first. You can contact me at those numbers and that email address."

They drove ten minutes without speaking before Louise exploded. "What in the fucking hell did you think you were doing? Did you even think?" The young policeman driving them to the airport shifted a bit in his seat up front. "Are you out of your mind, or what?"

"I'm sorry," he said. He started to lay his hand on top of hers, but Louise pulled it away viciously.

"I've been out at your parents'. Rønholt and I moved heaven and earth to find you. What could you have been thinking? You left Charlie out on the street!"

"Is he okay?"

"Yes, no thanks to you! It was pure luck I noticed him outside the market, where he'd been sitting for hours."

Eik's hands were folded in his lap. After a moment he asked, "What was in the house out there? You said the family was home."

"They came." Louise stared out into the darkness covering the landscape, at the narrow, winding roads and tall trees captured by the car's headlights.

"How was the daughter doing?"

Louise shrugged without answering. She leaned her head back.

The silence between them screamed, the mood so heavy that she literally felt she was being squashed down in her seat.

He tried again in the plane after takeoff. "The husband didn't see anything before the shot?"

"It was getting dark out. It's possible that Stephanie caught a glimpse of the killer, but the police got nothing out of her from the first interview. Now they're trying again."

"Stephanie?" he asked.

"The daughter, but she wants to be called Steph."

"What do you think of her?"

Louise exploded. "Were you even going to call?"

"What do you mean?"

"Were you even going to call me? Did you bother thinking for a single second that I was worried to death about you?"

Silence.

"Eik, what the hell's going on?"

"I'm sorry," he said again.

Louise said nothing, though she wanted to shake him, hold him, comfort him, and curse him out. Leave him. Stay.

"How much do the police know?" he asked. "Did something happen before the murder? Disagreements? Threats?"

"Stop it!"

"Was the family being harassed? What do the police have to go on? Come on, bring me up to date, we have a case here."

"Let me spell this out for you," Louise snarled as she turned to him. "*We* don't have a case. *I* have a case, and you are not a part of it. Got that?"

He was about to say something, but he sat quietly. Neither one of them spoke during the rest of the flight. Nor did they speak in the taxi to Frederiksberg.

Louise was still enraged. Not one single time had he even tried to explain. All she'd gotten was a pathetic "I'm sorry." But she couldn't care less about an apology. She wanted to know how he could do what he did, abandon her like that. Abandon Charlie. She had a right to more than a puny apology, but when she asked for an explanation, it was almost as if he wasn't listening.

"Talk to me, damn you!" she screamed, after fetching Dina and Charlie down at Melvin's and reassuring him that Eik was home again. "What's going on? I don't know, are you living with me or are you moving out? What have you decided? And what the hell is it with that basement room at Rønholt's building. I don't even know you!"

He spread his arms out in despair. "I'll walk the dogs."

Louise was about to ask if he was planning on coming back, or if she maybe ought to go out and start looking for him after an hour or so. Instead she started packing his things.

In the bathroom, she tossed his deodorant, toothbrush, and shaving supplies in a sack. She packed his clothes from the bedroom shelves she'd cleared for him. She stuffed everything into plastic bags. While she worked, she realized it wasn't Eik's dropping everything to go to his old girlfriend that hurt her most. She could understand that, even though he should have let her know what was going on. She had been through something similar herself. Shadows from the past can appear that need to be dealt with before you can move on. She also recognized that he'd been living with uncertainty for many years. Of course he would react.

But she wouldn't accept his silence and distance, when she was trying to understand and to show she was there for him. Instead of explaining, he turned away. Without a word.

After piling all his things in the hallway, she stood in the entryway with her forehead against the wall, overcome by a sadness almost too intense to handle.

Everything had been going so very well, and now this.

When his footsteps stopped outside, she opened the door and took Dina's leash out of his hand. She nodded at the bags and said it was best for everyone that he go back to his South Harbor place to sleep.

Eik looked at her dejectedly and nodded back. He grabbed the bags and herded Charlie back down the steps. "See you tomorrow," he said. He glanced back at her through the balusters of the banister. "It made me happy when I heard you'd come over there."

Louise stood listening to his footsteps for a moment as they disappeared down the stairway. Then she closed the door and went inside to call Camilla to tell her they'd found Eik and she'd thrown him out. She needed to cry. To be angry and dejected.

11

"This was exactly what wasn't supposed to happen," Sofie said, when her family doctor joined her in the hospital lounge. She had been parked there with a cup of coffee while her mother was being washed and turned.

Else Corneliussen swept her blond pageboy behind her ears and sat down beside Sofie. The home care aide had phoned and said she'd found her mother dead in the bedroom. She'd also found a farewell letter to Sofie in the living room, and a water glass and a saucer stood on the night table. The empty pill bottles were beside the letter, so there would be no doubt about what had taken place. That she'd wanted to die.

But her mother wasn't dead. Either she had been found too early or the pills weren't strong enough. Maybe they were too old? Sofie didn't know. She was so angry at herself for not helping her mother. For not making sure she'd taken enough. Now she lay unconscious in her room.

"She wanted so much to die," Sofie said.

The doctor nodded. "How do you feel about your

mother trying to take her own life?" She walked over and closed the door to the hallway; nurses coming in for the evening shift were walking by. She sat down.

"I'd accepted it," Sofie said. "We talked about it several times. It was difficult, right up to when I realized the alternative was so painful and miserable, that in a way it was worse than losing her. That's when a person understands, that's when you set her free. Out of love and respect, I think. But of course it was hard in the beginning when she talked about it. I didn't want to lose her. I wanted her to be with me. But finally I realized I was thinking of myself, not her."

Restless now, Sofie walked over to the window. A small, closed courtyard with raised beds and meticulously pruned bushes lay below; in the light from the offices on the other side of the courtyard, the bushes looked like black paperclips. "You know how much pain she was in." She turned to the doctor. "She was exhausted all the time. She couldn't get around because of her difficulty walking. This wasn't how it was supposed to happen, that's all."

She paused a moment. When she had stopped by her mother's apartment earlier that day, her blanket lay on the sofa as if she had just gotten up. She turned back to the doctor. "Do you think she was afraid when she took the pills?"

Dr. Corneliussen shook her head. "I think your mother felt at peace. She was setting herself free."

Sofie nodded. "I've always feared the day it would happen. The day she didn't answer when I called, like I usually do in the mornings. She was hanging around only for my sake, she knew how unhappy I'd be. But I did manage to convince her that I was ready to let her go. She said it herself, in just the right way: 'I'm not myself anymore.' "

The doctor nodded. She seemed to know exactly what Sofie meant. "If your mother wakes up, we will find a nursing home for her." It was still too early to know if she would regain consciousness. "She won't be returning to her apartment; you should prepare yourself for that."

"That can't happen, it can't! I won't have her stuck in some nursing home where she has to be fed every day. It would be so much against her wishes."

The doctor took her hand and pressed it. "I agree, one hundred percent. I've also spoken to your mother about these things. Several times. In fact, I expected her to ask me to help her get the right pills. And I would have helped, I want you to know that. But I couldn't offer to do it, she had to ask."

Sofie turned to her. "Would you?"

The doctor nodded again. "I know her wishes, and I also know she doesn't want life-prolonging treatment or to be kept alive by artificial means. But it's possible she didn't want to ask me, she knew it would put me in a dilemma, given my oath as a doctor."

"You should have helped her." Sofie said this quietly; mostly she was annoyed with herself. Why hadn't they talked about this before now, when they both would have helped? "Can we do it now, so she doesn't go through all this if she wakes up?"

The doctor's expression was grave. "I believe it's everyone's right to choose when they no longer want to live." She folded her hands in her lap. "When it comes to illness and age, I mean. When pain dominates and the will to live disappears. Or when they are entering a life without dignity. But to keep my opinion within professional limits, such a request has to come from the patient. On the other hand, as I said, I have spoken to your mother about it…"

Of course, Sofie thought. No one can suggest to another person that they die. "Will you help if I'm the one who asks? Will you help her to die?"

They looked at each other for a moment, then the doctor nodded. "But you're not the one I'm helping," she emphasized. "It's your mother."

Sofie felt something loosening up inside. She squeezed the doctor's hand. "How?"

"It's not something we can talk about," Dr. Corneliussen said. She stared until Sofie got the message. "But your mother won't be alone when she passes away."

12

"Come on, for Chrissake!" Camilla Lind leaned over the table in the editorial conference room. "It's a damn good story when a Danish woman disappears for eighteen years and suddenly shows up dead in England—murdered, and the police have absolutely no motive for the killing."

She ignored everyone around the table except Terkel Høyer, but the editor in chief didn't look convinced. "Let's put a hold on this," he said. "Because they *don't* have a clue as to motive, we can't know if the killing has anything to do with her past here in Denmark."

"No!" Camilla said. "But aren't you curious? Don't you want to know who she was, what she's been doing all these years, all this time when her loved ones thought she'd drowned?"

Ole Kvist, a seasoned crime reporter for *Morgenavisen*, finally woke up. "I could fly over there. I could try to interview the husband and daughter." No doubt he was eyeing the possibility of a few days in southern England, all expenses paid.

Camilla sighed. "We already know all that, damn it. You've already stolen it from the English newspapers. Focus on the woman, not the case, that story is history."

The first thing she had noticed when she returned to the paper was that not much had changed in the years she'd been gone. She wanted to do personal stories. Kvist wanted to travel and have the paper foot the bill. Only Jakob, who had been a trainee back then, showed the drive she'd had when she began as a reporter in Roskilde. But he was covering gang warfare, so he had more than enough to do.

"The police raided Christiania again last night," he said, when it was his turn to report. "Hashish, cash, gold bars. The value of what they confiscated is being totaled up this morning, and I'm in contact with the special operations leader."

Camilla leaned back and listened as Kvist spoke with renewed energy about flying to Bristol and seeing what he could dig up. She shook her head when Høyer told him to take it up with the international editor; they might have a man free in London, and it would be cheaper to send him out.

"The flight isn't over five hundred eighty-five kroners, round-trip," Kvist said. "That's less than a train ticket from London."

"Maybe." Høyer didn't even bother to look up. "But he wouldn't have extra travel expenses on Crime's budget."

Camilla left as soon as the meeting broke up. She was standing outside Høyer's office when he came down the hallway. "It's a damn good story for Sunday, a feature on the Danish woman," she said, before he reached the door. "We need to get over to Jutland, see where she comes from, find out who she was, why she disappeared. Find out what happened. Did you know she was married to a pastor before she disappeared?"

Høyer sat down and pointed to the chair across his desk. "I don't have the staff to do this type of story anymore. You know that, even though you've been gone. We're battling the online edition all the time; I have to deliver to justify our existence. This type of background story takes up resources I don't even have."

"That may be. But you'll lose ground if you give up the good stories."

"They take too much time."

"Then I'll do it myself," she said. "I'll do it on the weekend."

Høyer shook his head, though with a hint of a smile. "As long as you know I can't give you travel expenses; no meals or anything." He was back to looking like a man under pressure.

"All expenses are on me." Ironic, she added, that since she was no longer a freelance journalist, now that she was an actual employee, he, of course, wouldn't have to pay for the articles she delivered.

Camilla left the office feeling she had prostituted herself. But she simply couldn't let go of the story. And it was possible that her determination came from wanting to satisfy her own curiosity. On the other hand, she probably wasn't the only one interested in uncovering the woman's background. But she'd said nothing about the inside source she might be able to use if the background story was too thin.

On her way back to the office, she felt the old familiar tug of excitement. She was going out in the field, and she was so excited about the story that she caught herself smiling, despite having two articles by Kvist to edit and an email to answer from a freelancer in southern Zealand who was in an uproar because she'd changed the headline of his article. "Pushers Have Captured Lolland," he had called it, and an irritated Camilla wrote that the damn pushers have always been there, that he had to come up with something better. Now he was sore, and she had to smooth things over. But *Morgenavisen* wasn't going to be ridiculed for seemingly believing that hashish had first showed up in the Danish South Sea islands in 2014.

13

Louise had cleared off Eik's desk to ready it for Olle, who was moving in to help her on the case. She piled old case files on the shelves lining the rear wall of the office, then she folded up Charlie's blanket and laid it out in the hall for Eik to take back to his old office. Before she could text Olle to say that everything was ready for him, the telephone rang.

"Have you had a look at what I sent over?" Davies sounded excited.

She pulled her office chair out and sat down, and as she started her computer she said, "What exactly is it we're talking about?"

"The bank statement! We discovered that the deposits made into Sofie Parker's account all came from Danish account holders. It's obvious from the account numbers. We're still working on access to the Swiss account, and we're in touch with Europol as well."

"Interesting." Louise asked if Eurojust had issued an international letter of request. When another EU country originated the request for information from a foreign bank, a Danish court order wasn't sufficient to gain access.

"It's done," he said. "I sent the statement listing the account's movements to you. It's attached to the email, along with the international court order. We're hoping you can help us find out who made the deposits."

Louise opened the attached file, which was a scanned copy of the bank statement from the Zurich bank. Curious now, she leaned forward. "The amounts are very different," she said. One of the deposits was around twenty thousand euros, seven times larger than the next deposit. "Did you ask the husband what she might have been paid for?"

"He still insists he knows nothing about the account. And as he explained, his wife wasn't particularly open about her past. All he knows is that she grew up in Jutland, and both her parents are dead. She told him her father died shortly after her confirmation, her mother about six months before they met. He said his wife was an only child, and I must say he sounded convincing when he claimed she had no connections to her homeland. And he knows nothing about her disappearance from a boat outside Rome."

"But she must have had contact with someone here in Denmark." Louise made copies of all the bank papers.

"We've confiscated her computer and cell phone, and our tech people have just picked up his stationary computer at his business to have a look. Maybe something there will connect him to the Zurich bank. Unfortunately, it will be several days before we hear from them."

Louise glanced over the deposits. "No matter what, you should investigate what's on his computer," she mumbled. She couldn't understand why the English police hadn't confiscated the husband's hard drive and looked closely at all the correspondence and websites he had visited.

"We're going through his accounts," Davies reassured her. "We're looking for any irregularities. Perhaps his wife withdrew money and sent it to Denmark, to deposit in her own account."

"Isn't England one of the most tax-friendly countries? If they wanted to avoid taxes, wouldn't it make more sense to use an English tax shelter instead of sending the money over here, where the taxes are so high?"

"We're not thinking in terms of taxes," Davies said. "We suspect she might have been pilfering her husband's account. She might have been planning to disappear again."

Aha, Louise thought, letting the idea sink in.

"We still lack a motive for the murder," Davies reminded her.

"The deposits here aren't from a single Danish bank. It seems that several are involved. I'll look into this."

"Good. If they aren't her own accounts, we are, of course, interested in the identities of the people who deposited the money."

"I would think so," Louise said, hoping he could sense her smile. Of course, it would be nice to know who was depositing the money. She felt a devilish satisfaction at the thought that at least it wasn't Eik who had given his missing girlfriend all that money. If he had been making foreign deposits, the bank employee would have said so.

"I'll get back to you as soon as we contact the banks,"

she said, as Olle walked in carrying case files under his arm and a cup of coffee in his hand. "You'll hear from me," she promised.

She smiled at Olle Svensson and welcomed him to the Special Search Agency, a small unit in the Search Department. Under Louise's direction, the agency investigated the missing persons cases where illegalities were suspected.

"I hope you're not in the middle of another case, because we've just received a list of banks we need to contact." She handed him the printout.

"At your service," Olle said, reading the list as he walked over to his chair.

Eik's chair, Louise thought. She hadn't seen him this morning, didn't even know if he had come in. Maybe she should stroll by Rønholt's office? Hell no! He had to take care of himself.

"What about if we just divide them up?" Olle suggested. "That would be six apiece. I'll start from the bottom, you start from the top."

"Great."

"And I'm assuming we mail the court order and account numbers along with our requests, and wait for the banks to call us? Usually they want confirmation that they're giving out information to the police."

"Give them a call when you send out the requests, just to be sure. So they don't keep us waiting. We don't want these to end up with someone on vacation."

A few people in the department always made excuses, said they were waiting on a call when they were caught taking a case too lightly, but that didn't work in her agency.

"Of course," Olle said, in a way that revealed he wasn't one of those slackers.

"The account is part of the estate of Susanne Hjort Madsen," the Nordea employee said.

Louise wrote down the bank customer's personal identification number (PIN). She was told that the estate would end up with Susanne Madsen's husband, just as soon as the tax authorities were finished.

"And how much is in the account?" Louise asked.

"When the account was closed, it contained about thirty-eight thousand kroners."

"Which means that eight thousand is a large amount to transfer," Louise said. She then asked to have the bank statement mailed to her.

"The money was transferred a week before the customer's death," the woman on the phone said, "and the husband was aware of the money transfer. It was a joint account. The transfer was made through our foreign subsidiary, but there were sufficient funds in the account, and we had no suspicion of wrongdoing."

"There probably hasn't been," Louise assured her. "We're simply interested in clarifying the relationship between the deceased and whoever received the money."

She hung up and checked the CPR number. The family lived in Lynge. The widower was sixty-seven years old, five years older than his deceased wife.

Across the desk, Olle hung up. "An estate," he said, when Louise gave him a questioning look. "Christine Løvtoft, forty years old. Died just under ten months ago. She transferred one hundred thousand a few weeks before her death. I have her husband's name. They had separate accounts, and he didn't have access to hers."

After Louise had gone through four of the names, she raised an eyebrow at Olle. "Is there anyone alive on your list?"

He looked down at the paper and nodded. "Two of them. How about yours?"

She shook her head and said she was still waiting on the last two.

An employee at Sparekassen Sjælland reported that the account in question belonged to Kurt Melvang, an eighty-eight-year-old man living in a nursing home in Bispebjerg. "It looks like the account is being handled by a third party," the man at the bank said. Louise had already punched in the elderly man's CPR number and found the address. Rønnevang Nursing Home.

"For two of the names on my list, the survivor is dead, too, but the deaths occurred almost a year apart with one of them, and here"—Olle pointed at his monitor—"they were seven months apart."

Someone knocked on the door. Louise watched Eik take a step into the room before noticing Olle sitting in his chair. An awkward moment followed before Olle glanced at Louise for some sign. She heard Charlie sniffing his blanket outside.

"You're down in Olle's office now," Louise said. She glanced at Eik; he didn't look hungover or suffering from lack of sleep, though it had been very late when she threw him out. In fact, he looked like himself. A slightly distant version of himself. He nodded quickly and said he was fine with that. He closed the door behind him.

"Is something going on here?" Olle asked. Fortunately Louise's telephone rang at that moment. When she hung up, she told him that another account was part of an estate.

"Why are the people transferring money into the account dying?" she asked.

"Maybe the money is used for burials?" Olle said. "Or upkeep of grave sites?"

Louise nodded. "Expenses in connection with closing estates? But why a Swiss account for things like that? We need to find out what they paid for."

14

They parked on Tuborgvej and walked up the uneven flagstones to Rønnevang Nursing Home, a three-story redbrick building. There were patches of snow on the left side of the building, in a small sunny niche with benches, a few tables, and shrubbery.

It was quiet when they stepped onto the entryway's flecked terrazzo floor. The foyer was light and spacious, open all the way up to the ridge beam, exposing both upper floors. Galleries wrapped around the floors, all the room doors were visible. Green plants dangled over the railing at intervals. They stood for a moment and looked around, but there was no one in sight. Louise walked over and pressed the elevator button.

The second floor was a chaos of service activity. Coffee cups and lunch plates were piled onto wheeled carts just outside the elevator doors, and a young woman wearing a headscarf stood at a sink down the hallway.

She was sorting out dirty silverware under the running faucet, and she seemed friendly as they approached. "Hi. I just work in the kitchen, but Lis is coming."

She nodded toward a woman with short, curly hair bustling around the corner, a set of keys in her hand.

"Police," Louise said, as she stepped forward. "May we have a moment?"

Not really, the woman's expression told them, but she stopped anyway. "Of course, what can I help you with?"

"We'd like to speak with Kurt Melvang," Louise said. "Do you know where we can find him?"

"He's usually in the TV room with the others during morning coffee, but I don't think I saw him down there today. He's in room sixty-four, down the hallway. What's this all about?"

"Sorry, but I can't say," Louise said. Another staff member came along, watching in obvious curiosity from behind one of the wheeled carts.

"You should know that Kurt suffers from senile dementia. It might be a bit difficult to have a conversation with him."

"That's true," the other staff member said, "but he can be clearheaded at times, and alert. I'm his contact person; let's see if we can find him. Follow me."

Farther down the hallway, several residents were sitting at a table drinking coffee; some were playing cards, some napping. A large TV on the wall was turned on. "Has anyone seen Kurt?" the staff member asked.

"He's down with Inger," one of the residents said. "They don't want to share their cake with us."

"Oh, here he comes now," the staff member said, nodding toward a man bent over at the waist, pushing a walker. "Kurt, can we have a minute?"

The man stopped at the mention of his name and looked around in seeming confusion. Louise and Olle followed her over to him and stood discreetly behind her.

"I have to get to school here, now get out of my way," Kurt said. Just before ramming into his contact person, she grabbed hold of him; the staff was used to this sort of thing.

"Yes, let's go," she said. "We'll go with you."

Louise and Olle followed them to a nearby door. The woman told him that two policemen had come by and wanted to talk to him, then she joked around a bit with him, asking if he'd been getting into any trouble.

"Yeah, dig around a little bit, you'll find something." He spoke lightly, a complete turnaround from his tone a few moments earlier.

The woman left, and Kurt Melvang slowly turned and dumped himself into his chair. "You come here to put me in the slammer?" he said, still joking around. His eyes were moist.

"Not this time," Olle said. "We're here to talk to you about the sixty-five thousand kroners you transferred to a Swiss bank account."

"Ehhhhh," the old man sneered, irritated with them now.

"Don't misunderstand," Louise was quick to say. "We're not here to butt into your private affairs, but the person who received the money has been killed, that's why we're interested in knowing what she..."

The man struggled to get out of his chair, and before she or Olle could react, he had unbuttoned his pants and let them fall to his ankles.

Not knowing quite what to do, Louise said, "I'll get an aide." She hurried out the door.

"Unfortunately, things have been going downhill

rather quickly; his wife died earlier this year," the aide said, after pulling Kurt's pants up and reminding him that he had guests.

Louise sighed. She considered what to do for a moment before asking the aide if she'd heard about a considerable sum of money Kurt Melvang had transferred to a foreign bank account.

She was crossing a line; she knew that, but they weren't going to get anything out of Melvang. The question didn't seem to surprise the aide, though she stuck her hands in her pockets, as if she felt uneasy about being involved in a resident's private life.

"We can't hardly not hear, when his two adult children curse him out," the aide said sheepishly. "They've done it several times. I don't know how much money they talked about, and I don't know what he donated the money to, but they're mad at him for giving their inheritance away."

She pulled her shoulders up a bit. "This type of conflict shows up once in a while, when relatives realize they're not going to inherit what they thought they would. It's always very uncomfortable, but we never get involved in that type of family business."

"Donations," Louise said, after walking out of the nursing home. The sliding door closed behind them. "That explains why there's a big difference in the amounts of the transfers."

Olle got into the car. "Donations for what?"

"That's what we have to find out. Do you have the address of the man up in Birkerød?"

❧

The traffic was very light as they drove in silence up Kongevejen. It wasn't so much the donations that dominated Louise's thoughts. Mostly it was Eik and her frustration about how he dropped everything and ran off the moment the English police called him.

She didn't know what to think. Of course, anyone would act immediately if something came up in a case concerning a loved one, but how close could you be to someone after eighteen years? Louise couldn't make sense of it.

"We don't go all the way to Birkerød," Olle said, breaking into her thoughts. "We need to take the road to Bistrup after passing through Holte."

Olle was easy to get along with. Louise admitted to herself that she'd been too quick to peg him as being so pushy. He was the senior policeman in the Search Department, and once in a while his cheerfulness drove her up a wall. Not to mention that from the first day Louise joined the department, he had flirted with her shamelessly. He'd seemed aggressive. And then there were the drawings. Olle had drawn a cartoon figure of everyone in the department, and she had problems taking a grown man with such a passion seriously. Though she had to admit he drew well.

"It's number four," he said, pointing when the GPS informed them that their destination lay a hundred meters ahead and to the right. Louise parked at the curb and glanced at the house set back from the road.

"The lawn must slope down to the lake," she said, before getting out.

"It has to cost a fortune to live here," Olle said. He slung his lanky body out of the car. "They must have serious money."

"How much was it they paid in?"

"A hundred thousand." He swiped his hair back when the wind caught it.

The black front door opened. The man who appeared looked athletic, with a well-trimmed full beard and bristly white hair standing straight up, not unlike a brush.

"Erik Hald Sørensen," he said. He shook Louise's hand. She recalled a few things about him in her head: sixty-one, widower, wife died about ten months ago. Christine Løvtoft had been much younger than her husband, and the account from which the money had been transferred to Switzerland had been in her name. "Come inside." He stepped to the side.

Louise noticed the deceased wife's coat still hanging on a hook in the hallway, her high, black boots beside a row of men's shoes. They followed him into his living room. Several empty vases stood around, as if the fresh bouquets that once had been part of the room's furnishings had been forgotten. There were numerous signs of feminine influence. A copy of *Eurowoman* lay on the glass table beside the corner sofa and a modern designer blanket. Sørensen seated them on the sofa.

"Can I get you anything?" he asked, standing patiently.

They shook their heads and told him they wouldn't take up much of his time; they just had a few questions for him.

He sat down in the armchair across from them. Photos of him and a woman Louise's age stood on the windowsill. The smiling woman stood behind him, leaning forward slightly with her chin resting on his shoulder. Another photo showed them singing in a large choir, everyone standing in an open area. Louise noted framed vacation shots from the mountains of Norway; one showed them holding hands in a vineyard, mountains sloping in the background.

Sørensen's face fell as he followed Louise's eyes. "I miss her every single day," he said. He managed a modest smile. "I left my first wife for Christine, and I never regretted it a single second, even though my sons won't have anything to do with me now. They can't forgive me for choosing a woman barely older than they were, but you can't control love that way, now, can you?"

Olle shook his head. "No."

"I met her at the clinic." From the way he spoke, Louise sensed he was holding a great sorrow inside, with no one to share it with. "My ex-wife is a doctor, too. We had a medical clinic in Hareskovby, but Vivian left after we divorced. Later, when we found out that Christine had Huntington's, I dropped my practice. I wanted to stay home to take care of her."

For a moment he smiled broadly.

"And it's been ten months since she died?" Olle said, trying to steer the widower onto what they had come to talk about.

"Nine and a half. Christine was the one who got me started singing. I've always liked to sing, but I'd never done anything about it. I was the eldest of three boys, and I was pushed hard to finish my education."

He paused for a moment. "Christine wasn't like that. She felt you should do what you enjoy doing, and she also loved to sing. It was as if she wanted to show me that I could open up to life. We joined a large Nordic choir, and did several tours with them."

Now his smile was distant. "Then came her disease."

He looked at Olle as though he wanted this officer to know what had been taken from him. "Huntington's is a hellish disorder. Her mother had it, too, and Christine knew what to expect."

Louise tried to catch Olle's eye. They needed to get going, but he was leaning back in the sofa, allowing the widower to speak.

"Christine was a cheerful woman who loved life. She loved sex and warmth; it was natural to her. But it all disappeared after the diagnosis. She didn't want me to touch her that way. I didn't care that we couldn't make love anymore, she gave me so much else. But her body began to disgust her. Huntington's is an inherited brain disease that causes tics and muscle contractions, completely out of control. It also changes the patient's personality and behavior, and leads to dementia and total disability. There is no treatment; the patient dies within fifteen years. Christine felt that her body had betrayed her. She was a realist, she said. She'd watched the disorder slowly paralyze her mother's body, saw her rot away in a wheelchair. Until she was unable to do anything for herself."

He looked up.

"Your wife donated some money shortly before her death," Louise said. She felt a great sympathy for the woman's tragic fate, but they had to keep things moving. "Can you tell us what she was supporting?"

The question didn't seem to surprise Sørensen. He looked at Olle. "When you called, you mentioned an amount that was transferred to a foreign account." He shook his head. "I knew she supported several charities, but the truth is, I haven't looked closely at the estate. The executor isn't finished yet, either. Christine inherited a fortune from her mother, and she handled it herself. I've handed it all over to our lawyer, but I can ask him to see how much she transferred."

"That's not necessary," Louise said. "We know how much. What we're interested in is what she was donating to."

"I can't help you with that either, but I'll be happy to take a look and get back to you."

He had sunk in his chair a bit, but now he pulled himself together and slapped his thighs before standing up. "All right, then, I'd better walk Siggy. Otherwise he's going to tear something apart."

Louise had noticed the dog bed by the patio door, and she'd heard a bark when they arrived. She asked about the dog.

"He's out in the utility room. He goes crazy when people stop by; I put him out there so you wouldn't have to put up with it." He smiled wanly and followed them out to the hall.

"Thank you so much for your time," Louise said, even though they'd learned nothing new. "And give us a call if you find out what the donation was for."

"Okay, then, on to the next," Olle said, as Louise pulled out on the broad residential street. "It's down in Karlslunde or Greve. Are you up for it?"

Do we have a choice? Louise thought, as he punched in the address on the GPS.

Winnie Moesgaard led them into the living room. Muted music, light classical, came from the next room. Candles flickered all around.

In the car, Olle had told Louise that Mrs. Moesgaard was seventy-three years old. Her nearly white hair was loosely elegant, and she was wearing a soft skirt with a matching cardigan over a satiny, narrow-collared yellow blouse. Her eyes were red. The music was for her husband, Werner, who was six years older than she. He lay on his deathbed in the bedroom, as Louise and Olle had been told when they called and asked if they could stop by.

Less than two weeks ago, the couple had transferred just over twenty-six thousand kroners to Sofie's account in Switzerland.

"You can say hello," she said. She turned and led them into the bedroom.

"It's the police," she said.

Louise sensed the somber atmosphere. This wasn't necessary, she thought.

A narrow patio door stood near the foot of the bed, giving a view of a long stretch of winter beach, forlorn and frosty. Marram grass swayed, long-legged birds picked around in the sand, but the warm bedroom was quiet.

A vase filled with yellow tulips stood on a night table, and a woman holding a book in her lap sat by the window close to the door. She glanced up when they walked in. Though she looked twenty years younger than Winnie Moesgaard, she could have been her sister. Perhaps a sister-in-law. She nodded tersely and returned to her book.

The terminally ill man was asleep. His breathing was labored, but otherwise everything seemed peaceful. Louise nodded at the woman and smiled before walking back to Olle, who had stayed out in the hall. She wasn't going to stand there staring at a dying man she'd never met. It was simply too private.

Mrs. Moesgaard exchanged a few whispered words with the woman in the chair before leading them back into the living room.

"He has no strength left," she said, blinking a few times while she smiled a bit apologetically. "And we've known for a long time what would happen. It's still difficult to say good-bye to someone you spent most of your life with. We met each other when I was nineteen."

"Of course," Louise said. She prepared herself to listen, since the woman needed to talk, and she sat down and nodded at Olle to do the same.

"But you were interested in the donation," Mrs. Moesgaard said, this time in a stronger voice. She pulled a chair out and sat at the end of the table. "I don't know how I would have managed without the home hospice nurse."

The soft music from the bedroom began again after a short pause. "Unlike Werner, I'm afraid of death. I can't be alone with it, I don't dare. I'm ashamed of that, but I've never seen a dead person."

She glanced at them uneasily until Olle smiled and said that it was nothing at all to be ashamed of. "It's completely natural to feel that death is difficult."

"That's why I was very grateful several months ago, when my husband told me he'd contacted a nurse a close friend had recommended. The friend had lost his wife to cancer, and he'd been very grateful for professional help."

"A home hospice nurse," Louise said. Now she understood who the woman in the bedroom was. She didn't realize home hospice care existed anymore; she'd thought it was something from the past. But she still didn't see the connection with Sofie Parker in England. "So the money transferred was for a nurse to come and sit with your husband on his deathbed?"

"You could put it that way," the woman said. "But it isn't exactly a payment for services. A bill was never sent. We decided ourselves how much to give. You give what you can, or at least an amount you feel is reasonable."

"Is it possible for us to have a few words with the nurse?" Louise asked. "Then we'll have someone to contact in the home hospice service if we need more information."

"Of course, but there isn't anything wrong, is there?"

"Not at all," Olle quickly assured her. "We just need to be able to contact the service. We're lacking information concerning a case we're assisting the English police with."

"I see," Mrs. Moesgaard said. She went in to get the woman.

The nurse joined them in the living room. She had cool hands and an open expression, and she moved with a natural grace. Not that she was transparent, but there was something ethereal about her. It felt comfortable being around her.

"I'm Margit," she said. Mrs. Moesgaard asked her if she'd like a cup of coffee. "Yes, thank you very much."

She turned back to Louise. "You wanted to ask me about something?"

Louise nodded. "We'd like to know if you've seen…"
She thought about what Kurt Melvang's aide had said. "If
heirs ever become offended, perhaps even angry, because
your service receives such large donations? In some cases
even an entire estate has been given away."

"Oh. Well, the fact is I know nothing about this. I'm a
volunteer in the home hospice service; I have nothing to
do with finances."

"Certainly, I understand." Louise asked how long they
usually stayed when called to a deathbed. "Of course, I
realize how difficult it is to generalize; sometimes death
is quick and sometimes not."

"You are so right about that." Margit smiled. "But most
often it takes longer when the person dying is alone and
without a family. They want us to come early, before they
start feeling lonesome and insecure. When the terminally
ill person has relatives around, usually we give the ones
providing care some breathing room. We relieve them at
night, for example."

"I assume there must be some sort of rotation, where
volunteers take shifts?" Louise said. "Or do you stay with
the same person for the most part?"

"We have a duty schedule, but we're shorthanded in
this district, so we always work it out ourselves. It *is* best
if the person dying and the relatives don't have to deal
with too many volunteers, so we do try to arrange it so
only one or two of us can handle an individual case."

Louise nodded. "Could we get the name, address, and
telephone number of the home hospice service, in case we
need to know more?"

"We don't actually have an office. We take turns man-
ning a telephone; you can always contact us that way."

She gave Louise the number and wrote down her name and home address underneath.

"I'm thinking relatives," Olle said, on the way to the car.

"You mean, the killer is one of the relatives?"

"Some of them must be pretty disappointed about their entire inheritance being donated to an organization. You never know how people will react in situations like that."

Louise nodded. That line of reasoning made sense. Given such large donations and the home hospice nurses working for free, it stood to reason that someone must be raking it in. Judging from the Swiss bank statement, this could be where Sofie Parker entered the picture. But she couldn't figure out how some heirs had uncovered her identity.

"In any case," she said, "Ian Davies and his people should investigate this." She was pleased that already, after one day, they could offer a possible motive to the English police.

15

Louise finally caught up to Ian Davies on the phone. "I think we've found something. We'll email you a list of names and contact information."

At first, she had tried the Nailsea Police Station, but he had been out. Then she called Jones, who was also out. She was in the Search Department lounge when Davies finally returned her call. She'd expected he would be happy to hear what she had to tell him, but his reaction was surprisingly brief.

"We'll also send a summary of some interviews we've conducted." It annoyed her when he mumbled something she couldn't understand. "Is this a bad time? Should I call back later?"

"No, no. I'm sorry! It's just because the Parker daughter has disappeared. We've been out looking for her since early this morning."

"Stephanie?" Louise walked over and sat down in the windowsill, worried now. "What happened?"

She had the feeling Davies wasn't alone. A door slammed in the background.

"We brought her in for an interview yesterday evening after you left. In fact, she called us." He sounded preoccupied again.

"And?"

"She told us she saw the man who shot her mother. She'd remembered. She'd been in shock when we first spoke with her, that's understandable."

Louise gestured to Olle to stay when he walked in holding his coffee cup. "Stephanie has disappeared," she said, adding that the daughter had seen the killer. She put her cell phone on speaker and held it up.

"Can she identify him?" Louise asked. "Did she give a description?"

"She agreed to come down to the police station today after school, so we could put together a description and send it out. But she never showed up. We drove out to the house, but her father was the only one there. It looked like someone had gone through her mother's office. We still don't know if anything was taken. We're afraid the perpetrator returned, that he might have been inside the house. He could have taken Stephanie, because he knows she can identify him."

Eik had been standing in the doorway, but he stepped aside when Rønholt stopped out in the hall. Annoyed, Louise shushed them.

"Our entire force is out looking for her, but no one has reported having seen her," Davies said, his voice audible in the room.

She sensed Eik's eyes on her. It bothered her that he and Rønholt were listening.

"Fill me in later," Olle whispered, and he left to give her privacy, but the others didn't take the hint. Louise punched off the speaker and stood by the window with her back to them.

"As I said, we followed up on the donations," she said. She filled him in on the home hospice service and the volunteers working for it. "We suggest you take a closer look at the relatives of dying people who gave most of an inheritance away. And it might be interesting to check the amounts withdrawn from the Swiss account, to find out what they've been used for. But, of course, the first priority is to find the girl. Please keep me informed of any news."

She ended the conversation. Eik was gone when she turned to go back to her office, but Rønholt was waiting for her.

"Take a look at this," he said, handing her a blue sheet of paper. It was a job application.

"Slagelse?"

"Yes. Of course I'll put in a good word for you. I know the police chief down there."

She laid the job application by the coffee machine. "I'm going nowhere. If someone has to leave, talk to Eik." She walked out.

It was almost 5:30 p.m. when Louise, sweaty from ninety minutes of intensive training in the police fitness room, walked up to the department in her workout clothes. She didn't like running in the winter, but she did it anyway. Today, however, it had been easier training on the machines.

She was late. Jonas would soon be home from boarding school. There was an introductory meeting at Frederiksberg High School at eight, and they had to eat before then.

On her way to the office to pick up her bag, she heard a whining sound. For a moment she stood listening before walking slowly down the hall to the door of Olle's old office. Her skin tingled at the sound of Charlie on the other side.

She opened the door while talking to the German shepherd, and he wagged his tail while trotting over to her. The desk was empty, the computer monitor black. Eik's jacket wasn't hanging over the chair. He had left the office without the dog.

For a long moment, she gazed around the office. Then she lifted Charlie's leash off the hook behind the door and took him with her.

Her phone rang as she walked to her car. She was so angry that she almost didn't answer, but then she reminded herself it could be Jonas, who might be home by now. She took the phone out of her pocket; it was her son's number.

"Hi!" She stopped abruptly when she didn't recognize the dry voice or the name of the woman who introduced herself as Bente, who lived on the second floor of their building.

"Your son asked me to call you," the woman said.

"Has something happened?" Louise couldn't control her voice, which sounded like a hoarse whisper.

"Melvin fell down out in the hallway; your son found him. He's doing CPR. You'd better come home."

Louise had reached her car, and now she leaned against the front grille. She felt as if someone had punched her in the gut. Images flew by of Melvin on the steps, maybe after walking Dina in Frederiksberg Gardens. No, it was too dark, she thought. Maybe he'd been down shopping.

"The ambulance is on its way."

"I'm coming," Louise said. She let Charlie hop in back.

16

When Camilla reached Korsør, the pylons of the Great Belt Bridge rose high above the foggy winter landscape. On the slope to the bridge she glanced in the rearview mirror before passing a truck; a BMW was coming up on her as if she were standing still. She swerved back into the right lane. She'd planned on taking the passing lane, zipping over the bridge as fast as possible—she had a fear of heights. Camilla cursed loudly when her car hit the bumps at each pylon. She glanced to her left when she reached the West Bridge; Language Island and its old lighthouse looked ghostly. On the last stretch she drove alongside an IC4 train, and suddenly she was on the island of Fyn.

Terkel Høyer had caved and let her check out the story, as long as she traveled to Jutland on a weekend. But he had steadfastly refused to allow her travel expenses, and she hadn't argued with him. While driving across Fyn toward Sofie Bygmann's small Jutland hometown, she caught herself humming, even when a semi in front of her sprayed gravel on her windshield. It had been ages since she'd hit the road to investigate an intriguing story. It was the type of article Camilla loved to do, though the thought of arriving unannounced to try to convince people to talk also sent a chill or two down her spine.

Her GPS told her to turn right five hundred meters farther ahead, and she slowed down for a moment. A church stood off to the left. White, traditional, and actually quite big, she noticed as she slowly drove by. Big in relation to the size of the town, anyway. For a moment she stopped at a T junction to get her bearings. Left or right? It looked deserted both ways. She turned right when a car behind her honked.

She passed by a grocery store that also functioned as a post office, bakery, and flower shop. She continued past the town's beauty salon, located in a fine-looking white brick building. And suddenly she was out of town.

Farther on, she turned off on a gravel road, backed onto the highway again, and returned to the T junction. She spotted a bicycle shop; the facade and the bicycles in the window looked as if they had been there since Sofie left.

Camilla signaled and parked over by the curb.

The bicycle mechanic, a small man with tousled gray hair and a mustache, stood for a moment in the doorway of the repair shop, drying his hands on an oily rag. He flung the rag down before walking over to the counter. He didn't seem thrilled at the sight of a customer, Camilla thought, before introducing herself.

"I'm from *Morgenavisen*, and I'm very interested in

speaking to someone who knew Sofie Bygmann." She let that hang in the air for a moment, hoping for a reaction, but he didn't respond. "The preacher's wife who disappeared," she added.

Finally, he reacted, but it was difficult for her to interpret. Maybe he was rebuffing her, maybe he was acknowledging that he knew the wife. They stood for a moment without speaking.

"Did you know her?" Camilla said.

The bicycle mechanic pushed his glasses above his forehead and laid his palms on the counter. He nodded as he leaned forward. "Her folks bought her first bicycle here."

Camilla smiled and nodded to encourage him.

"She rode up and down the street here, singing, 'The light works, the light works!' But that's thirty or forty years ago." He shook his head ever so slightly.

"What do you remember from back then?" Camilla said.

"I'm thinking she went to high school in Vejle, or maybe it was business school. My son was in vo tech, sometimes they rode together in the mornings. He had a driver's license; he drove her in."

He paused, as if biting back the memory.

"I'd like to speak with him if I could," she said.

The man's expression changed. Finally he said, "That won't be easy. He died a month short of twenty-one."

Camilla's hands fell to her side. "I'm so sorry."

He just looked at her. Then it seemed as if he decided to accept her condolences. "The grocery man's daughter was Sofie's best friend. Henriette was some years younger, but they hung out a lot together."

He pointed toward town and said she lived in an apartment above the grocery store.

Camilla smiled and thanked him for his time. Then she asked if it was okay to use his name in her article. He nodded. He didn't care.

The bell above the door jingled as she left the shop. The grocery manager's daughter wasn't home, so Camilla went into the store and asked for her. At first the store looked deserted, but to the left, beside the bottle recycler, sat a woman in a tiny open room, a mini post office. She shook her head when Camilla asked if she knew where the manager's daughter was.

Camilla was about to leave when a storage room door opened. A stocky older woman pushed a cart full of wares into the store, mumbling to herself as she wrestled the cart over a small step without spilling anything.

"Excuse me," Camilla said, clearing her throat. The woman in front of her didn't look up, but her lips moved.

"Excuse me," Camilla repeated a bit louder, finally catching the woman's attention.

"Yes?" The woman's voice sounded just service-minded enough not to be clearly dismissive, but it was absolutely not cordial.

"I'm a journalist," Camilla said. Presenting herself as an editor was irrelevant, she'd decided. "I'm writing a story about the preacher's wife, who disappeared several years ago. Did you know her?"

The woman nodded slowly, as if she was thinking that the smart thing might be to keep her mouth shut. "I went to church. Well, I still do, but things changed without a preacher's wife."

"Changed how?"

"When she left him, all the joy in the church disappeared. Everything was different."

"What happened back then?"

The woman shook her head slightly. "Hard to say. There was all that business with her mother. So yeah, it's hard for us to say what happened exactly."

"With her mother? What happened to her?"

The woman peered at Camilla as if she'd just remembered this journalist was an out-of-towner who didn't know all the local stories. "She took seriously ill. She didn't want to keep on living, but the pills she got her hands on didn't work. They did more harm than good, if you get my drift."

Camilla didn't, not exactly, but the woman explained before she could ask. "She died soon after anyway, at the hospital, and then Sofie disappeared. These days you'd probably say she was depressed. Back then, no one really supported her, or we just didn't know how bad a shape she was in. I don't think her husband understood just how hard she was grieving, either, though he must've been used to that sort of thing."

She cleared her throat noisily. "But now I see in the paper she didn't kill herself. That's likely what most people thought happened."

"No," Camilla said, "she'd been living in England. And she was murdered."

The woman nodded and straightened out her blouse. "I feel sorry for the preacher. He doesn't deserve all that business coming out again."

The cold wind bit into Camilla's cheeks out on the sidewalk. The shutters on a beat-up old hotdog wagon across the street rattled, and a bus headed for Vejle drove by, splashing water on her boots before she could step back. She stood for a moment; should she visit the preacher now, or wait until she'd spoken with more people?

Her cell phone rang. *Terkel Høyer*, she thought instinctively, *calling to hear how things are going…or no, he probably doesn't think he has the resources to even make a call anymore.*

It was Frederik. She said hi, but the second she heard his voice, she knew her husband wasn't calling just to see if she had arrived safely in Jutland.

"I just got an email. I have to go to Los Angeles this week. They want me to meet the other writers and the series producer."

"That's great," Camilla said. "Everything's getting started."

"It's not great at all. I told them I wanted to work from Denmark. That all the meetings had to be on Skype."

"But it's obvious that the other writers need to meet you in person."

"Sure," he said, "and I've got nothing against going over and meeting them. But apparently they expect me to stay."

"I'd think it would be better for all of you to start out together. Also for you. So you're sure they know your thoughts about the story and character development."

He sighed and admitted she was right. "But the least they could have done was give us more time to plan. Now we're going to have to stay at a hotel first, then we'll have to start looking for a nice apartment, or maybe a house out on the coast."

"We?"

"Yes, and you'll have to look around for a place for us to live; I'm going to be working a whole lot for a while. But, of course, it's important to find a place that suits you."

"Honey, hey! I'm not going to Los Angeles, and anyway, what about Markus? We can't just leave him here in boarding school. And what about my job?"

She laughed. Then she realized he was serious. That *they* should move. But that hadn't been part of the deal. Certainly not now, just when she was beginning to enjoy her job at *Morgenavisen*. Besides, it felt surreal talking to Frederik about L.A. while she was in a small, wind-blown village on the edge of the Jutland Bible Belt.

Farther down the sidewalk, a woman around Camilla's age approached pushing a stroller. She stopped at the front door of the apartment above the grocery store. She dug into her pocket for her keys, then she lifted the travel sleeper out and secured the rain cover before pushing the stroller snuggly against the wall.

"I've got to run, we'll have to talk when I get home," Camilla blurted out. She hung up with the sense that this sudden situation would be difficult to handle. She didn't want to be away from Frederik. She *really* didn't want to. But her time as a rich man's housewife was over.

She put her phone on mute and walked over behind the woman, who was opening the front door with a shopping bag under her arm while holding on to her baby's sleeper.

"Let me give you a hand," Camilla said. She held the

door as she introduced herself and asked if she was Henriette, and could she speak with her for a moment?

"You'll have to come up with me," the woman said.

The scent of cinnamon rolls and wet coats filled the stairway. Sofie's old friend led the way up the stairs, struggling with the travel sleeper while Camilla carried the shopping bag. Inside the apartment, Camilla had the impression that the woman lived there alone. No large coats hung in the entryway, and only women's shoes and boots stood on the shoe rack. Also, her name was the only one on the front door's nameplate.

"Go on into the living room," Henriette said, as she unwrapped the homemade woolen scarf from around her neck. Long blond hair fell down her back. Her cheeks were rosy red, and Camilla saw no anger or rejection in her blue eyes.

"I'd like to talk to you about Sofie Bygmann, if that's okay? I'm writing an article about her."

Henriette seemed a bit puzzled about the last name. "She took back her maiden name," Camilla explained. "Did you see her after she left Stig Tåsing?"

The baby slept quietly in the sleeper. Henriette laid it on the double bed in her bedroom, then she walked into the kitchen, tore off a paper towel, and blew her nose. "Left him?"

She returned to the living room and gazed at Camilla for a moment. A hint of a smile lifted a corner of her mouth. "Sofie never left her husband. Stig threw her out because she and the doctor helped her mother die." She gestured for Camilla to sit down on the sofa. "When Sofie disappeared, everybody focused on finding her. Nobody cared about how that asshole treated her."

"What do you mean, helped her mother die?"

"Her mother tried to commit suicide, but she screwed it up. She ended up laying there like a vegetable. We don't know exactly what happened, but the talk was that the doctor and Sofie agreed to help her mother end her life, since that's what she'd wanted. They probably turned up the morphine drip, and the pastor didn't think they had the right to do that."

This surprised Camilla. She straightened up. "The impression I had was that they were the perfect couple; everyone liked her and got along well with the pastor. I've heard nothing about him treating her badly. Was he violent?"

"Violent." Henriette smiled, as if the thought was absurd. "Not really, he just refused to bury her mother because she decided to end her own life. Or tried to, anyway. And because the doctor and Sofie helped her take the last step."

"Can pastors really refuse?" That also surprised Camilla. She knew of several cases where pastors refused to bury suicides, but the clergymen were from free churches, those not funded by taxpayers like the mainstream houses of worship, if she remembered right.

Henriette shrugged. "The whole town knows he's sort of a maverick in the church. He won't marry people who were married before, and he won't have anything to do with gays. But he's also just a really nice guy, very well liked. And he was a big shot in the local sports organization."

"Did it end up in court?" Camilla had her notebook out and was taking notes.

Henriette shook her head. "It never got that far, it was only a big deal here in town. He threw her out before anything more happened."

"And what about the doctor?"

"He couldn't prove anything, but he made life hell for her, she had to move away."

A small grunt came over the baby alarm, but Henriette didn't move. The sound disappeared.

"Do you remember the doctor's name?"

Henriette thought for a moment, but then she shook her head. "It was so long ago."

Camilla nodded slowly.

"I think what Sofie couldn't really accept was that her mother couldn't be buried in the churchyard when her own daughter was the pastor's wife. When her husband didn't mind burying the bike mechanic's son, a drunk driver who killed himself and the baker's son in an accident."

She shook her head again. "But I didn't even get a chance to talk to her. All of a sudden she was gone." She stared straight ahead, a sad look on her face. "And the next thing we heard was that she disappeared, down in the Mediterranean."

Stig Tåsing didn't seem particularly surprised when Camilla showed up at the manse. She understood why as they walked into the kitchen.

"Tove down at the grocery called and warned me that a journalist from the capital had shown up, digging into the old story about my wife's disappearance. But it's no shock," he added with a smile, "considering that Sofie has apparently been found."

The pastor's hair was chestnut brown; Camilla suspected that he dyed it. He was tall and stocky, somewhat southern European in appearance due to his brown eyes and full eyelashes.

"I admit I was surprised when the police all of a sudden stood out here in the hall and told me she was the Danish woman shot in England."

"And you haven't been in touch with her since she disappeared?" Camilla said. It had been eighteen years since his wife left him—or he threw her out. What would be the natural reaction after so long a time? she wondered.

He shook his head. "Let's sit down in the living room." He opened a double door into three high-ceilinged rooms.

Though his expression was dark, he seemed more curious than annoyed at Camilla showing up out of the blue. He invited her to sit down, adding that he had just brewed a pot of tea. "Would you like a cup?"

Camilla thanked him. She tried to capture the atmosphere of the room. The furniture was a bit heavy, like heirlooms, and paintings hung from every wall. She guessed that much of it came from the previous pastor, but of course he might have picked it out himself, because it fit the large rooms well.

"Milk?"

She shook her head, and he handed her a large, flowered porcelain cup that looked like it came from an English tea service.

"I don't mind talking to you, but I'd like to read the article before it appears in your newspaper." He waited for her to answer.

Camilla nodded. "Of course." He seemed very straightforward and easy to talk to. She had no trouble seeing him on a soccer field with the town's young boys; it was more difficult envisioning him standing above the congregation in the pulpit. She didn't doubt, however, that his dark, resonant voice was effective inside the church.

She studied him as he slowly stirred his tea. How had Sofie's abandoned husband felt, living in uncertainty all these years, only to be told that his missing wife had been killed in England? Stig and his wife had never been divorced, yet she had married another man. So many questions remained. Camilla tried to prioritize them for her interview, but the one that dominated all others was the first one out of her mouth.

"Why did you refuse to perform the funeral service for your mother-in-law?" She saw at once that the question startled him, so much that he couldn't hide it.

He folded his hands and sat rubbing his thumbs together a moment before looking up. He sent her a thoughtful, appraising look, as if he were considering whether or not to talk about this. Then he nodded slowly.

"I won't deny that I condemn suicide. Or perhaps I should say," he added, as if he were only now checking his feelings on the matter, "that I refuse to accept it as an option. It's a selfish act, one I cannot support here in my church." His voice was deep, as if he wanted to emphasize his point.

He took a sip of tea and looked at Camilla. "It's not an acceptable solution. I strongly believe that God decides when we should die. God alone."

Camilla concentrated on writing his words down verbatim.

"As I understand it, your mother-in-law was very ill. Her pain had become too much for her to stand. Shouldn't we have the right to decide when to die in such cases?"

"How do we know when the decision is well considered? When are people able to judge they're ready to die? Those who commit suicide are only handing down their own unhappiness to their survivors."

His questions weren't posed in anger or with any desire to further discuss them. Camilla had the impression that he was very interested in the subject. "I suggested a memorial ceremony for my wife's mother, but she rejected that idea completely. She wanted the services performed under the auspices of the Church, and I couldn't go along with that. Just as I can't treat individuals in my church differently."

His teacup empty, he glanced at his watch. "I assume the people you've talked to here have told you the services took place in our neighboring town's church?"

Camilla shook her head. A heavy silence fell between them, then he leaned forward and rested his head in his hands for a moment, as if he needed a break. He ran his fingers through his hair and straightened up, his head shaking ever so slightly. "Everyone spoke up. Everyone had an opinion. Everyone thought they knew what happened, because after all, they knew us."

"What *did* happen?" Camilla asked quietly.

Another silence followed. She had the feeling he might stand up and end the interview, but he leaned back in his chair, crossed his legs, folded his hands over his stomach, and took a deep breath.

"What happened was, after we argued, my wife decided, as I said, to have her mother's funeral service in another church. She made several accusations against me and my theology, and it ended up becoming very personal. As conflicts caused by deep sorrow often are."

Camilla nodded. Her parents were still alive, but even though she was a married adult with her own son, Markus, she still feared the day she would lose them. She had almost lost her father several years earlier, after an assault disabled him.

"Sofie was very close to her mother. They spoke together several times a day. The loss was very difficult for her, and she didn't act rationally."

He paused a moment. "I don't know what it was, but in any case she wasn't herself. And two days after the funeral, that morning, she packed her bags and waited in the kitchen for me to come downstairs. She said she was leaving me. She needed to get away. And I admit thinking that she was right. She needed to put her mother's death behind her, but I had absolutely no idea I'd never see her again. I thought she might have plans to borrow somebody's summerhouse, or visit a friend on Zealand."

"Did she have any money?" Camilla had noticed a newspaper on the pastor's desk; the open page showed a photo of Sofie from when she had disappeared. Young, smiling, hair pinned up in a loose knot in back. "To get by on?"

The pastor nodded. "She was going to inherit a lot of money when her mother's estate was settled. Her father had been very successful, he'd started a factory that manufactured valves for pumps used on the big oil platforms. He sold it all when he turned sixty and retired. The family was quite wealthy."

Camilla had barely touched her tea. The doorbell rang, and Tåsing excused himself and walked out in the hallway. He returned shortly after, his expression serious, sad. "I have a visitor I'm going to have to receive."

She stood up at once and gathered her things. A woman was crying, and Camilla picked up fragments of sentences. An accident at work, a fall. Died in the ambulance. Self-conscious now, she pulled her coat off the hook and thanked him for his time. He joined a young woman out in the kitchen; she sat with her back to Camilla, head buried in her hands.

"We can never know when death will arrive," he spoke into her ear. "But it will come when God decides our time on Earth is over."

Chills ran down Camilla's spine as the door closed behind her.

17

February 1996

The voice thundered down at her. "You killed your own mother! You robbed her of life and made yourself the master over life and death."

His anger with Sofie was like a hot cloud surrounding him. His eyes blazed with contempt.

"I didn't kill her. I respected her wishes." She pulled her legs up to her chest.

Sofie had just gotten out of bed and was holding a hot mug of tea where she sat on the corner of the sofa. An empty feeling lay heavily inside her after having cried most of the night. It had been the right decision, but the finality of it and the loss had made her deeply unhappy.

"I'm not asking you to understand," she said. "Well, actually, yes, I am. Please, won't you hold me?" Her voice was small. She felt like she was on the edge of a deep chasm; her sorrow had robbed her of the energy and will to defend herself. She just wanted to explain her actions, and for him to understand. Or at least see things from her side.

"I'll report her to the police," he continued. "I'll report that damned doctor who thinks she can play God."

"No you won't!" Sofie said. "You'll keep her out of this. If you're going to report anybody, report me. I respect people's rights to choose—"

"*You* have no right. *We* have no right to play God in our own or anyone else's life. How could you do this to me? To *us*."

"This isn't about you." Now Sofie was angry. How could she have been so naïve as to think he would understand? "You of all people should be able to show compassion. I believe in death with dignity, and I won't stand for you judging me."

For a second she thought he was going to kill her. He rushed over to the sofa, his dark eyes lit with rage, his voice icy. "You will never talk about this to anyone, ever. I will not accept your voicing an opinion so strongly against everything I stand for and what I preach in church. Jesus died on the cross for us. Was that a dignified or undignified death?"

He jammed one knee on the sofa, his face so close that droplets of spittle spattered her cheeks.

Though she was close to tears, Sofie stared back at him in defiance.

"I can't have a wife who so openly defies God's will," he continued. "What could you possibly have been thinking?"

"I'm no longer your wife." Her voice was flat, and even now, as she was cornered in the sofa and not reacting as she should, filled with defiance and anger and despair and sorrow. She wanted to talk to him about Christian charity and understanding. But she couldn't. She didn't have it in her. She felt as if she were falling. Over the edge of the abyss.

He kept raging at her, but she didn't listen. She thought about her mother and the evening in her apartment when she had emptied her bottle of pills. Alone.

She thought about the suicide note. It was her hand-writing, no doubt about that, yet it was different. A bit shaky, not as firm as usual.

To my beloved daughter.
    I can't go on any longer, I'm asking you to un-derstand and accept and forgive my (selfish) way of saying good-bye to you.
    Good night.

When the police had arrived to check the apartment, after her mother had been taken to the hospital, one of the officers wanted to take the note with him, but Sofie had objected. They took a photocopy of the letter and left the original with her.

"You're my wife for better or worse," he said, biting off his words, "and we agreed to love and honor each other till death do us part." He stood by the window with his back turned defiantly to her.

She was about to say something about the capacity for understanding, but instead she quoted another part of the marriage ritual. "Bear with each other and forgive one another if any of you have a grievance against someone. Forgive as the Lord forgave you."

He whirled around and pointed an accusing finger at her. "Don't you speak the words of God after what you've just done!"

Sofie tried to fight off her sobbing, but it rose out of her like a gusher. Grief from her mother's death, his anger, her sense of being completely alone, but most of all the injustice of being attacked for keeping a promise.

She stood up. "You can't refuse to officiate her funeral service. She lived in this town all her life, she was christened and confirmed in the church. My parents were married in our church. What kind of a person are you?"

"It's no longer your church."

The look he gave her was so cold that she felt her love for him collapse inside her. "You can't do this to her," she whispered. Her hands felt icy.

"You can't do this to me." His voice sounded completely flat, his words might as well have been spoken by a stranger. "Until you regain your senses, you will not set foot in my manse. You will leave, and you will not even *try* to put me in a situation where my congregation can doubt all that I stand for."

He left the room, and a while later, after Sofie pulled herself together and walked into the kitchen, he was gone.

18

S he's the person I'm closest to," Melvin said, pointing to Louise from his hospital bed.

Something tugged at her deep inside. She had spent most of the weekend at the hospital with Jonas, until he had to return to boarding school Sunday evening. To her great relief, her ex-boyfriend Kim had offered to take care of Dina when he heard that Melvin was in the hospital. Kim had given them the dog, and he and Jonas still kept in close touch. He lived in a beautiful half-timbered house on the outskirts of Holbæk, so he had suggested that she drop Dina off on the way to the boarding school in Odsherred.

The drive to Holbæk the previous evening had been long and dark, but she enjoyed spending time with Jonas in the car, just the two of them. And it was good to see Kim. He had a pot of coffee waiting when they arrived. It had felt so nice, so familiar to sit in the low-ceilinged living room, listening to Jonas and Kim talk about dogs, school, and a sea kayak jaunt that Kim was trying to convince her son to go on.

"It's up in Sweden, and we'll be gone only a few days," Kim had said. Louise smiled and sank farther down into the sofa when Jonas said it was a long time until Easter, you can't plan that kind of stuff so early. What if he got a gig or something? Kim nodded in acknowledgment and asked if Jonas had something going on.

Without Louise really understanding how it happened, Jonas had made a name for himself in the dance music scene. It had begun with some remixes he'd uploaded on YouTube. In no time his music had been shared an incredible number of times, and it hadn't gone unnoticed. His artist name was JoeH, and his first success, "Back to Normal," had been on the Top 100 DJ rankings for a few weeks—something Louise knew only because Camilla's son, Markus, had bombarded Facebook with the news. Jonas would never mention something like that himself, but last year he had been asked to perform on the Apollo stage in the days leading up to the Roskilde Festival. That entire week he had been difficult to bring down to earth. She hadn't even tried, because she was so proud of this young, introverted guy who so early in life had lost his parents, and yet he kicked ass, so much that he was known even outside the country. An online music magazine had recently compared him to the world-famous Swedish DJ Avicii, but Jonas had forced Markus to take the quote off Facebook. It was too braggy.

While sitting in Kim's cozy living room, Louise had almost been able to set aside her anger at Eik. And she had accepted Kim's offer to drive Jonas the rest of the way to Odsherred, which freed her up to return to Copenhagen.

She stepped over to Melvin's bed and took his hand.

He'd been unconscious most of the time in the hospital, but early that morning he had started to come out of it.

Earlier, before anyone really knew how badly Melvin was doing, the neurologist had told Jonas to pat himself on the back, that Melvin Pehrson wouldn't be alive if he hadn't reacted so quickly.

Louise's heart had swollen to twice its size. Her son had just turned sixteen, and he'd saved someone's life. Melvin's life! She had practically crushed Jonas with a hug.

A nurse stood at the foot of Melvin's bed, marking off a checklist in his medical file. "Do you want to be resuscitated in case of cardiac arrest? It happens once in a while during treatment, so you two will have to decide."

Louise couldn't speak for a moment as they looked at Melvin. The left side of his face still drooped from an earlier stroke. Suddenly he looked tiny in the white hospital bed. And old, Louise thought. He was seventy-eight, and he'd already made it clear that he hoped to God he didn't get too old to take care of himself. He so much wanted to keep living in his apartment, to not have to go to a nursing home.

Melvin took her hand. He tried but failed to turn his head.

"Louise's son is the reason I know how to answer that." Melvin's voice was weak, and it trembled somewhat. But his eyes were smiling. "If he hadn't found me, I wouldn't be here today. That would've been that. But now I know how happy I am to still be around, so I want everything possible done to keep me around if the ticker goes out again. I'd thought I'd done it all, but I'm not ready to check out yet."

The nurse made a mark without looking up. "Do you have any allergies?" she asked.

Louise had to step back. For a moment she feared the years were turning her into a weepy old aunt, but then she thought about all the levels of emotional pressure she'd been under lately. The broken relationship with Eik. And now Melvin in the hospital. Louise hadn't had time to process it all.

Someone knocked quietly on the door. A gray-haired woman cautiously stuck her head in the room. Her face was pale and serious as she peered at the bed and then recognized the patient.

"Well, I'll be!" Melvin seemed truly surprised and a bit self-conscious as the woman approached his bed. "You're here?"

Mrs. Milling took off her gloves. "You gave us quite a turn. Don't do it again."

Melvin smiled at her and nodded. "I'll try not to." Grete Milling clearly wasn't going to be doing any light bantering. Even though the immediate danger had passed, her face still showed signs of shock. She shook her head and stroked his cheek.

"Thank you for calling," she said to Louise. She unbuttoned her long wool coat. They had spoken several times that weekend, and Louise had promised to call her the moment Melvin woke up. The senior lady seemed a bit confused and uncertain, so Louise brought a chair over to Melvin's bed and took her coat for her.

"Sit," she said. "I'll see if I can find a doctor who can tell us what's going to happen now."

It had gone better than Camilla had expected on Monday morning, when she presented her idea for an article on a Swiss suicide clinic to Terkel Høyer.

She sat in the retro-blue chair across from her boss and told him what had happened in Jutland. "Assisted suicide. Sofie and the family's doctor helped her mother kill herself."

Høyer seemed interested. "Did you talk to the family doctor?"

Camilla shook her head. "She left after Sofie disappeared. The pastor made it difficult for her to practice in town after his mother-in-law died. He didn't even try to hide his contempt for what she'd done, either."

"Did he report her to the police?" Høyer pulled his chair closer to Camilla. Earlier she had laid a stack of printouts on his desk, information on assisted suicide, and before their meeting he'd had time to skim the papers.

"No, she was never charged, he couldn't prove anything. But he definitely made things hot for her."

On the drive home, Camilla had realized it wasn't so much Sofie's story that interested her as the dilemma surrounding a person's right to decide when he or she would die. Several years earlier, her own father had been the victim of an ugly assault and had suffered serious brain damage. If his rehabilitation hadn't been successful, he would likely have ended up a vegetable in a hospital bed—how much personal dignity is there in such a life?

"It's so enormously interesting, whether it's okay to help another person die." She was caught up in an enthusiasm she'd thought had disappeared years ago. "There are all the ethical questions, and then there's the problem of being able to judge yourself if it's time to go. I understand the pastor, too. Suicide is wrong. A person committing suicide can cause terrible suffering for the people left behind. It's not permitted to actively be involved in death. But damn it, we *are* involved!"

Høyer tipped his chair back and nodded thoughtfully. "When we help the sick or terminally ill, we're involved in deciding whether someone lives or dies. But the purpose in that is to extend life. When children are prematurely born, we intervene." This was something he knew about; his youngest child, Josefine, was born two months early, and it had been a struggle to keep her alive. "On the other hand, we've chosen limitations on abortion, which you can agree or disagree with. And we can switch off life support."

"Exactly. We're involved already. When we extend lives, it's okay to play God, but when someone suffers and lives in pain, and everyone knows it's not going to change, when this person can be released, our right to play God stops, we condemn it. Or at least we think the ethical questions are too difficult."

She sank in her chair and swept her straight blond hair behind her ears. "It's so interesting."

"Where do you stand? What's your opinion?"

Camilla thought a moment, then shook her head. "I don't know. I'd like to think I could help somebody I loved very much, but I'm afraid I'd be too egotistical. I'd be thinking about my own loss. I don't know if I'm brave enough, either."

She shrugged. "There's a recent case of a woman, a mother of two, who went to Switzerland to commit suicide. The family knew about it, and everybody accepted it. She had a fatal illness that would slowly take her life.

She didn't want a painful, undignified death. I understand that. And I have great sympathy for it. And I can imagine you don't want your relatives and loved ones to see everything you go through."

They both sat for a moment, staring straight ahead in silence.

"But you can't forbid people to take their own lives," Høyer said thoughtfully. "They do it, no matter if God forbids it, or a clergyman condemns their choice. It happens every single day."

"But suicides often put the people around them, their loved ones, in the position of discovering them," Camilla said. "I'm sure that's something a lot of people could do without." She began framing a number of scenarios that would be interesting to include in her article. "Surely many people involved would prefer a suicide in a peaceful and well-controlled environment, not done in loneliness and desperation and maybe even shame. And surely someone wanting to die would like to have his or her loved ones there when it happens? It could be less dramatic, less traumatic, maybe even a good farewell, plus there are those who commit suicide because they're unhappy, not physically ill. Desperate people who feel shame or some sort of inner chaos jump in front of a train, hop out of a skyscraper, hang themselves in a park—"

Høyer raised a hand to stop her. "That's something else. Those are desperate people, unhappy, mentally ill people who don't have a fatal illness. Should these people be able to order a suicide? Bullying, a broken love affair. Where are the limits?" He raised an eyebrow at her.

"I don't know, really I don't. But I could try to find out by going to Switzerland and talking to them. I thought I went to Jutland to track down Sofie Bygmann's past, but this is the story. So if you want to send Ole Kvist to England to cover the killing, go ahead. I'm going to switch directions and concentrate on what might have been the reason for her disappearance. Of course I can't claim that the doctor assisted with the mother's death, not in an article, but I can get into the general subject."

As she was about to leave, he asked, "Which way are the winds blowing politically here regarding assisted suicide?"

"It's not being considered. It's the same with euthanasia. But I'll find out what the arguments are. There's also something shameful about how only those who can afford to travel to Switzerland can commit suicide in peaceful surroundings. Is assisted suicide only for the rich? That doesn't sound right at all." Her head was swimming with angles for her story.

"Good. Set up a meeting with the clinic in Switzerland as soon as possible, and this time the paper is covering your expenses."

"I'm meeting with the director at five o'clock today. My flight leaves a few minutes past noon."

Just before the door closed, she heard Høyer say, "I should've known."

19

Something in Davies's voice set off alarm bells in Louise's head.

She had just turned on her computer and put water on for tea. Charlie was in Eik's office; he could take over caring for the dog when he found time to show up for work. His office looked exactly the way it had Friday afternoon, so she had filled the German shepherd's water bowl and given him a dog biscuit to chew on.

She rolled her chair over to her desk and sat down. Davies's voice was distant and aloof in a way that disturbed her. "I'm calling to inform you that we have arrested Eik Nordstrøm this morning for the murder of Sofie Parker."

She couldn't hold back a short burst of laughter. "What in the world are you talking about?" She nodded distractedly at Olle, who had just walked in and was unpacking himself out of his enormous down coat.

"Yesterday evening Nordstrøm broke into the Parker family home and demanded to see the daughter's room.

That led to a nasty confrontation with Nigel Parker, and we were called in."

Louise was too stunned to speak. The idiot had gone back to England without saying a word? The pain was so bad that her skin crawled. They had lived together for six months, but apparently he didn't trust her enough to share his thoughts with her. And she had no way of knowing what the hell was going on in his head.

"What's more, Mrs. Parker's office has been searched again, though at present we don't know what, if anything, has been taken."

She felt Olle's eyes on her from the other side of the desk. She tried to concentrate and push her own frustrations away for a moment. "But his being over there is hardly a reason for a murder charge. I admit I wasn't aware he'd returned to England, and I'll make sure he doesn't bother you again in your investigation."

"From what you've said, I have to believe you haven't received the latest information from Europol. Late yesterday we learned that Eik Nordstrøm was in Zurich at the time that Sofie Parker opened her Swiss bank account. According to information supplied by a Danish bank, he made withdrawals from the Danish bank on that date. Therefore it's quite probable that he knew about the account."

Olle was at her desk now. He mouthed, *What the hell is going on?* She pressed her lips together and held her breath while her brain raced to process what Davies had said. She felt helpless, blind to what else the English officer knew. She steadied herself and said, "It's very probable that Eik was in Switzerland at the same time as Sofie Parker. They were traveling together before boarding the boat she disappeared from. But that doesn't connect my colleague with the account she opened, and I know for a fact that nothing in his own bank account points to money being deposited from a foreign country."

At once she regretted what she had said. Stupid, telling him she had knowledge of Eik's bank account! The English police didn't need to know they'd had reason to check his bank account. It would be too complicated to explain that they'd been searching for Eik before he showed up in the Nailsea jail. And it certainly wouldn't put him in a better light.

"What's more interesting," Davies continued, as if he hadn't heard her, "is that our techs have finished searching the hard drive of the deceased's computer. I'm looking right now at a printout of several emails."

He paused long enough for Louise to feel the stiffness in her body. She forced her shoulders down and straightened up. Olle's cell phone hummed on his desk; it sounded muffled, as if it were packed in cotton. Louise felt trapped in a bubble where time stood still and sound couldn't really get through to her.

"It seems that Nordstrøm sent several threatening emails to her."

The bubble around her burst. "Now you listen! He hasn't been in contact with Sofie Bygmann since she disappeared in Italy!"

Finally she sensed a crack she could squeeze through. In her mind she was already tearing down his accusations, though she was also enraged at Eik and felt like letting him sail his ship alone.

"That doesn't seem to be the case." It took a moment

for that to sink in for Louise. "The two of them have been in touch by email regularly."

"You're wrong." She sat up straighter, something flickering inside her. "Someone must have hacked his email."

After a moment, Davies asked, "Is this a personal thing for you?"

She stared down at her desk, trying to run through various scenarios for what might have happened.

"We verified both accounts," he continued. "One of them is his work email at National Police Headquarters, the other is his private email. It's certain that he sent the emails the deceased received."

He was holding something back; Louise could hear it. He wasn't going to let her in on all the details. "And when did this email correspondence take place?" She concentrated on controlling her breathing. She needed to calm herself and think clearly. Most of all she wanted to redirect the conversation to Rønholt and wash her hands of the whole case.

"The last email was sent a little over a week before Sofie Parker died. Up to now we only have a temporary summary of what was written, but when it's all been translated and we've read through it, I will forward the emails to you."

After they hung up, Louise stared straight ahead. She tried to recall what she and Eik had been doing a week before Sofie Parker was shot, but nothing came to her. The days were a blur, and she had no idea when he had emailed the woman she hadn't even known was still alive.

She couldn't look at Olle when she stood up and left the office.

"Louise...," he said, but she was already out the door.

Hanne was on the phone when Louise marched through the secretary's office without so much as a glance and barged into Rønholt's office. He was in a meeting with two gray-haired men she recognized, officers from the National Police.

She ignored the two men. "I have to talk to you."

She and Rønholt stepped out of the office, then she towed him into the lounge. "What the hell is going on?" For a moment she feared she would start talking and never be able to stop, but suddenly her thoughts cleared. "Eik has been arrested. Again."

Rønholt raised an eyebrow, but before he could speak she said, "I've just spoken with the English police. They suspect him of murdering Sofie Parker, and it looks like they have a very good case against him."

"Eik didn't kill anyone," he said, with a certainty that caused Louise to regret not redirecting Davies's phone call to his office.

"That may be, or it could also be that we're the ones in the dark. Like I had no idea he's been emailing Sofie Parker for some time now. I didn't know they'd been in touch. And I didn't know he had some reason to send her threatening emails. Not that I know what he threatened her with. Or why. I didn't even know he knew she was alive."

She felt dizzy, thoughts swirling in her head.

Rønholt was standing close to the window in the kitchenette. He leaned back and rested his hands on the countertop. "But they'll have to release him when they hear he has an alibi for the weekend she was shot. You were together, weren't you?"

Louise slowly shook her head as she pieced together her memories of those days. "No. I was visiting my parents in Hvalsø, and he wasn't home when I got back Sunday evening, after driving Jonas to boarding school. It was late. I was asleep when he got in."

Rønholt stared at the floor.

"They're charging him with assault against the husband and breaking and entering," Louise said. "He might even have taken something from Sofie's office; they haven't determined that yet. What the hell is going on? Is there anything else besides that fucking basement room you haven't told me about?"

He shook his head. He still looked calm, but his expression was serious now. "I would be very surprised if Eik actually were in touch with his missing girlfriend. This doesn't sound at all right to me."

"Apparently he sent the last email to her no more than two weeks ago." She had been racking her brain. Some evenings Eik had been sitting in the living room with his computer on his lap when she went to bed. Could he have written the emails then? Or was it late at night after opening a bottle of red wine, even though she was tired and was in bed with a book. Maybe she hadn't noticed if he had occasionally seemed quiet. She didn't know, and she couldn't make sense of it, either, considering all the kissing and sex, and how close they had been during the six months they'd lived together. That he had been writing threatening emails, that something so significant had been happening in his life without her noticing it, made absolutely no sense to her.

"He didn't do it," Rønholt said. He walked over and put a hand on her shoulder. "You know Eik. Of course he didn't kill anyone. But it definitely sounds like he's gotten himself into serious trouble."

"You take over from here," she said, unable to control her emotions now. "Charlie's in Eik's office. You'll have to take care of him. And if there's anyone you feel should be informed about his arrest, do it. His parents, Ulla out in South Harbor. I'm signing out. I'm all done with this." Her throat tightened.

He nodded. A deep furrow cleaved his forehead, and he ran his hand through his thick gray beard. "I'd better call the English police. Did they send us the emails he supposedly wrote?"

Louise shook her head and said Davies would send them immediately after they were translated and read. She didn't want to see them anyway, not at the moment.

Her phone rang; it was her son. Thankful for the interruption, she put the phone to her ear. "Hi, Jonas. Are you on break?"

She almost couldn't understand him. He was crying and speaking so fast that his words flowed together. "I'm sorry," he sobbed. "I'm sorry, I need you to come up here."

20

Damn thing! Camilla pounded the wheel when the GPS for the second time led her onto the wrong entrance ramp. The flight to Zurich had gone quickly, and picking up her rental car had been relatively painless, but the GPS was confused by the various levels of the city and the bridges crossing each other. Right now she was headed in the wrong direction.

The suicide clinic was outside the city. It had moved several times, most recently because several people opposed to assisted suicide had vandalized it after the address had been made public.

When she slowed down to get her bearings, a blaring semi tailgated her. She had to get back to the airport. The semi honked feverishly before pulling up beside her. Camilla ducked and turned off onto the next exit ramp.

Ten minutes later, she was finally headed in the right direction. The clinic was just under an hour away. The roads were cleared of snow even outside the city, and the black asphalt of the road grid spread out before her like a giant web spun onto the white landscape. A thick layer of snow covered roofs of houses and church spires; the city looked like an oversize toy Christmas scene, the surrounding mountains rising up like enormous dikes protecting the city. She savored the view of the snow-covered mountainsides as the roads became narrower. Zurich was visible to one side of the road, and the other side was flanked by occasional warehouses and small industrial buildings.

It had been a lousy Monday morning. Frederik had been busy packing, and he'd planned on surprising her with lunch at Nimb before leaving for the airport and Los Angeles. But her flight was already booked and her appointment at the clinic scheduled, and she'd had to hurry.

Camilla checked the clock on the Punto's dashboard. Frederik was probably checking in now. She slowed after passing a city limits sign, but three hundred meters farther she was already out of the town. He had asked if she could delay her flight to Switzerland until he left, but she'd explained that she couldn't change her appointment with Dr. Sigmundt, who had time to speak with her only today.

"Turn left in two hundred meters," the GPS jabbered.

Dreary buildings with large, empty parking lots appeared when she entered an industrial park. Everyone had gone home. She'd been told she might have to wait until someone had time to talk to her. They had a client that afternoon, and it was impossible to say how long it might take. And another client would be arriving that evening, so she would likely have to settle for an hour's interview at most.

They had explained that people were given however much time they needed. That went for the person dying as well as the person's family. They'd also had a client that morning, and if the process dragged out, the next one would be delayed. Therefore it wasn't easy to schedule an exact time, she'd learned. When a client was dead and after the family said their farewells, the police and a doctor were called in to provide proof that it had been a "free death," the term they apparently used instead of assisted suicide.

Camilla neared a residential area, and she spotted the hotel where she was to wait. They'd mentioned an Italian restaurant close by if she got hungry while waiting. Food was the last thing she had on her mind, though.

Frederik hadn't been angry when she left. *If only he had been*, she thought, as she pulled into the hotel parking lot. He tried to hide his disappointment after realizing they wouldn't have time together before he left; that made her feel worse than anger would have. He wouldn't be home for at least two weeks.

Maybe she should have waited, but her opportunity was here and now. Sofie Bygmann had aroused her curiosity, and she wanted to understand her. Or no, not actually understand, Camilla mumbled as she parked. She already understood her. Of course Sofie had wanted to help her mother; it was her wish. But Camilla wanted to learn about the clinic's procedure when someone had decided to die.

She was fired up, and it had been a hell of a long time since she'd felt that way about an article. The freelance work she'd done in Roskilde the past year focused mostly on subjects of local interest—pony shows, anniversaries, business portraits, events in the town. Usually she handed in only a few short articles a week, and when she took a good long look in the mirror, she knew very well she was doing it only to maintain a portion of self-respect. She hadn't wanted to be only a rich man's full-time house-wife.

But now she was back, and unfortunately the price she had to pay was saying good-bye to her husband in a decent manner. They could survive that. She was certain that Frederik also had stood in front of the mirror and stared into his own eyes, and he'd decided that being a rich man's son and running his father's business, a job he'd never wanted, wasn't enough for him. He was back in the film business, and the joy his work gave him stood out on him like a halo. Of course he felt she also should grab her chance when it came along.

She shut off the engine and sat for a moment, staring into the blue. It was strangely deserted there. Farther down the road stood the large house where someone had just chosen to leave this world. The family might still be inside. Camilla imagined them walking around, packing their things. Or maybe they had already left; the house looked empty. She could see the front door and a window half-hidden by a hedge. Someone would call when Dr. Sigmundt had time for her, she'd been informed.

It was snowing now, and Camilla trotted up to the hotel's main entrance. Inside the foyer, the snowflakes in her hair melted quickly, and a few drops of water crawled under her collar. The lobby was empty, and the restaurant appeared to be closed. A bit bewildered now, she looked around for a moment until a young girl walked up to the reception desk and asked if she could help her.

"Could I get a cup of coffee?"

The girl nodded. "Latte, cappuccino, espresso?"

"Just plain black." She pulled out her credit card after the receptionist opened a door and disappeared. Camilla's phone rang, and a woman said they could see her now at the suicide clinic, if she had arrived.

"I'll be right there," she said. She waited by the door the girl had opened. Five minutes later she still hadn't shown up, and Camilla took a few Swiss francs out of her purse and laid them on the desk. *In case she ever came back*, Camilla thought.

Camilla stood under an overhang for a moment before ringing the doorbell of the two-story house. Quickly she checked to see if her phone was charged—it might be needed to record—and she also made sure she had a pen and notebook. She'd already checked all of this back in the airport. *Nerves*, she thought.

Throughout her many years as a journalist, she had done tons of interviews all over the world, had spoken with people in all sorts of situations and positions. She had interviewed people who had just lost loved ones, she'd even spoken with a voluntary minesweeper in Kosovo who had lost a leg. It wasn't because she suddenly felt unqualified to interview the leader of the suicide clinic. But she was nervous about doing it properly, writing about it so readers would understand those who supported Sofie Bygmann's position. Also, knowing someone had chosen to die inside the house within the last hour or two probably added to her unease. *Sort of a weird situation*, she thought. But beautiful in a way, too, that someone who wanted to end their suffering had been allowed to do so.

She stepped outside. Snowflakes landed on her shoulders and coat as she turned and strode back up to the door. Before she could press the doorbell, the door opened to a tall, broad-shouldered man with neat salt-and-pepper hair, a pair of stylish eyeglasses pushed up above his forehead.

"Camilla Lind, I presume? I hope you've had a comfortable flight from Copenhagen?"

They had spoken on the phone the day before, and the conversation had been odd. When she'd finally gotten through to Dr. Sigmundt, he had been dismissive at first. He told her to contact the clinic's representatives in Denmark. He couldn't speak with journalists on such short notice. His calendar was full, and besides, he would soon be leaving the country on a long trip. In other words, he would be unavailable until late spring.

But Camilla had ignored all his objections. She talked about Sofie, who had helped her mother die several years earlier, Sofie's husband's attitude, and the breakup that followed their dispute. She had been every bit as insistent as he had been dismissive.

"Now the woman's dead," she'd said. "And I would very much like to show our readers what caused Sofie Bygmann to leave Denmark. I would also like to take advantage of all the attention on her murder to focus on assisted suicide, which is illegal in Denmark. The authorities here oppose it, even though seventy percent of the Danish population apparently support euthanasia."

She had done her best to sway him, and she didn't

really know what she'd said that had convinced him to squeeze her into his schedule the next day.

"We have about an hour," he said, after shaking her hand. He exuded calm; he looked relaxed, serene. He knocked on a door, opened it, stuck his head inside, and said something she didn't catch. Then he held the door open for her.

"This is where it takes place," he explained. He introduced her to an older couple who volunteered at the clinic.

"Elin and Werner greet people when they arrive and get them settled in. It could be said that they are the dying person's hosts."

The woman was replacing tea light candles in small holders, and the man smoothed a comforter before spreading a yellow blanket over the recliner bed.

Camilla considered bringing out her notebook, but she decided it wouldn't be necessary. She could remember this room.

It looked like a living room with a bed, plus a table with chairs, a sofa, and a high-backed armchair. Christmas decorations lay scattered around, even though it was well into January. Small elves, a team of reindeer. A small crib and bands of angels. Camilla remembered hearing that Christmas decorations in this part of Europe traditionally weren't taken away until after Easter—in other words, it wasn't a sign of a careless staff. She took note of the yellow walls, the paintings, a CD player on a small bureau. Books, magazines.

"It's up to the people dying if they want to lie in bed or sit on the sofa or an armchair," the doctor said. "Their conditions can vary widely. Some prefer to sit up, but most would rather lie down, because they simply fall asleep after drinking the lethal dosage."

His guileless manner suggested that fear or anxiety about death was completely foreign inside the clinic. Camilla nodded and said she was ready to move on.

"Nowadays I spend all my time doing paperwork—there's a mountain of it involved with every death. But down here, the dying person is greeted and settled in to the room you've just seen. We have another room nearly identical to it, sometimes it's also in use. My office is upstairs."

They walked down the hallway toward the stairs. The floor tiles were dark, and nature photographs in small, dark frames adorned the walls. Nothing in the house gave the impression of it being a hospice or private hospital. It felt like a home to Camilla, one that someone had just moved out of without taking anything along.

His office was in the gable end of the house. A large window stretched across the entire wall. The sunlit room was filled with loose-leaf binders, journals, and stacks of thick folders. An old IBM computer stood on the desk beside a typewriter—it had been ages since she'd seen one of those.

"Please, have a seat," he said, and turned to the door when Elin walked in with a thermos and two cups.

Camilla had just brought her notebook out when Dr. Sigmundt leaned forward and asked what had happened to the Danish woman who had been killed. He looked concerned. "I don't know, of course, if Sofie Bygmann is a common name in Denmark. But a woman with that name worked for us once. I truly hope she's not the victim."

She put the notebook down and stared at him. "A Sofie Bygmann worked here at the clinic?"

"Yes, many years ago, shortly after we started. She showed up unannounced at my office in Zurich. It was a late afternoon, I remember, the day before my daughter's birthday, and my wife was angry because I couldn't come. The whole family was there to celebrate. But we were expecting a couple from England, and the clinic was very new, we had only a few volunteers. I had to be there. Sofie offered to help, she wanted to work as a volunteer, and the timing couldn't have been better. At first she couldn't be there alone, of course, but I began training her at once. Besides all the practical details, someone has to make sure the terminally ill person doesn't feel alone, if there's no family there. And Sofie was extremely good at that."

"I had no idea she'd worked here," Camilla said.

He pulled open a drawer and brought out a photo of Sofie as a young woman. Her hair was up in a bun; the end of the pencil stuck through it was visible. She was shielding her eyes from the sun and smiling at the camera. A tiny baby lay on her arm.

"Is that her?" He sounded hesitant, pensive.

It was Sofie, Camilla was certain, but she studied the photo a few seconds before nodding. His expression fell, and he turned and gazed out the window while absorbing the grim news.

"She worked here until the little one was two or three years old, but we kept in touch with each other after she left." His wistfulness disappeared. "I even received a Christmas card from her in December."

"Is this her daughter?" Camilla asked. She felt she was being meddlesome, but he simply nodded.

"It turned out she was pregnant when she arrived," he said, his meek smile fatherly yet lenient. "She was more surprised than anyone when she realized why she was beginning to bulge. We have an apartment for guests over our garage at home, so she moved in there. My wife took care of the baby when Sofie was at the clinic. She was very well liked, and the families were always pleased with her. Once in a while people come back to us. For example, one woman was with her husband when he was dying. A year later she came down with a fatal illness and chose to return. It was touching to see how happy she was when she learned that Sofie would be sitting with her."

"So what made Sofie leave?"

He sat for a while and looked out the window again. Snow had turned to sleet.

"I don't really know. I think it was just time for her to move on. She'd inherited quite a bit of money from her parents, and she looked on her time here as a sort of leave of absence. We're so pleased that volunteers spend their time and energy helping us. No one has to stay any certain length of time here, though of course we can't suddenly be without help. Sofie's daughter was old enough for her to travel fairly easily, too."

Camilla nodded. Another piece of the puzzle surrounding Sofie's disappearance was in place now. This was where she lived in the years between Rome and England.

"Elin and Werner also worked at the clinic back then. Our organization relies on many strong people, both those who make sure everything operates smoothly, and those who take care of the administrative details. As I said, every single death requires a lot of work."

"Could you elaborate on that?"

"Do you want me to go through the whole process, or just what takes place here at the clinic?" He looked dejected again as he fidgeted with Sofie's photo.

"The whole process, if you would. I'd also like to know how you decide who gets to come here. Can anybody who is tired of life contact you and set up an appointment?"

He sighed, but though he obviously had answered that question countless times, he didn't seem annoyed. "Not everyone is approved; far from it. We're not here to kill people. Our doctor evaluates every single application, and, of course, it's not enough to simply be tired of life. Our country's laws must be obeyed. We are here to help people who have very good reasons to leave this world. We give them a dignified death."

"The ones approved are in extreme pain, or have some terrible fatal illness that robs them of their dignity, or soon will, is that right?"

"They must be diagnosed with a fatal illness before we can help them. We also have to be certain it's what they want, and that they're in their right minds when they decide." He straightened up and stuck the photo back in his desk drawer, then pushed an information sheet over to Camilla.

"First they enroll," he said. "That costs about five hundred Swiss francs. We have to be convinced that people are serious when they contact us. Then they have to send an application in, with a copy of their medical records, birth certificate, proof of residency, and a valid passport, to make sure the person is who he or she claims to be. After that, they pay a deposit of four thousand Swiss francs. This is returned if they aren't approved."

Camilla nodded and wrote everything down.

"We handle all the formalities involving the local authorities here in Switzerland. Those who apply aren't involved in that. But this administrative work is expensive. Also there are things to be taken care of after the death."

She asked him to wait a moment while she brought out her phone; she wanted to record him to make sure she got everything. "And when everything is approved, what happens next?"

"Before applicants arrive, we ask them to write two personal letters. One about their lives, their life histories, a little bit about who they are, and the other about their illness and how it has progressed. And when we have the letters and the doctor's approval, they make the final payment of nine thousand Swiss francs. Then we set a date."

"So at that point everything has been planned down to the smallest detail?"

He nodded. "But once in a while we have to change to an earlier date, if the client's condition worsens."

"Do they arrive on the day of the suicide?" Camilla could hardly imagine how the time leading up to the day must be for those about to die.

"Usually they come three or four days in advance. But some choose to wait until the day before. It varies, depending on the client's situation and wishes. They know in advance what time they should arrive. If a person comes alone, we can arrange for them to be picked up. Once in a while a contact accompanies them, usually someone who has been involved before and knows the process. Elin and Werner greet them, get them settled in, and then wait out in the kitchen while the family says their good-byes. If there is a family."

"Do you also arrange the travel and the hotel?" Camilla felt uncomfortable at the idea of a package tour: a one-way ticket to death. Suicide vacation.

"The client has to arrange for transportation and hotel, at their own expense."

He asked her if she would like a cup of coffee. Camilla shook her head. There was something surrealistic about listening to him explain the details involved in the suicides, while knowing one of their clients would be arriving soon. Clients had to pay over more than thirteen thousand Swiss francs, plus transportation and hotel. Camilla tabulated in her head, doing a quick conversion to Danish kroners. In other words, not everyone could afford an assisted suicide.

"When they arrive, we have papers for them to sign, then the client is asked several times if he or she is certain of their decision. We also ask some very simple questions, such as, do you know your name, where you are, the date of your birth. The relatives in the room are required to give their names, addresses, and telephone numbers, which we forward on to the police."

Camilla changed her mind and poured herself a cup of coffee.

"When they are ready, a video camera is turned on so the authorities know they have chosen to die. If the family is there, this is when they say good-bye. Sometimes all of them stay there to the end, sometimes only a spouse stays. When people come by themselves, Elin sits with them if they want her to."

"How does it take place?" she asked.

"The terminally ill person drinks a sedative. The lethal dose of sleeping medicine is then ingested within fifteen minutes, to make sure it stays down."

"And they take the lethal medicine themselves?"

He nodded. "That's essential. If they can't drink it, a tube is used. All they have to do is squeeze a soft plastic bag and press the fluid into their body. If they are paralyzed, we have a special gadget where a switch is placed in the mouth, and they bite down on a button that releases the medicine."

He leaned forward in his chair, folded his hands on his desk, and looked straight at Camilla. "We don't kill people. We help sick people die with dignity. Most of them choose to hear music while they fade out. We have a CD player, and they can bring their own music. Some people also bring flowers. Or something that makes them feel secure. Something nice that they're used to. People prepare themselves for this, they look forward to it. They're here because they've made their decision, and death is a relief in comparison to the alternative."

"How long does it take after they drink the medicine?"

"They fall asleep within a minute. After that, it takes about ten minutes. It can vary a bit."

"And then you call the local authorities?"

He shook his head. "No, first the relatives are given all the time they need. Only after they've left the house do we call the police to report we have what we call a free death, or an assisted suicide. The police and a doctor arrive. We have to go through this procedure. Then our undertaker arrives and takes care of the cremation and the urn, and sends the remains home."

"So you take care of that?" She'd imagined the families themselves had to arrange the transportation of the corpse.

He nodded and smiled, as if he'd read her thoughts. "This is one of the things our clients pay for."

The sound of voices came from below. Dr. Sigmundt stood up and apologized for having no more time. Camilla thanked him profusely for meeting her on such short notice. He asked her to keep him informed of any breakthrough in the investigation of Sofie's murder. They walked out to the stairs.

"I'm very sorry to hear it's our Sofie who died," he said. "I had a bad feeling about it when you called. But I feel terrible for her daughter, now that she has no parents."

"So there was no contact with the father?"

"I asked her once, but she didn't want to talk about it. I admit thinking that she probably didn't know who the father was, she never talked about him. Maybe she was one of those women who want a child so much but could never get pregnant."

They passed by the room where the next client was getting ready to leave this world. Low voices mumbled behind the closed door. Just as they were about to say good-bye, a middle-aged woman in a brown wool cardigan opened the door and walked out. She was pale, but she didn't look like someone close to breaking down. Classical music streamed out the doorway, and Camilla heard the sound of weak laughter inside. The woman returned from the kitchen with a bottle of wine and two glasses.

For a moment it seemed she was about to explain, but Dr. Sigmundt simply smiled and stepped aside to let her by. The door was open long enough for Camilla to see a man lying in bed with his face turned to the door. Nothing in his expression led her to think he was afraid about what was going to happen. He was simply waiting for the woman. A younger woman stood beside the bed, and another man sat in the armchair. Candles were lit, the curtains closed.

It looked like a living room furnished with a sickbed. Nothing was sterile or hospital-like about the mood.

"People have very different ideas about their final good-byes. Some people drink a glass of wine together, others want it over with as quickly as possible. Occasionally it's gloomy and depressing, but most of the time it's a relief for the person dying, and the end isn't so sad."

The door closed, and they stood for a moment in silence.

Outside in the snow, Camilla thought about the people who soon would be saying good-bye in there. Then the man would be dead, and in an hour or two the family would be leaving. The hallway would be filled with police, the doctor, and the undertaker, and it would all be over.

Tomorrow or next week, everything would be repeated. Others would be released from their suffering. And relatives would travel home alone.

She crossed the street to her car. Briefly she considered getting something to eat in the hotel, but instead decided to head for the airport. She wanted to go home.

21

Expelled from boarding school. Jonas had been caught with another boy in his class, smoking behind the gymnasium.

No, Louise didn't know that her son smoked. And yes, she knew the school's rules against smoking, she told the vice principal, when she called to ask how a boy could be expelled for a single offense. Jonas had received no warnings; he had never been late to breakfast, had never skipped a class, had never been written up for not having done his homework.

"We have a zero tolerance policy on smoking, drugs, and alcohol" was the answer she received.

Louise had been so flabbergasted that she almost asked if they were mistaking her son for someone else. But then she recalled her conversation with Jonas. He had freely admitted that he'd been caught with a pack of cigarettes from the nearby filling station. He'd sounded shook up, but Louise sensed it was mostly because he felt he'd let her down.

"He will be sent home," the vice principal had said. "He's upstairs in his room packing now."

"I'll pick him up this evening," she'd said, without any idea of the consequences his being expelled would have for the rest of his school year. She would have to see if he could return to his old class.

"He has to leave the school immediately. You have to come now."

"I can't do that. And I can't take all his belongings in my car. He has a bicycle there, too."

"Then you'll have to come get the rest of his things later. We have a lot to consider this coming week. This is a big shock for all of us; a lot of people are upset."

"Listen," she said. "Jonas saved someone's life Friday, doesn't that make any difference? He nearly lost one of the people he is closest to."

She explained how Jonas had resuscitated one of their neighbors. "He was shook up all weekend. Maybe he's even been in shock. You're all aware that he lost both his parents. You could even say it's my fault that he suddenly decided to smoke. I should have kept him home until he'd had time to deal with what happened to him. But Jonas didn't want any absence on his record, and insisted on returning to school. You can't throw him out. Can't you just give him a warning?"

"We have to be consistent in how we treat our pupils," the vice principal said. "Others have been sent home for smoking; it wouldn't look good to make an exception in his case. We all like Jonas very much, he's a great kid. That's why we're so disappointed in his actions."

Louise sensed the vice principal was loosening up a bit, though it still didn't sound like she might change her decision.

"We're having a special meeting this afternoon with the two students' contact teachers, so we'll have to see what happens. My very best advice is for Jonas to immediately write a letter to the principal, to describe the episode with your neighbor and try to convince us why we should keep him on. But I can't promise it will help. Our principal makes these decisions, not me."

Louise cursed after she hung up. She had considered asking Kim to drive up to get him, but now she dropped the idea. This was something she had to go through herself, together with Jonas.

By the time she turned off the freeway at Holbæk to get to Odsherred, the shock was gradually wearing off. She was starting to get good and pissed off. Not at Jonas, but at the school's rigid principles. Of course they had rules and prohibitions, she respected that fully. At the same time, though, she was having doubts about her son staying at the school, even if they permitted him to. Jonas hadn't hit anyone, he hadn't bullied anyone, hadn't stolen anything, which in Louise's book were much more serious offenses than a sixteen-year-old smoking a cigarette because he felt terrible about something.

"No way," she said out loud. This school wasn't for him. If a student who normally behaves himself—takes care of his schoolwork and is a good classmate—can't make a single mistake when he's under considerable pressure, without being punished so severely that he has to leave the school immediately—that school's values were too different from hers. If Jonas had been a troublemaker, a bad student, and a bad classmate, clearly he should be thrown out. But damned if she and Jonas were going to crawl on their knees and beg them to take him back. The only stupid mistake she could see he'd made was not getting farther away to smoke.

On the last stretch of road, she was stuck behind a red Toyota that slowed when they neared the boarding school. Probably the parents of the other boy who broke their smoking rules, she thought.

Her son was standing out in the school's parking lot when she parked beside the red car. Several of his classmates were there to give him a hug and say good-bye to him. Seeing his face made Louise sad. He looked white as a sheet among all his friends.

She said hello to the other boy's father, but the mother ignored her. She strutted over to her son without a glance at Jonas or the others in the group, as if everything was Jonas's fault.

Before Louise reached Jonas, he grabbed his bag and started toward her. A man with unruly curly hair approached her from the other side. Louise hadn't seen him before, but he seemed to be on the verge of tears. He reached for Louise's hand and said he was Jonas's French teacher and that he was terribly sorry for what had happened. He couldn't at all understand how Jonas could have done what he did. And again it was as if her son at the very least had robbed the local bank or committed a serious assault.

"I sincerely hope he'll think about his actions."

Louise almost replied, but instead she studied him for a moment. Was he being ironic behind those curls? But all she saw was a very sad expression.

"I'm sure he will," she said, though mostly she wanted to argue for some sense of fair-mindedness.

"Are we ready?" Jonas said. He'd already thrown his bag into the car and was getting in.

"I'm really sorry," he said, as they headed back toward the freeway. "I feel bad about what I did."

"It *was* dumb," Louise said, "but it wasn't any worse than that."

She felt his eyes on her, but she kept staring straight ahead at the road. There was no reason for him not to feel sorry for acting so dumb, she thought. Even though she felt the school had overreacted.

A while later he asked, "How's Melvin? Have you been in to see him?"

Louise nodded. "He's conscious now, and thanks to you it doesn't look like he's going to have any permanent damage from the heart attack."

"So he's going to be okay?" He was very worried, that was obvious.

"It seems that way. He's tired, but it looks like he's doing fine. It wouldn't surprise me if the hospital released him soon. But he's going to have trouble walking up the stairs to the fourth floor," she added. She asked Jonas where he learned first aid.

"There at boarding school." They had taken a two-day first-aid course before Christmas, he said.

At least the school had been good for something, she thought, though she was still pissed off. Maybe she was being unfair, though. Jonas had been so happy at the school, and the teachers had been so much more committed than last year, back in lower secondary school. She probably just needed to calm down.

"I didn't know you smoked," she said, taking advantage of the mood of openness between them.

"I've only done it a few times." He looked down at his hands, as if he expected to be bawled out or be sternly told to forget about getting a driver's license.

Instead, she asked, "You want to drive by the hospital and see Melvin?" She slipped into the outer lane of the freeway.

"Yeah, thanks." He asked if she'd heard from Eik.

Louise thought shortly about telling him that Eik was in jail in England, but she decided he could do without knowing that for now. He had enough on his plate.

She clenched her teeth. She didn't even know if she would ever see Eik again. In private life, that is. She knew what had come between them, but she still hadn't considered what it meant for their relationship.

"Can you remember Melvin's ward?" she asked, trying to hide how badly she felt that Eik had kept something vitally important a secret from her—that the girlfriend he reported missing eighteen years ago had been alive.

Jonas nodded and said he still had the slip of paper with Melvin's ward and room number written on it.

"Think it over about that letter to the principal," she said an hour later, when she let him off at the hospital.

Louise had cleared the table after dinner and was about to plop down on the sofa when Camilla called. Louise had given Jonas permission to visit a friend from his old school. Maybe she should have grounded him for breaking the boarding school's rules, but when he came home from the hospital, he looked overwhelmingly relieved at not losing another person he was close to. She didn't have the heart to discipline him.

"What are you doing?" Camilla asked.

"I'm down for the count," Louise said.

"How about a beer at Svejk?"

"Now? No way, it's Monday! Today has been totally insane, and I don't feel like talking about it."

"I really need a beer," Camilla said. She explained that she'd just returned from Zurich. "And I know what Sofie Parker did all those years when no one knew where she was."

"I don't give a damn about Sofie Parker! I don't want to hear one more word about her." Louise wasn't sure if her outburst came from Eik's contact with his ex-girlfriend or if she just felt snubbed by Eik's returning to England without her knowing what the hell was going on.

Suddenly the words gushed out of Louise's mouth like a bucket turned upside down. She told Camilla about Eik and his arrest, then about Melvin being hospitalized.

"And now Jonas has been booted out of boarding school for smoking a cigarette," she added.

"Yeah, I know. Markus texted me. He thinks it's *so* unfair."

"It is, too." Louise's heart sank. "I can't understand why they don't take into account what he's just been through."

"I really think you'd like to hear what I found out," Camilla said, her voice even. "Maybe it can help clear things up a bit for you."

Louise sighed. "Yeah, maybe I do need a beer after all. I'll meet you there."

"Where's Frederik?" Louise asked, as they sat in a corner with two tall, foamy Czech beers.

"He flew to Los Angeles to meet the producer and studio people who are making the TV series."

Louise took a sip of beer. What she wanted most was to just sit with her old friend and make small talk. About whatever. "Unbelievable that they kick someone out for one single mistake." She asked if Markus was doing well at boarding school.

Her friend nodded. "He has a girlfriend up there who's suddenly the most important thing in the world. You can't tear him away. He stayed this weekend, too."

Louise smiled. Jonas had mentioned that. His friend and his blond Julia had become inseparable, and Louise sensed it was beginning to wear on her son.

"What the hell is going on with Eik?" Camilla leaned over the table. "They can't charge him with murder!"

Louise stared down at her beer, turning it in her fingers. "Actually I think they can. Especially if he doesn't have a really good explanation for turning up at the crime scene twice now, and why he sent threatening emails to the victim. The police over there also know Eik was with Sofie right before she disappeared, so you can't blame them for putting him at the top of their list."

"Threatening? How?"

Louise shrugged. "Dunno. I didn't even know the two of them had been in contact after she disappeared. In fact, I wasn't even aware that he knew she was alive."

"And when exactly did it happen?" Camilla hadn't even touched her beer. "When did she disappear, I mean."

An image of Eik suddenly popped up in Louise's head, and she felt leaden, sad. His dark, longish hair, blue eyes, sharp cheekbones. It all came at her at once; she'd thought she'd found her man, but now the dead woman had taken him from her.

"Honestly, Camilla. It's just too much for me to talk about now. I feel terrible."

"When exactly is it that no one knows where she was?" Camilla asked, as if she hadn't heard her.

"From the summer of 1996, when she disappeared, until she met Nigel Parker in the spring of 2000."

"I can clarify that. In September '96, Sofie showed up at the suicide clinic in Zurich where I was today. She worked there as a volunteer until late 1999."

"Why was she there?"

"To learn how to take people's lives, is the short version."

Louise didn't understand. She looked at her friend.

"When I looked up her first husband," Camilla said, "the pastor in Jutland, we talked about her mother's suicide. Or attempted suicide, I should say. She tried to kill herself, but ended up as a vegetable in a hospital bed. She didn't die until the local doctor gave her a helping hand."

Louise sat motionless, her hand on the fogged-up beer glass.

"Sofie and her husband had it out," Camilla said. "He refused to bury her mother because of her attempted suicide and the help she finally got in dying. He condemns suicide, he believes only God can decide when our time is up, but Sofie supports the right to choose. I think she felt let down by her husband, big-time. I have to admit, talking with him made me think a lot of things over. It's damn interesting, and it's an important dilemma, too. I can understand her preoccupation, after experiencing the dilemma firsthand. And that must have motivated her to stay in Switzerland."

"Who was the doctor that helped her mother die?"

"I found her name, Else Corneliussen, but she moved away shortly after Sofie's mother died. I've tried to find her, but no one knows where she moved to, and anyway it was a long time ago. It seems the pastor drove her away. Maybe he threatened to report her for euthanasia or accessory to murder."

Louise folded her hands pensively.

"But there's something else," Camilla said. "I think Eik is the father of Sofie's daughter. And if he is, I can damn well understand his going over to be there for her, considering what she's been through. The girl was born six months after Sofie started at the Swiss suicide clinic. That was in March or April of 1997."

Neither of them spoke as they counted the months backward.

"Damn," Louise mumbled. She stared into space for a moment while gathering her thoughts. Eik had a daughter! Now that she thought about it, they did resemble each other. Dark hair, the eyes, the brash attitude. Why didn't she notice it before, and why the hell hadn't that idiot told her?

"Hello, anyone home?" Camilla said.

Louise nodded distractedly, then she excused herself and walked outside to call Rønholt.

"There's something I need to tell you," he said, before she could explain why she was calling so late. "I just read through the correspondence between Eik and Sofie Parker. Apparently the two of them had a child. I thought you should know, because it puts their connection in a different light."

"I know about it. And now you've just confirmed it. What I don't understand is, why didn't he say anything?" Louise shuddered; it was freezing out there. Two young guys in big coats had stepped outside to smoke. They casually checked her out before turning their backs.

"I don't think he knew about it until recently," he continued. "Four months ago, Sofie emailed him and said she wanted to meet. Two weeks went by before he wrote back, he said he wasn't interested, that she didn't exist to him. And that's all he wrote."

"He didn't ask why she suddenly contacted him? And where she'd been all these years?" Louise stepped aside to let the two men go back inside. Through the window she noticed Camilla sitting with her phone in her hand, apparently texting someone.

"No, his answer was short. He wanted nothing to do with her. The fact that he waited two weeks indicates that he thought everything through before answering her. But then she wrote him again, a long email. She didn't blame him for not wanting anything to do with her after so many years, but it wasn't about them. She informed him they had a daughter who needed to meet her father."

Rønholt cleared his throat. "Eik didn't take that well. I'll spare you the details of the email he sent back to her. Let's just say it could be read as brutal and threatening. Sofie then wrote another long email. She grilled him about his life, his work, whether he was married, his family, his apartment—all sorts of things. As if she had to approve him before deciding to allow him contact with his daughter."

"And that pissed Eik off," Louise guessed.

"Yes, you could say that. He demanded to know where they lived, but Sofie wouldn't tell him. She hadn't told her husband about tracking down her daughter's father. She and Nigel Parker had apparently agreed that he would be Stephanie's father, even though she was born before they met. That's what he told the English police, anyway. He'd promised Sofie not to tell Stephanie he wasn't her biological father. At some point Sofie decided to take her daughter to Copenhagen to meet Eik. But of course he didn't want to wait, he wanted to see his daughter immediately."

"Do we know why she suddenly thought it was time for the two of them to meet?" Louise's anger with Eik was slowly seeping away.

"It appears the girl and her stepfather didn't get along. Possibly that's why Sofie thought it would be good for her daughter to meet her biological father. In hopes that they would get along better."

"So it was because of the daughter that Eik dropped everything and flew over there, when he heard that Sofie had been shot," Louise surmised.

"Probably. I've put in a request to talk to him over the phone. Hopefully we'll know more then. Also about why he went over there the second time."

Louise shook her head when Camilla signaled through the window, asking Louise if she wanted her coat brought out to her. The last time she'd seen Eik had been in the Search Department's lounge. He'd seemed distracted and distant since she'd thrown him out of the apartment. She'd believed his distraction came from their breakup, when his thoughts had of course been with his daughter in England.

She'd been so self-centered. But why hadn't he said anything? He could have let her in on the situation.

"I think I know why he went back to England," she said. "He overheard my conversation with Ian Davies, when he told me that Stephanie had disappeared and the police were looking for her, because she'd seen the killer and possibly could identify him. They feared she was in danger, and I think he went over there to protect her. But he can't do that sitting behind bars. Damn!"

For a few moments they mulled over what they had learned.

"You've got to go over there and try to straighten things out," Louise said. "There's a small chance they'll believe you more than they believe him."

"First, I'll see if I can talk to him, hear his side of things. Don't forget, they believe they have good reason to suspect he's guilty of murder. Which is why they aren't being very cooperative."

Louise paced up and down the sidewalk to keep warm. "If they intend to pin this killing on Eik, we're going to have to find out who really killed Sofie Parker." She stepped back to the bar's entrance, which was partially shielded from the wind. "I sent the English police the list of names of those who deposited money in the Swiss account, but I don't know if they've followed that up."

"I doubt it, now that they have Eik," he said, his voice spiritless.

Before hanging up, he told her to look into the case again; he wanted her and Olle to systematically go over the witness statements, to find who had been in contact with the hospice nurses and the service itself. And he would try to get into contact with Eik.

"I've ordered another round," Camilla said, when a half-frozen Louise returned to the table.

"Stephanie *is* Eik's daughter." Louise warmed her hands between her thighs and shivered. Drops of condensation drew stripes on the beer glass in front of her. "Damn it! If only he'd said something."

She summarized what Rønholt had said. "What kind of a woman was she anyway, this Sofie?" she mumbled. "If only he'd never met her!"

"That's not how I see her." Camilla's tone of voice caused Louise to look up. "She seems like a strong woman to me, and brave. She fought for what she believed in, and she paid the price. She deserves respect for that. You can't see all this objectively, you're too involved."

"That may be, but she didn't tell her daughter who her father really was. It's damn hard for me to respect that!" That came out more forcefully than she'd intended.

"Maybe she had her reasons," Camilla pointed out. "It's clear to me she wanted a new life after what happened to her mother. And when she and Eik broke up, she didn't know she was pregnant. Should that stop her from following her plans?"

"She went underground and let him initiate an enormous time-consuming search for her. She'd been missing for years!"

Camilla didn't respond to that. "How much time goes by before someone receives an inheritance?"

Louise shrugged. "I guess it depends on how complicated the estate is, after someone dies. If there are stocks or bonds, back taxes, unknown heirs, and things like that, things that require extra time. But it has to be settled within two years."

"If I understood the pastor in Jutland correctly, Sofie inherited quite a bit of money from her parents. Do you know how much?"

Louise shook her head.

"I think it was her plan all along to go underground," Camilla said. "Most likely she'd received an advance on the inheritance before she left. Imagine her traveling around while waiting for the rest of the inheritance."

Louise shrugged again. "But then why would she start a new life? How tempting is it to live in a small English town, married to a dull optician who doesn't get along with her daughter, when she has enough money to do so much else?"

Camilla slumped down in her chair and drank her beer. Louise had always been fascinated by how her friend could drink a humongous glass of beer as elegantly as if she were sitting at an exclusive New York bar, nipping at a dry martini.

Louise looked out the window at the darkness, the glistening wet asphalt of Smallegade. It was all starting to make sense. It seemed very likely that Sofie had traveled after leaving the pastor. And that she had arranged for her inheritance to be transferred to a Swiss bank account, because she'd already decided to leave Denmark. That fit well with her opening the account back when she met Eik.

Louise wrote a note in her cell phone notepad, to check where and when the inheritance had been paid out.

"So you think she volunteered at the suicide clinic after getting her money?" Louise said.

Camilla nodded. "And she spent the next few years as a volunteer for the organization." She nodded again.

"But why there?" Louise took a few very inelegant slurps of beer.

"I think she felt very strongly about it," Camilla said. "She felt the issue was vitally important. After experiencing how badly it went when her mother tried to kill herself. Sofie supported the right to choose when to die."

Louise nodded thoughtfully. Something that had happened at the suicide clinic in Zurich might have caught up to her now. At any rate, it should be looked at in connection with finding the actual killer.

Oh God! she thought, when the realization suddenly hit her.

"What?" Camilla said, annoyed now at Louise's silence, her look of distraction.

But Louise's thoughts were so far away that she barely heard her friend. Sofie returned to Zurich after disappearing from the boat. Partly because her money was there, but also to work at the suicide clinic, so she could learn how to assist with a suicide, learn all the practical details involved. What if the home hospice nurses were more than just that? What if they were helping people here in Denmark to die? In comfortable surroundings, in their own homes! All of it managed by Sofie Parker from her office in England. They needed to contact the home hospice nurse service again. Her thoughts were swirling as she stood up to pay.

22

At seven thirty the next morning, Louise drove down a January-dark residential street in Hvidovre. She had tried to call the organization several times from home, but all she'd gotten was an answering machine. Before going into Police Headquarters, she drove out to see Margit Østergaard, the woman who had given her the number.

She crept slowly down the street, trying to spot the house number. Finally she parked in front of a small, white, single-story house.

A light shone from inside, though the outside of the house was dark. She got out of her car, straddled the dirty snow piled up against the curb, and walked up to the house.

The sidewalk had been shoveled, and several bird balls hung from trees in the front yard. Louise rang the front doorbell and stared at a wreath with small red berries hanging from a thin nail.

She waited a few moments before ringing again and leaning over to look in the kitchen window. A television appeared to be on in a room behind the kitchen. Maybe the living room, she thought. She rang one more time, this time holding the button down. Maybe Margit Østergaard was in the shower. No one answered.

She called again and once more got the answering machine. She stepped down and walked around the house on a narrow tiled path hugging the wall. Through one of the three windows in back, she noticed the television was still on in the living room. Louise approached the window, then immediately jumped back a step.

A standing lamp glowed beside an armchair. A plate of food had been set on the coffee table. In the middle of the room the home hospice nurse lay facedown on the floor, the back of her head shot off.

Shit shit shit! Louise caught herself wishing that Eik or even Olle were there. She pushed the handle of the terrace door with her elbow. Locked. Now she noticed the bullet hole in the big window, like a spiderweb, the threads sparkling in the light, the midpoint dark, dead. It didn't look like much, compared to the extensive damage the woman had suffered from the shot.

Louise's heart pounded; quickly she glanced around before calling 112, the police emergency number. On autopilot now, she gave the address and name of the victim. Described what she saw and knew: single woman, middle-aged, no obvious signs of break-in, no sign of a struggle in the living room—presumably the perpetrator hadn't been in the house. Then she described the bullet hole in the window and the trauma of the victim visible from where she stood.

After the call, she looked around, her senses alert as her breath hung in the light from the living room. The

sky was turning brighter, though it looked like it might
be one of those days without a real daytime. Clouds
hung heavy in the sky, shrouding everything in a dark
gray haze. Temperatures had risen in the night, a thaw
had begun; it would be difficult to find clear tracks, unfortunately. Maybe it would be a different story when
the techs arrived with their equipment and began fine-
combing the small pathway and the flower bed under
the window.

She hurried back to her car and sat down to wait.
Thoughts ran through her head, all the questions she
would have asked the nurse. Now it was too late. She sank
down in the car seat and pulled the hood of her winter
coat up around her head. She wished someone were with
her.

Louise had expected the female head of Homicide of
the Western District Police to show up with her team,
which is why she was very surprised when Thomas Toft
knocked on the side window of her car. She jerked up and
hurriedly pulled her hood down. It had been a long time
since she'd seen her old colleague from Homicide. She
wondered if he had been transferred to the Glostrup police without her knowing.

"Hi," she said, after she stepped out of the car. She was
about to shake his hand when she noticed her former partner, Lars Jørgensen, and Detective Michael Stig, standing
over by a white Ford. "What in the world are all of you
doing here? The last time I checked, Hvidovre was in the
Western District."

Toft nodded. "When Emergency heard it might be a rifle, they contacted us. It's the third shooting of this kind within the past two months, not counting gang shootings."

Louise was startled. "What?"

Her old colleague nodded again. "The first homicide was our case, and when ballistics showed the same rifle was used in the second homicide, they gave us that one, too."

"And you think Margit Østergaard could be a third victim?" Louise looked over at the house.

"We can't know that yet," Toft replied quickly. "But we still haven't established a motive for the first two homicides; we haven't even connected the two victims. So we asked to be called in on any report that could be related to the two homicides."

Louise nodded thoughtfully. "You might be interested in a shooting in England." She greeted Michael Stig when he walked over to them.

He had been an investigator at Homicide while Louise worked there, and it had been his knife-sharp elbows that had spurred Louise to accept Rønholt's offer to head up a small new unit in the Search Department. Possibly it had been a step down the career ladder, but it had sounded awfully attractive when she'd heard that Stig had been promoted and would be her new boss following her old boss Willumsen's death.

Good that she left, she thought, seeing him standing there with his meticulously knotted tie and his arrogant attitude, which had thoroughly pissed her off when they had worked together. And things probably wouldn't have been better when it turned out that Hans Suhr was retiring and Stig would be heading up the Personal Crimes Department, still known as Homicide. Success wasn't treating him particularly well, apparently; he was thinner and ragged at the edges. It gets lonely at the top, also in the police corps.

"What's this about England?" he asked, ignoring Toft, who wanted to know how Louise was doing. "You're saying the shooting of a middle-aged woman in Hvidovre has international connections?"

Louise straightened up and smiled at him, refusing to be provoked. "I didn't say that. But as I was about to say, there *could* be a connection. The woman inside the house with the back of her head blown off has a connection to a Danish woman shot in England some weeks ago. The two homicides resemble each other, too."

The head of Homicide approached them from the tech's car.

"And this case resembles our first two cases," Toft told Stig, as Louise walked over to meet Suhr.

He smiled at her. "What are you doing here? Are you transferring back to us and no one told me?"

"I'm the one who called the homicide in." Louise explained that she had met Margit Østergaard the day before and had driven out for more information. "She's involved in a case I'm working on."

They stepped back onto the sidewalk when the forensic pathologist drove by. Traffic on the street was heating up, with people on their way to work, children heading for school, but many curious onlookers were standing on the sidewalk and watching from doorways. Uniformed police had set up barrier tape, technicians were at work inside the house and in the backyard. Several police officers were already taking witness statements, both from onlookers and from people in the surrounding houses.

"What's this case you're working on?" Suhr asked, as they walked away from the crowd.

Louise told him about Sofie Parker while considering whether to tell him about her suspicion she'd driven out to Hvidovre to confirm. "Both women were associated with a home hospice nurse service, and dying people they cared for have donated money to an account in Switzerland. Completely voluntarily. And the account was managed by Sofie Parker. That's why we're interested in other people who have been involved in the nurse service, because we see a motive among relatives who might not like so much money being given away."

"Interesting," Suhr mumbled. He seemed to clutch the straw she'd handed him that finally might connect the victims.

"There's no question the two women were linked through the nurse service. It's less certain they knew each other personally." Louise decided to confide in him. "Besides all this, I suspect that the nurses not only sat with the terminally ill, but also played a part in providing them with a dignified death in their homes. That's only my suspicion, of course; we haven't confirmed it yet. We're about to do another round of questioning. That's why I came here to talk to Margit."

"How long has your department been working on the case?"

"Since the murder of Sofie Parker."

"But why did they contact you when they discovered the woman was Danish?" Suhr sounded confused.

Louise began to explain about Eik Nordstrøm, how he

had reported Sofie missing, and that the department still had the case, since it had never been closed. "It's a long story."

"Sounds like you've made good progress in that part of the investigation. It'll be interesting to see if the first homicides are also linked to the nurse service. What would you say to joining us on a temporary investigative team on this case? Of course I'd have to clear it with Rønholt."

"Thanks, but I think I'll pass." Louise watched Michael Stig cross the street. "I'm happy at the Search Department, and anyway we can help each other on this."

"If you suspect this has something to do with the killing in England, that makes four homicides in two months. And who says it ends here. We need to get organized to stop this."

Louise clenched her teeth as she weighed the pros and cons of joining Suhr's team. First and foremost she would be in the middle of an investigation quite possibly focused on hunting down a serial killer. Working again alongside Toft and Lars Jørgensen was also appealing. Suhr too. But—and it was a big but—Michael Stig headed up the team. He would be absolutely unbearable to work with if she barged in and stole some of his thunder. And he would gloat if it turned out to be a coincidence that Sofie Parker and Margit Østergaard were both involved in the home hospice nurse service. He would make her out to be an idiot.

"Call Rønholt," she said.

This case was too serious for her to let Michael Stig stand in the way. Also, she realized it gave her the opportunity to withdraw from Eik's case. Even though she almost had forgiven him. He had chosen to distance himself from her, and she had to respect that.

"The new team will be meeting in my office after lunch," Suhr said, apparently confident that Rønholt wouldn't object to his stealing one of his people. *And he probably won't*, Louise thought, as she walked to her car.

It was like déjà vu as Louise logged on to the computer in her old office and sat down across from Lars Jørgensen. Her former partner's bulletin board was up to date with photos of his Bolivian twins; they had grown from a pair of charming, mischievous terrorists to a pair of healthy adolescents. Louise hadn't seen them for a year, and they looked twice as tall now.

Toft sat at the end of the desk. An e-cigarette stuck up out of his checkered shirt pocket. He had been one of Headquarters' hard-core smokers, but a total smoking ban had chased all the nicotine addicts down to the street every time they had to have a smoke.

"How will it be when you move out to Teglholmen?" Louise asked. "Will there be smoking balconies or cabinets?"

Toft peered at her over his glasses. "When's the last time you heard of anyone taking smokers into account when they plan new offices?"

She smiled. "Poor you, having to go down to the wharf."

As yet, no one knew what it would be like when Copenhagen Police moved into the new building by the Fisketorvet mall, but there had been talk. The Personal

Crimes Department was one of the departments slated to move. Louise had expected her old colleagues would be sad about leaving Police Headquarters, but it sounded as if they were looking forward to it. She understood them; no one denied the old historic building needed a thorough renovation.

Michael Stig walked in carrying a cup of coffee. Louise offered to find him a chair, but he said he wasn't staying long.

"We were just about to check where we are on the first cases," Toft told his young boss, who sat on the bookshelf just inside the door. He'd set his coffee down, and now he was drumming his pen against his thigh.

Louise started by telling what she knew about the murder of Sofie Parker. "Shot through the kitchen window. No witnesses other than the daughter, who is missing. No motive."

She sketched out the family's situation, the daughter, the husband, and the past history in Denmark.

"How long had Sofie Parker been missing?" Toft asked.

"Since disappearing in 1996 and up until recently." She told them about the email Eik had received. She added that the Swiss bank account was the only thing linking Sofie Parker with Denmark.

Michael Stig nodded as she spoke, as if he had heard it all before. "And the child's father is the Danish man the English police arrested for murder."

Louise was surprised. He'd wasted no time in getting up to date.

"Eik Nordstrøm," he continued, "is the man you share an office and an apartment with." He looked over at Toft and Lars Jørgensen. "I told Suhr it's a bad idea for Rick to work with us on this case."

Louise detested him, but she fought to keep her head down, and her feelings under control. "We don't live together, but it's true that we were in a relationship. And I'm not involved in his case."

"No?" Stig asked.

"The English police are working on it." She stood up to face him eye to eye. "The case on my desk is still the case the Search Department opened after the disappearance of Sofie Bygmann. I've been asked to find out what she did from the time she disappeared from the boat until she showed up in England. That's what I'm involved in. And we did find out, in fact."

"Let's hear it." He nodded at her.

Having to justify taking part in the investigation annoyed Louise, when Suhr was the one who had headhunted her. "She went to Switzerland to work at a suicide clinic." She explained about the home hospice nurse service and the donations, which they presumed that Sofie Parker had managed.

"I believe the nurse service is actually an organization providing assisted suicide," she said. "I would have spoken to Margit Østergaard about it, but obviously I arrived too late. And the motive for the killings could be that someone feels they've been cheated out of an inheritance. Some of the donations to the organization are big."

"And this organization was supposedly led by the woman shot in England." Stig sounded doubtful. He asked what she had on the homicide in Nailsea.

"It's all in here." She slid the file onto the desk.

Stig opened the file, leafed forward to the description of the murder weapon, and read for a few moments before looking up at Louise. "This makes it look like we have a perpetrator." He fanned the air with the file. "I'll have our technicians compare this rifle with what we've already examined. It'll be interesting to hear Eik Nordstrøm's explanation."

Now she was irritated. "Like everyone else, he's innocent until proven guilty!"

"But he can't be ruled out, either." He gave her a condescending look, as if *she* were the one he was looking to take down.

Louise bit her tongue.

Stig stood up and turned to Lars Jørgensen. "Call me when you're caught up on what we've got. But send me a few emails along the way, so I'll know where you're at." He left with her file tucked underneath his arm.

Louise caught the look her former partner gave Toft. "What?"

Jørgensen shook his head slightly. "It doesn't exactly save us time, emailing him about everything said after he leaves. It would be a lot easier for all of us if he just stayed and listened."

"You mean you sit there and email him, every time something is said he might want to hear? That he would have heard if he'd been here?" Louise couldn't believe it.

Jørgensen looked over at Toft, who shrugged. "You have to choose your battles."

"Helle Frederiksen, forty-five, lived in Tårnby," Toft said, as he began going through the Danish homicide cases. "Shot in the head and killed on November 19. The shot was fired through the living room window from just under eight meters. The weapon was a hunting rifle, the perpetrator must have been out on the street. No footprints found in the hedge or on the lawn. No unaccounted fingerprints in the house. A boyfriend lives in Oslo; he came down to visit when their days off matched up. We corroborated his alibi, he was at work. A sister has a key to the house, her prints are of course inside, too. She was home with her husband and children, working at her computer."

"All we have is what the techs found," Jørgensen said. "She was a healthcare aide, well-liked. Outgoing, worked out in the local fitness center, ran twice a week with a few coworkers. During the winter she taught cooking at an evening school." He threw up his arms.

"Are her parents alive?" Louise asked, thinking of Sofie.

Jørgensen nodded. "They live in Tårnby, too, not far from her. Her sister lives close by in Kastrup."

"Healthcare aide," Louise said, "that's a perfect fit. She might have joined the nurse service."

"We need to ask her sister if she knows anything about that," Toft said. "I'll handle it. I was out there a few times right after it happened."

"Who's the second victim?" Louise asked.

"Niels Boe, a master carpenter from Lynge. Lived alone on a farm on the outskirts of town. Shot in his living room with a hunting rifle, and according to ballistics it was the one used in Tårnby. The homicide in Lynge took place five weeks ago."

Louise was surprised. "I can't recall hearing about any connection between the two homicides."

Toft shook his head. "You didn't hear about it. When we found out it was the same murder weapon, we shut the lid on the Lynge case. We questioned family and friends. Spoke with the two workers employed by the victim, went through all his business connections. Nothing pointed to a motive or any link to Helle Frederiksen. Just as nothing in the investigation of her murder pointed to any connection to the carpenter."

"But," Jørgensen said, "we don't believe they were chosen randomly by some crazy killer. That's why we showed up so soon when we heard about the homicide this morning."

Louise leaned her elbows on the desk and folded her hands under her chin. "Two things. We need to look for some link to the home hospice nurse service. If we find one, we'd better find the others associated with the service, damn quick. I'm beginning to think someone out there is picking them off one by one."

Jørgensen nodded, but Toft seemed more skeptical. "It still could be coincidental that the two women in England and Hvidovre knew about the service. We're not even sure they knew each other."

"That's true." Louise was about to say more, when the door opened and Stig stuck his head inside. "They've just extended the custody period in England. The suspect doesn't have an alibi for the homicide. Find everything you can on Eik Nordstrøm."

Louise jumped up. "What the hell! He's not the one we're looking for."

Suhr showed up in the doorway.

She couldn't believe her ears. "You can't be serious. We're supposed to spend time and resources checking one of our colleagues, while the perpetrator goes about his business? For Chrissake, Eik is in jail in Bristol, he can't have shot a woman in Hvidovre this morning; use your head!"

"Point taken!" Jørgensen said.

"But we still don't know if she was shot with the same weapon, and until we do we're going to ignore that case and focus on what we do know." Stig was short of breath. "And what we do know is, the hunting rifle used to kill Helle Frederiksen and Niels Boe was used in another homicide, the one Eik Nordstrøm is being held for. That's a fact, and that's what we're going to investigate."

Louise ignored Stig and looked at Suhr. "How quick can Ballistics finish if we light a fire under them?"

The Homicide chief nodded. "They're working on it."

Stig drummed his fingers against the door frame, impatient to leave. Beads of sweat stood out on his forehead.

"Do you have a moment?" Louise asked Suhr, after Stig had left. He nodded, and she followed him out into the hall.

"If this is how it's going to be," she said, angry now, "I'm going back to the Search Department to find out if Helle Frederiksen and Niels Boe had any ties to the nurse service. Maybe everyone here thinks it's a shot in the dark, but show me one other thing that links these cases together!"

Suhr lifted his hand. "Easy now."

"It's totally okay that you investigate other angles," she said, ignoring his admonition. "But I'm out if we don't work fast to uncover any connection between the victims and the nurse service. And if there is, priority number one must be to find out how many people are at risk of having their heads blown off in their living rooms."

Her eyes pleaded with him. "We have to identify them, to stop this from happening again. We need to work together to find them quickly, everyone with some work-related link to the service, and how many nurses are involved. Are there others on the business side, doctors involved in providing the lethal medicine? Undertakers? We have to identify the people in danger of being killed."

Suhr nodded. Finally her heart slowed, and her voice was calm now. "Or else we work separately. In which case Olle and I will focus on talking to all the relatives of those who made deposits, and we'll contact the home hospice nurse service, too."

Suhr nodded again and waited to be sure she was finished. "I agree. We have to follow up on your lead."

"Of course we have to consider other motives," Louise quickly added. "But I'm already involved in this case, and that's what I'm going to concentrate on. So it's your decision if it's with you or my own department."

Once more he nodded, and he stuck his hands in his pockets. "We'll do it here. Right now I have twenty men working on the homicide in Hvidovre. I'm putting Stig in charge of them, even though he has a lot on his plate. So you, Jørgensen, and Toft will follow your lead. I can't spare any more officers, you three will be on your own."

"Fine." Three was better than one, and she understood that Margit's murder required every body he could scrape up. Now the three of them could go to work and find the motive.

The Homicide chief walked back to the office and held the door open for her. "You three dig in and try to find what links the victims, based on the information Rick has brought in," he told the two others. "We have a briefing this evening at six, and of course again early tomorrow morning. We have to locate the perpetrator—now."

He turned back to Louise. "I'm assigning two people to work with the English police. We have to keep abreast of what they come up with over there."

She nodded. Of course, they had to cooperate with England, she knew that. Just not in Michael Stig's biased fashion.

23

The first person Louise called was Winnie Moesgaard in Karlslunde. She waited an unusually long time before the woman answered. The elegant elderly lady's thin, feeble voice nearly broke.

"My husband passed away this weekend," she said. "The undertaker just stopped by."

"You have my deepest condolences," Louise said. "I'm so very sorry to bother you at such a sad time, but unfortunately it's very important."

"What's it about?" Louise could barely hear her.

"Last week," Louise began, searching for the right words, "I met Margit Østergaard, the woman who sat with your husband."

"Yes." She sounded hesitant.

"I'm sorry to have to tell you, but this morning she was found murdered. I'm well aware that you have a lot on your mind right now."

The woman gasped.

"She was shot in her home sometime between midnight and seven a.m., so I would be very appreciative if I could ask a few questions, if you can handle it."

Silence. For a moment she was afraid that Mrs. Moesgaard had hung up. Finally Louise said, "Would you prefer that I come out to you, so we can sit down and talk about it?"

"Heavens no! I just can't understand how this could happen. It makes me so terribly sad. Margit was such a fine and warm person."

"Unfortunately we don't know much, and that's partly what I'd like to talk to you about." Louise decided it wasn't a good time to ask if her husband had received help in dying. It was best to stick with what was most important right now.

"When you and your husband used the home hospice nurse service, did you meet any other nurses besides Margit?"

It sounded as if Mrs. Moesgaard blew her nose and cleared her throat while covering her phone. Finally she said, "I very much liked Margit. So after the first time she was here, I asked the service to send her regularly. That's one of the things the nurse service offers. Once in a while another nurse spelled her, of course. They all have jobs and families."

"So there have been others?"

"Yes, once another nurse took the night watch. But I didn't speak much with her."

"Do you remember her name?" Louise was ready to write the name down.

"Hmmm. Just a moment."

Louise heard her footsteps, and in a moment she was back on the phone. "It was Esther, but I didn't write her last name down."

"Do you know anything about her? Where she lived, where she worked when she wasn't a home hospice nurse?"

"No, I don't know anything about her, but she was also very nice. We didn't speak very much, I didn't learn much about her as I did with Margit. It meant so much to me when we sat with my husband, talking about this and that. It took my mind off things."

"Of course." Louise felt sorry for the charming lady. She was all alone now.

"But can't the nurse service provide you with her name? Surely they know it."

"Yes, they must. Do you have a number we can call?"

"I have it somewhere here..."

A few moments later, she was back. Slowly she read a telephone number.

"Thank you so much for all your help." Louise felt she'd made a bit of progress when she realized it was a landline number, not the one to the emergency hotline.

Toft had also just finished talking to someone, and he reported that Helle Frederiksen's sister didn't know of any home hospice nurse service, but she knew her sister took evening and night shifts once in a while.

"The sister didn't think any extra money was coming in, but she didn't want to ask Frederiksen if she was doing something else those evenings."

Louise called the landline number Winnie Moesgaard had given her. No one answered. She looked the number up on her computer and was informed that it was an unlisted number. She called down to the tech boys and asked them to run it through the system.

"Bingo!" Jørgensen said, as soon as he hung his phone up. "The carpenter's daughter says her father had been sitting with terminally ill people once a week since her mother's death. The daughter thought it was creepy, and she asked him if he could volunteer to visit the elderly. But apparently it was important to her father to sit with the dying."

He had their attention now. "But she didn't know anything about it, she moved away from home a year ago, and in fact it sounded like she didn't care if he sat with dying people or went to soccer matches. She was just happy he stayed active and was around people after her mother died."

Louise felt her scalp tingling. "Jesus! They *are* being taken out one by one."

"But how many are there?" Toft asked.

"I have no idea," she said. "But we have to find out, fast."

Suhr had walked in and was leaning against the door frame, listening without saying a word.

"We have to focus one hundred percent on identifying the others," Toft said, looking at Louise.

She nodded. "I'll talk to the people I've already contacted, to get names and hopefully addresses. You two get on the list of the other relatives of donors to the Swiss account. Let's not mention that we suspect someone helped the deceased person in their families to die, they might not even know what went on. And we can't risk them clamming up on us."

The phone in front of her rang. It was Nis, the tech

who had traced the unlisted number. "Margit Østergaard," he said. Before he could give her the address, she cut him off.

"Thanks, I was out there this morning, I know the address. Damn it!"

Jørgensen looked at her in anticipation. "It was Margit's private number that Mrs. Moesgaard wrote down," she said. They were back at square one.

Before she could say more, Toft stood up. "I'm going out there to search the house. If there's any lists of names or anything else with names on it, I'll find it. She had to have been in contact with some of the others."

Louise smiled at him. Typical Toft. He was thorough as he could be, and stubborn; you could rely on him to do the grunt work.

On the other side of the desk, Jørgensen was already calling the next on the list. Louise listened to him explain and ask for the names of the home hospice nurses who had sat with the dying relative.

Louise thought about Eik for a moment. Imagined him going to England to find the daughter he'd never met. Now the daughter was missing, and he was in jail. Somebody should tell him that the man who shot Sofie was back in Denmark. She couldn't be sure, but she felt certain that Eik had gone to England to find Steph, that he was afraid the perpetrator might be after her.

She texted Rønholt and asked him to tell Eik about the homicide in Hvidovre, if he got permission to talk to him.

"Niels," Jørgensen said, after he had hung up. "The son didn't remember the last name, but he'd thought it was a bit inappropriate for a man to sit with his mother while she was dying. But his mother brushed him off, told him she felt safe with Niels at her side."

"Surely there's more than the few we have now?" Louise said.

Her former partner shrugged. "Honest, I thought the home hospice nurse service was a thing of the past. And I have no idea how many of them there might be. How do people even find out about it?"

"There has to be a doctor involved! They get the medicine somewhere. Like, if it's morphine, that's not something most people can get their hands on. And how do they make sure they can prove it's an assisted suicide, not murder, if they get caught?"

She thought again about Else Corneliussen, who had helped Sofie's mother to die. She'd asked Olle to find her, but as yet he'd made no headway.

"If it's true that they help people die, like you're saying," Jørgensen said, "at the very least they risk being charged with euthanasia. I just don't understand how they dare do this. Dying people have to make it crystal clear they want to die, otherwise it's murder."

Louise thought about Melvin. If he had ended up as a vegetable, or as someone who just laid there looking at life without being a part of it, could she have convinced herself to help him? "Probably they do it because they think it's wrong that people suffering from a fatal illness, people in great pain, have to leave the country and pay a fortune for an assisted suicide. And also it's about the right to die with dignity. I'm certain they've all experienced something that made them willing to run the risk, just like Sofie Parker."

Jørgensen nodded, apparently agreeing with her. He

called the next person on the list. After talking to them for a few moments, he said, "Is there anyone else in the family who might remember the name?"

After hanging up, he said, "Looks like it wasn't a topic of conversation. This woman explained that her aunt had wanted a home hospice nurse, so the rest of the family stayed away."

"Damn it!" Louise was afraid the perpetrator was way ahead of them. "We have to talk to people in person, not just call them up. I'll get Olle to help us. Otherwise it'll take too long to go through the list."

She called him and filled him in on why she needed his help. "Can you go back to the nursing home and talk to Kurt Melvang?"

He didn't hesitate. "Sure. I've still got everything right in front of me on the desk here. It's the senile old guy who dropped his pants, right?"

"That's him. And if he doesn't remember the name of the nurse, ask his two adult children. They were pissed off at the nurse service for robbing them of their inheritance. I'll try to set up a meeting with him in Birkerød."

"You doing okay?" Olle asked, as Louise was about to hang up.

His sudden concern made her pause, and she sank in her chair. "I don't know. I think so."

24

Camilla wasn't about to wait for Terkel Høyer to return from his meeting or answer her text. She hopped in her car and headed for Jutland.

After arriving at work, she'd barely had time to pour a cup of coffee and sit down in the editorial office to get ready to work on the Switzerland story before Stig Tåsing called and asked if she could come by the manse.

"It's not something we can talk about on the phone?" she said, thinking about her deadline. If the article about the suicide clinic was going to be in tomorrow's paper, she had to get busy.

"No," he'd said. "You have to come over here."

She was on the Great Belt Bridge when her editor in chief called and asked where the hell she'd gone off to now.

"I had to leave," she said. She explained what had happened. "He wouldn't tell me what it was about, but I'm guessing he's ready to say more."

"And how did you *guess* your way to that conclusion?" Høyer didn't sound all that confident in her judgment.

"I'll pay the toll and gas," she said, while passing a semi.

"Right now I'm more interested in hearing how you're going to get that article written. I'm holding a two-page spread for tomorrow."

"You'll get your story. But if we can get something more out of the pastor, it'll damn well be worth it. The Switzerland story won't be any worse the day after tomorrow. What the hell's wrong with you, Terkel, what's happened to your nose for a story?"

"All right," he mumbled. "I guess I just have to get used to you being back."

From a distance she spotted the church and the beautiful, whitewashed manse with its red tile roof. The bare crowns in the tall trees surrounding it looked like thin, bony arms reaching for the sky. She signaled to turn off and slowed down.

Several texts had beeped in on the way, so she pulled over and checked her phone. Frederik asked if she had time to Skype. Camilla was about to answer that it would be a while, when she realized he was probably in bed. It must be night in Los Angeles.

Suddenly her stomach knotted, and instead of texting she called him, mostly just to hear his voice.

While waiting for an answer, she looked out over the brown fields. Snow clung to the hedgerows. She missed her husband, so much that her chest ached. Maybe it was all this talk about death, her imagining how it would be to travel to Switzerland and send the person she loved most on his final journey. She couldn't shake her experience at the suicide clinic; she longed to snuggle up to Frederik and hear his thoughts about all this.

His answering service kicked in. She left a message, explaining that she was in Jutland and that she loved him and missed him very, very much. She would do everything she could to talk Markus into flying to L.A. during winter vacation, if it was humanly possible to separate him from his girlfriend. She parked in front of the manse. Otherwise she'd have to invite Julia to go with them. No matter what, she was going to spend a week over there with Frederik.

Stig Tåsing stepped outside. He wore jeans and a T-shirt, his chestnut-brown hair combed back. He still had his slippers on, as if he hadn't really started his day yet.

They greeted each other. His mood was serious, and he seemed eager to get her inside. On the way, Camilla had tried to guess what was so important that he would ask her to drive over. Now he took her arm and led her to the manse, as if they were coconspirators.

"Early this morning," he said, his voice barely above a whisper, "the doorbell woke me up. It was Sofie's daughter. She thought I was her father. She came here to Denmark to find him."

Camilla gaped in surprise. "I'll be damned," she said, forgetting that he was a pastor.

"She has the same way of looking at people as her mother, only her eyes are darker."

His unexpected guest had shaken him up; she could see that.

"Of course I told her I'm not her father, but she's very

upset. And very determined to find him. Somebody simply has to help this poor girl, and I thought about you."

Camilla nodded. "Good thinking." She followed him inside, her thoughts racing—how much should she tell the young girl? She didn't know for certain that Eik was the girl's father, and also, how could she tell her that he was in jail in England, being held for the murder of her mother?

Maybe she shouldn't say anything, maybe she should just call Louise. While taking off her boots in the hallway, she decided it wouldn't hurt to hear what the girl had to say. Then she could call.

He led her through the house. The girl was sitting on the sofa in the living room, wrapped up in a blanket. Camilla stopped in the doorway and looked the girl over. It was almost comical, how much she resembled Eik. Or was it just because she was looking for it? She walked over and introduced herself. The girl surprised her by speaking Danish, asking if Camilla had known her mother.

"No, I didn't, but I think I can help you find your father." She nodded when the pastor asked if she'd like a cup of tea.

"Mum taught me Danish," Stephanie said, after he left the room. Camilla's surprise had apparently been obvious. "She didn't have any ties left to Denmark, but it was important to her that we could speak Danish together."

"A wise mother," Camilla said. She studied the girl's pale face, her dark eye makeup. On the surface, Eik's daughter looked like a tough girl. If she were scared or crushed by her mother's death, she was certainly hiding it well.

"I'm here to find my real father," she said, without bothering to explain why she had shown up out of the blue at a manse in Jutland. "I ran off because I can't stand the complete idiot my mother married, and I know he'll never help me find my biological father. I don't understand why they didn't tell me a long time ago."

"Tell you what?"

"That I had another father!" She threw up her hands. "They could have just said, then I wouldn't have had to stay there and listen to him yell at me all the time. She just told me for the first time a month ago." She shook her head and bent over, her fists under her chin as she stared straight ahead.

The pastor returned with a tray carrying a teapot, biscuits, and buttered rolls. Camilla wondered if he kept these things on hand, in case someone suddenly showed up needing to talk. "How did you find me?" he asked.

"I searched my mother's office for some clue of where to look in Denmark." Stephanie straightened up again. "I found your marriage certificate and the address here."

"She kept it?" The pastor's eyes clouded over.

"That's why I thought it was you."

"How did you get here?" Camilla asked. "Did you fly to Copenhagen?"

The girl looked at Camilla as if the question were ridiculous. "I'm sixteen. I'm perfectly able to buy a plane ticket. I took a flight from Bristol, and my mother had a lot of money stashed in her office. I can take care of myself for now."

"Of course, you can," Camilla replied quickly. How could she win a stubborn teenage girl's trust in record time?

"Will you help me?" the girl asked, before Camilla had time to think out a strategy.

"I absolutely will."

"Stephanie explained that her mother had plans for them to visit Denmark, so she could meet her father," the pastor said. "Which didn't happen. So now she's here to look for him."

"Steph," the girl said. "My name is Steph, and I'm going to find him."

"How much do you know about your father?" Camilla asked.

"Nothing." A hint of vulnerability showed through her mask, which made her look very young. "I don't know his name or where to look. But I'll keep trying until I find him, I'm not going back to live with Nigel."

"Has he done anything to you?" The girl's utter contempt for him concerned Camilla.

The girl flashed a smile, and suddenly all the black shadows couldn't hide how pretty she was. "No, he'd never do that, he's just so…irritating. He criticizes me constantly, nothing I do is good enough. Mum promised me she'd talk to my real father, see if maybe I could live with him for a while, at least until I could move away from home. I think he irritated her, too, because she started defending me."

Had she considered whether her biological father was as anxious to meet her as she was to meet him? It didn't seem so to Camilla. At least until Steph said, "And if he didn't want anything to do with me, she promised she'd find a boarding school for me."

The pastor poured tea for all three of them. "Please, eat."

"You were married to my mother. Why didn't you keep in contact with her?" Steph sounded like a child who suddenly discovers that she's completely alone.

The pastor laid the tray down without answering. Instinctively, Camilla sat down beside the girl, put her arm around her shoulder, and pulled her close. Had anyone even comforted the girl after her mother's death? She should have been offered help from a therapist, after having gone through such a brutal, traumatic experience. Camilla's impression was that she'd had to deal with everything herself, now that her mother wasn't there to take care of her.

The girl's body felt tense under her arm. Her breath was ragged, but she didn't push Camilla away. After a few moments, her body slumped into Camilla. "I don't know what to do, now that she's gone." Her voice was small, but she wasn't crying.

"You can stay with me in Copenhagen while we try to find your father." Camilla thought about all the empty rooms in their enormous Frederiksberg apartment. "But I want you to talk to the police. You can help them by describing the man who shot your mother."

The girl looked surprised, but she nodded. Her stubborn expression had returned. "It's a deal. Will you promise I won't be sent back to England?"

"I can't promise you that. But I know someone who will fight for you, that I can guarantee. She works for the Copenhagen Police. Her name is Louise Rick, and you've already met her."

25

Revenge, triggered by economic loss, Louise thought, as she parked in front of the Birkerød home. Erik Hald Sørensen was the first of eight people on the list Louise was going to look up. On the way there, Jørgensen had called and asked if they should shuffle the list according to size of donation, with the families of the deceased who had donated the most at the top. Louise had rejected the idea; a small amount could mean more to poor families than a large amount to the wealthy. The only thing important now was finding the names of everyone involved in the home hospice nurse service, to prevent any more killings. Suhr had assigned an extra man to call and make sure the relative was home when the police arrived.

"I'll only bother you for a moment," Louise said, when the widower invited her inside. His wife's coats were no longer hanging in the hallway, she noted. Her high boots were also gone.

"No bother," he said. He asked her to follow him, as if he looked forward to having some company. He offered to make coffee.

"No thank you," she quickly replied, though she didn't feel she could let him in on why she had to hurry. She looked around the living room; something was different in there also. A box. She sensed him watching her.

"I'm packing up all the dog things." He blinked his eyes rapidly a few times. "I found a good home for him in southern Zealand. I can't keep him, I don't seem to care much about anything anymore, and it's unfair to him."

His shoulders slumped; he looked lost standing there in the middle of the room, eyeing the dining room table and the lambskin, dog brush, tick tweezers, and heavy, black leather dog leash. "He's a good dog, but he needs his exercise."

Louise let him speak. He walked out of the room, and a moment later he returned with an elegant, heavy wool trench coat. "It's a Max Mara. I gave it to my wife for Christmas last year. Could you use it?" He held it out to her.

Louise smiled at him. "Unfortunately I'm not allowed to take gifts." She laid the coat over the back of an armchair. "I'm here in connection with an investigation. Someone was murdered early this morning in Hvidovre. It turns out the victim was a home hospice nurse, working for the service that helped you when your wife was dying. Right now I'm trying to find all the volunteers who work for the service, since we have reason to believe their lives may be in danger, too. So I'm hoping you can give me the names of those who helped you."

Hald Sørensen rested his hand on the high back of a dining room chair and gazed out the window. He cleared his throat. "I don't remember much about those days, I'm sorry to say. Christine's last days are a blur. But I wasn't happy about having a stranger in our house near the end."

He paused for a moment, then took a deep breath. "I wanted to sit with her. Alone. But it was her decision, and naturally I went along with it. I believe she mostly wanted to spare me her body's decay, as she called it."

He looked sad as he stroked his full beard.

"So it wasn't you who arranged things with the service?" Louise asked, steering him back to the subject.

He shook his head. "Christine took care of it all. But of course I called them when she asked me to."

"Do you remember the name of the person who came?"

"Unfortunately not. But it was an older woman. She was my age, anyway." He smiled.

"Did you speak with her?"

He nodded. "Not much, though. The first time she came was the day before my wife died."

"Of course. Did she mention anything like where she lived, or what she did when she wasn't working as a home hospice nurse?"

She was hoping for something, some tiny clue that could lead her to the woman's identity. Her age suggested it was someone they hadn't heard about. She could also be the Esther who had sat one night with Werner Moesgaard in Karlslunde. They still didn't have her address.

"She didn't sit there talking about herself," he said. "We played music for Christine, but when I was in the room, mostly the nurse sat and read."

"Did she have a car? Did she drive here herself?"

He shook his head. "She took the train, and I'm certain she came here from somewhere in Copenhagen. That would fit with her using a five-zone train card. I remember we talked about that."

Louise's phone rang. She excused herself and fished it up out of her bag. Suhr told her that a woman from the nurse service had shown up at Police Headquarters. "She thinks her life is in danger, and she's begging to talk to someone who's investigating the shootings. She also believes the homicides are linked to the work of her organization."

"I'll leave right now."

Again Louise felt the elderly man's eyes on her. "A witness has shown up. She'll give us the names we're lacking," she explained. "Thank you so much for your time, and I'm very sorry to have brought up all these painful memories again."

A thin, gangly, late-middle-aged woman with red-rimmed eyes was sitting in the office with a cup of coffee when Louise returned. Toft sat across from her.

The woman stood up and held out her hand. She seemed a bit uncertain of herself. "Else Corneliussen," she said, to Louise's great surprise. Her voice boomed, in contrast to Louise's impression of her as a frail woman.

She gazed at the doctor who had helped Sofie's mother die. Olle hadn't been able to track her down, but no matter, now that she'd shown up on her own.

The woman sat down again; her dark brown eyes looked tired, and she clasped her hands on the desk in front of her. She seemed determined and eager to get started, though.

"I feel horrible about not coming in much earlier. Not

only because I'm at great risk of being shot myself, but it might have prevented Margit's death."

She bit her lip before continuing. "It wasn't until Sofie was killed over in England that I began to suspect a connection."

Louise had already taken her coat off and dropped her bag. She pulled out a chair and grabbed the thermos that Toft slid over to her. He was at the computer now; she assumed he wanted her to do the talking.

"I just couldn't understand it," the woman said, trying to control her wavering voice. "It's beyond me, what's going on. But after hearing the news this morning, there's no longer any doubt in my mind. There is a connection." She threw her hands up in dismay.

"Can you explain," Toft said, "how you're so sure about who was killed. The name of the Hvidovre woman hasn't been released." He looked over at Louise, who shook her head.

"I don't need to hear the name. I know it's Margit." She looked up. "I called her when I heard about the killing, and she didn't answer. She didn't answer the emergency service phone, either. So I called the cell phone we use only among ourselves. She didn't answer that, either, and she never turns it off. It's her personal emergency number. So I contacted the daughter of an elderly man; Margit was supposed to be sitting with him, starting at eight this morning. The daughter said she hadn't shown up. So I came here at once."

"More coffee?" Louise asked. The woman shook her head. "What's your connection to the home hospice nurse service?"

Else Corneliussen closed her eyes and took a deep

breath, as if she were gathering strength. But when she opened them again, she seemed neither nervous nor unsure. She looked like a woman who was deeply unhappy and afraid.

"I'm a doctor. I established the home hospice nurse service, along with Sofie Parker. I'm involved with assisted suicide. Please, let me explain everything from the beginning, and hopefully we can put an end to this insanity."

Louise nodded and glanced quickly at Toft. The doctor's explanation was to be in the report.

"I was Annelise's doctor—Annelise, Sofie's mother. She died many years ago." She asked Louise if she knew what had happened back then.

"Let's hear your version."

"Annelise wanted to die. At the end her pain was intense, and she'd just come home from a long, exhausting stay in the hospital. There wasn't much left of her, and several times I expected her to ask if I could help to end her life. And I would have done so, but she beat me to it." The doctor looked up. Maybe to show that she still felt the same way, Louise thought.

"Annelise emptied her medicine cabinet, and she was admitted to the hospital with serious damage to her liver and kidneys. But she didn't die as she'd hoped. I offered Sofie my help at the hospital, so her mother could finally find peace. I knew it was what her mother wanted. Besides my practice, I had two shifts a week at the hospital, so I knew the staff, I was used to working with them. I knew which nurses shared my feelings about helping those who wanted help, and we decided to be generous with morphine in the drip. I doubt it would surprise anyone to know it's a merciful way to free people of their suffering, and it's often used." She spoke the last sentence with authority; clearly she was prepared to defend her medical decision.

"Later it caused a lot of trouble for Sofie with her husband. He was so set against our way of thinking. He wouldn't tolerate Sofie's wanting a dignified death for her mother, an escape from all her pain. On the contrary, he thought she should have talked her mother out of it. Then he made serious accusations against me in the local press; he believed that I misused my authority. And of course it was his right to believe that. We live in a country where the government and most members of the Danish Council of Ethics are dead-set against what more and more Danes now support. Assisted suicide and euthanasia aren't allowed, but that doesn't mean it doesn't take place. Just not out in the open."

She reached for her coffee. "In the home hospice service we've formed a circle of well-educated, skilled people who help others die in peace, at home in familiar surroundings, without risk of something going wrong as it did for Sofie's mother."

"And who are *we*?" Louise asked.

"After going through her mother's death, Sofie decided to help others in the same situation, the terminally ill and elderly, like her mother. People who don't want to live any longer because they have no strength left, they live a life of pain and total dependency. She inherited a large sum of money from her parents, and she went to Switzerland to learn as much as she could. Not just the practical details, but how to support relatives who had to deal with the terminally ill person's decision. There are serious ethical questions with assisted suicide, and she was very conscious of that."

"So you were a part of it from the beginning?" Toft asked from behind his computer monitor.

The doctor nodded. "But I can't provide the medicine. That would be far too easy to discover. We decided that Sofie would take care of that. Which is why she settled in England, where you can live without all the registration we have here. You could say she went underground."

"How did she get hold of so much medicine?" Louise asked.

"There are pharmacies in Mexico that sell medicine normally not sold over-the-counter. It's more expensive without a prescription, and you have to pay in dollars, but the medicine comes from the same pharmaceutical companies, the quality is the same."

"But that's illegal," Toft said.

Else Corneliussen shook her head. "Over there you can walk in off the street and buy these products. Outside their stores they advertise Valium, Viagra, strong pain medication, sleeping pills, so it's no more illegal than that."

"Sofie bought it and had it shipped over?" Louise asked. She thought about the package sent from Cozumel, Mexico.

The doctor nodded. "Yes. The past several years I've gone to London about every other month to meet with Sofie and bring the medicine back to Denmark."

"So it started with just you two?"

"And the nurse who helped that evening when Sofie's mother passed away. Several others joined us, though some of them have stopped. How it happens is, the terminally ill have to be able to take the necessary dosage themselves, but we help them. That's why most of the home hospice workers we accept are educated nurses. It's not a requirement; the most important thing is, of course, that they share our ideals and offer their assistance."

"But the terminally ill pay you to help them?" Louise made no attempt to soften her tone.

Again she shook her head. "You don't pay to be permitted to die. No one in the organization receives money for what they do. No one profits. The money the terminally ill or their relatives donate to the home hospice service goes to buying medicine, the shipping, my travel expenses to get the medicine, our transportation to and from the homes of the terminally ill. There are also expenses in connection with the videos made at the deathbed, in which the person dying says they want to die. The income and expenses go through an account in Switzerland that Sofie took care of."

"How many are there in your service?" Toft asked.

The doctor's red eyes moistened. "Our group covers North Zealand, metropolitan Copenhagen, and mid-Zealand, and we have seven hospice workers, two doctors, and one undertaker. Or at least we had, until all this began."

She lifted a handkerchief from the pocket of her dark blue cardigan.

"May we have the names of these people?" Toft asked. His expression when looking at the doctor told Louise that he didn't at all care for the woman's mind-set of helping people to die.

Dr. Corneliussen took a piece of paper out of her bag. "Anita Nielsen, Fleming Sau, Lise Rasmussen, and Esther

Larsen—all four of them have been with us for quite some time. Also there's Tone Frost; he's the undertaker, and he's new to the group. And Erik Hald Sørensen and me, though we're not on the regular schedule. Here are the names, telephone numbers, and addresses." He laid the sheet of paper on the desk. "The last number below each name is their emergency phone. I've already left a message on the phones, to let them know you're probably going to contact them."

"Erik Hald Sørensen! From Birkerød?"

The doctor nodded. "He's a doctor, but he hasn't been with us very long. Do you know him?"

"I just came from his house," Louise said. "But he didn't mention that he'd joined the home hospice service."

The doctor leaned her arms onto the desk. "Erik contacted us not long after his wife asked us to help her die. Everyone in our group has at one time or another been part of an assisted suicide. That's how people hear about our service, and in fact they often volunteer afterward. We have to be able to trust people before we allow them into our network."

"It's just that it sounded like Hald Sørensen was against his wife's decision," Louise said, thinking about the conversation she had with him.

"Losing her made him very unhappy," the doctor said, nodding. "But later on, when he offered his help, he'd reached the point where he respected her decision. What he didn't like was her choice to die so early. He had trouble accepting that she didn't want to be with him as long as possible—that's normal for the people who love those who are dying."

"What do you mean, so early?" Louise asked. "I had the impression she was exhausted from her disease."

"Christine would probably have lived another year, maybe two. But her condition would have worsened, diminished her abilities. She knew what was going to happen, she'd seen what her mother went through. And she didn't want that for herself. That's why she decided it was time. So even though Erik's loss was difficult, he offered his help. He explained that it was his way of honoring the memory of his wife."

Louise nodded; it made sense. "It just puzzles me that he didn't say anything; he knew I was there to try to find all of you, so you could be protected."

"We have a lot of members, not only active volunteers, but others who support us financially. They all want to show their sympathy for the work we do. But as long as it's illegal here, they all feel sworn to secrecy. It also happens sometimes that someone dying doesn't tell relatives of their decision, because they already know their family will be against it. The only reason I'm sitting here asking for your help is, I'm afraid that four of us have been killed for being in our group, and several more are at risk. I simply can't be responsible for that happening."

Toft went out to find Lars Jørgensen, to help him send patrol cars to everyone on the list.

"Will they all be brought in here?" the doctor asked, confused now.

"Yes," Louise said. "We need to talk with all of you, but our first priority is to get them out of their homes and find out if they have family or friends they can stay with."

Toft and Jørgensen came back in. "They're being brought in now," Toft said. "The only one we couldn't get hold of is Erik Hald Sørensen. He didn't answer any of the numbers. I contacted the North Zealand Police, they've sent a nearby patrol car to the address."

His phone rang, and he stepped out into the hall. A moment later he was back. "The patrol car is out there now. The house is empty, but a patio door is open."

"Damn it!" Louise stood up. She had a bad feeling about this. "Let's go."

"Do you ever regret leaving Homicide?" Jørgensen asked, as they sped up Kongevejen, the road leading to Birkerød. Something in his voice made Louise think her old partner might be putting feelers out. They hadn't seen much of each other since she transferred to the Search Department, but once in a while they lunched together. She just couldn't recall him talking about leaving, only saying that he got tired once in a while of having a boss like Michael Stig.

She shook her head, then she got in the right lane and signaled to turn off at the road to Bistrup.

"Rønholt is a great boss, I haven't regretted it one second." She didn't mention the times she'd been at a crime scene and had to withdraw because she was no longer an investigator. Sometimes she missed the rush that came with working in Homicide, but she kept that to herself.

"Are you happy there?" she asked.

Jørgensen had been left alone with his Bolivian twins several years earlier. It had been difficult for the chief of investigations at the time, Willumsen, to accept that one of his male investigators had to pick up his kids every day. For a while he had ridden Jørgensen so hard that he'd had to go on sick leave. Willumsen died soon after, and Michael Stig rose up in the ranks.

"You probably never thought you'd hear me say this," he said, looking out the window, "but I'd rather have Willumsen as my boss any day, no matter what, instead of Stig. I can't even imagine how it's going to be when he takes over from Suhr at the end of the month."

He shook his head. "Stig was a good investigator, no doubt about that, even though he got on everyone's nerves. But he's not a good leader. You know the type that when something goes wrong, he makes it look like it's someone else's fault?"

Tell me about it, Louise thought. It was easy for her to imagine Michael Stig passing the buck.

"It's like he's always a step behind, and he tries to make it look like we're the ones not keeping him informed. I don't understand how he gets away with it."

Louise sensed it was difficult for Jørgensen to speak up like this. Maybe he felt disloyal, but he had absolutely no reason to. She'd known from the start that Stig wasn't a team player. She turned her head when Jørgensen pointed out a flock of ducks, rocking back and forth on a small lake they passed by.

"That's Michael Stig for you, right there," he said. "Calm on the surface, but underneath he's scrambling like crazy to stay afloat."

Louise turned onto the street leading to Erik Hald Sørensen's house. At the corner she noticed the police car parked out in front of the hedge, and she tensed up again, sharpened her focus.

She parked behind the North Zealand Police vehicle and spotted the two officers, waiting up by the white-washed house. Before they got out, she checked her shoulder holster while Jørgensen called Toft to say they had arrived and were ready to go inside. They walked up to the black front door and greeted their two colleagues, a man and an unusually tall woman with short, blond hair.

"Have you been inside?" Louise said.

The male officer answered. "We were only told to show up here, so we've been waiting on you. But we walked around the house, the back door is open."

"Good," she said. "And no sign of anyone having shot through the windows or doors?"

The female officer shook her head. "No sign of a break-in, either."

"Stay here. We'll look behind the house."

A couple out walking their dog stood staring at them from across the street.

She walked around one side of the house, and Jørgensen walked around the other. Several times on the way, Louise cupped her hand to a window and peered in, but she couldn't see anyone. She hopped over a low stone fence and went around the garage to the backyard. Before reaching the patio and the door to the utility room, she peeked in two windows, one of them a bedroom window. A pile of Christine's clothes lay on the bed; apparently he had started sorting them.

Jørgensen showed up and shook his head. "The house looks deserted to me."

He pulled out a pair of plastic gloves and handed them to her. Louise no longer carried them around with her.

She remembered the dog that had been shut in the utility room both times she'd been there. "There might be a dog inside, be ready for that." She opened the door the rest of the way and checked the utility room. A countertop with two sinks lined the wall, like in a scullery. A washing machine, dryer, and a large sack of dog food stood at one end of the room. The rest of the room was filled with storage shelves, and there was also a hook for coats. The slippers Sørensen had worn earlier that day were under the hook.

"Hello," she called out. She walked over to the kitchen door. Her skin crawled, and she sensed Jørgensen right behind her as she entered.

Her breathing seemed to roar in the dead silent house.

"Let's go in," she whispered, flashing on an image of Margit Østergaard on her living room floor with a bloodied head. Though Louise was reasonably sure that Sørensen had left, it was still possible he was lying inside.

The house was empty. Everything looked exactly as it had several hours earlier. He'd been packing things up for the dog, but he hadn't made progress.

"The two rooms in back are empty," Jørgensen said. He returned to the living room.

Louise was in the kitchen. A coffee cup and buttering board had been laid out, as if he'd started making lunch but had been interrupted.

"And the room on the other side of the living room is empty, too," Jørgensen said. He followed her out to a short hallway with three doors on one side, leading to rooms facing the street. The first door opened to a bedroom with stacks of clothes and things waiting to be sorted. The next room contained a hospital bed and a tall night table; a wheelchair was folded under the window, two crutches leaned up against a wall.

"This must be his wife's sickroom," she said.

The bed was without sheets, and a folded comforter and pillow lay at the foot. A blue pack of Ga-Jol licorice still lay on the night table beside a portable alarm clock. A few photographs had been thumbtacked beside the head of the bed; one of them depicted Sørensen and his wife, the other a woman—her mother, Louise guessed. The room had been emptied and cleaned, but it seemed as if he'd lacked the energy or will to take these final things out.

Louise was about to leave the room when she heard steps in the living room. She glanced at Jørgensen, who already had his hand on his holster.

"It's only me," a female voice said. The tall officer appeared in the doorway. "The car is still in the garage. We talked to the neighbors across the street. They just came home, so they haven't seen anything going on over here."

"He must have taken his dog with him," Louise said. It dawned on her that Sørensen might be out walking the dog, and he might have forgotten to shut the patio door. She looked around the living room. Her skin crawled again when she picked up one of the small, silver-framed photos on the windowsill.

Sørensen stood on a hilltop, his arm around his smiling wife. Christine leaned on a crutch under her right arm. They were both tan, the wind whipped their hair.

"Maybe after you stopped by, he realized he could be in danger, too," Jørgensen said.

Louise nodded and carefully slid the photo into her coat pocket. "We need to keep this house under surveillance. And if he's not back in an hour, we'll have to put an APB out for him. I want to be sure he's under our protection the moment he shows up."

The house had a view of a large lake that disappeared behind a forest thicket.

"He might come in through the utility room. He could be down at the lake with his dog, so be aware of that," Jørgensen cautioned the female officer.

"And inform him that he'll be offered police protection," Louise added. "And mention that it might be best for him to stay with family." She nodded when Jørgensen asked if he should write her cell phone number on his card, so their North Zealand colleagues had both numbers.

Louise's phone rang on the way back to Copenhagen. It was almost two; they had decided to stop someplace to pick up a few sandwiches.

"I'm sitting here with someone who wants to talk to you," Camilla said. "Are you at the office?"

"I'm on the road. Can I call later?"

"Where can we meet? It's important."

Louise had the impression her friend was also driving somewhere. "Where are you?"

"On the freeway, but we'll be in town in half an hour. Would it be better if we stop by your place?"

"Who's with you? We're busy as hell." Louise was annoyed; Camilla always wanted things to happen right here and now.

"Stephanie Parker is sitting beside me. She came to

Denmark to look for her father, and I think it's a really good idea for you two to have a talk. As I understand it, you've met before. Steph saw the man who shot her mother; she'll be able to help you."

"Stephanie! What in the hell is she doing here?" Louise blurted out, before she realized that Stephanie also could hear her. "Police Headquarters, in a half hour." She hung up.

"Jesus! Stephanie Parker is in Denmark," she told Jørgensen. Adrenaline surged through her body; she was worried.

"Sofie Parker's daughter? Why is she here?"

The nagging doubt she'd been trying to bury was back. Of course Eik hadn't shot his ex-girlfriend, she was sure of that. But what did she actually know?

"Steph is Eik's daughter. She disappeared from her home several days ago. She's Jonas's age, but she's never met her father. Eik didn't even know he had a child until recently."

Her old partner looked over, obviously startled by the news. But she was grateful he didn't ask any more questions.

26

They'd just arrived back at Homicide when Suhr stopped Louise and asked her to come into his office. His forehead was deeply furrowed; he looked tired. And old, Louise thought, as he told her to sit down.

"Michael Stig has gone home." He sank into his high-backed office chair. "It's serious. I've had this feeling that the pressure was getting to him, but whenever I asked him about it he convinced me he could handle it. These shootings have been brutal on all of us. And now there's another one."

He seemed sad, as if he were responsible for the head of investigations letting them down. *But then he is, of course*, Louise thought. Responsible. He had recommended Michael Stig for the job after Willumsen's death.

"What happened?" she asked.

"We were in my office, preparing for the press briefing later this afternoon. He was going to update the media, also on the Hvidovre homicide. Suddenly he stood up and left the office, and when he didn't come back I went out to look for him. I found him sitting at his desk, staring into space. He didn't react when I came in, he just sat there clicking his pen, like he always does when he's listening. But no one was talking."

"Did you send him home?" Louise was surprised and a bit shaken.

"I called Jakobsen, the stress counselor, and he put him on sick leave, starting today. He's out of the picture."

Louise didn't know what to say. Stig going down from stress was the last thing she'd expected. Not that she doubted Homicide's stress counselor and his diagnosis, not that Stig couldn't have too much on his plate. But her ex-colleague had always been disapproving of human weakness. And now he was showing it.

"Can you head up the investigation on the hospice nurse homicides, while I calm my bosses down? Naturally they're very worried, what with Stig taking over after me, as I'm sure you've heard. And you already head up a department, you're qualified," he added, before she could object.

"As long as Rønholt goes along with it, it's okay by me." Louise scanned her emotions for some small rush of joy, but nothing showed up. All she registered was Eik. She put that aside and asked Suhr to inform the rest of the team that they would be reporting to her, and that they all would meet after the briefing at 6:00 p.m.

A message was waiting for Louise when she returned to the office: Jørgensen and Toft were questioning the three hospice nurses who had been brought in to the station. They were in the offices next door. The undertaker had just arrived, but there was still no sign of Sørensen. North Zealand Police had pulled the officers stationed at his house, but they would drive by again that evening. And they still hadn't found the last hospice nurse, Anita Nielsen, who lived in a house in Hedehusene. Else Corneliussen had agreed to scan her photo of the woman and send it to them, after which they would put out an APB for her.

Louise had just sat down when the front desk called and said she had a visitor.

"Hi, Steph," Louise said, walking up to the black-haired girl. Steph had pulled her hands up into the sleeves of her leather jacket, and her scarf was pulled tightly around her neck, covering the lower half of her face. "Good to see you again. Are you cold?"

Louise herself felt both warm and cold inside at the sight of Eik's daughter standing there, shuffling her feet in the freezing weather. Suddenly she saw how much the girl resembled a young Eik in the photo his parents had. At the same time, she looked like a desperate, insecure young girl in black makeup, with no one to hold on to. She had left home without knowing the first thing about who she was looking for. What if she didn't like Eik when she met him? What if she was disappointed because she'd been expecting something else? And what if she was rejected? Louise couldn't bear the thought.

"I promised Stephanie I'd help find her father," Camilla said.

"Steph! My name is Steph, not Stephanie," Steph mumbled, without looking up.

Louise nodded. Before she could ask how Steph and Camilla had found each other, Camilla explained that

Steph had made her way to the manse in Jutland, where
some of her mother's old documents were still stored.

"This young lady is awesome," Camilla said. "I explained about us being friends and all."

"Are you hungry, Steph?" Louise said, waiting to see
if they should drop by the cafeteria before heading for her
office.

The girl shook her head.

Back in the office, Louise said, "We'd better tell the
English police you're here and you're safe. They're worried about you. I understand you saw the man who shot
your mother."

"Yes." Steph sat down on the chair Camilla brought
over to her.

"You can probably imagine I have a lot of questions to
ask. Are you okay with that?"

The girl nodded.

Louise sat down at her desk. "I'd like you to look at a
photo, so we can clear up whether it was the man you saw
that evening."

"Fine." Steph nodded. Suddenly she looked like a small,
lost girl wearing way too much makeup. Her emo look—a
full purple skirt, black leggings with neon-green polka dots
with holes in them, a large zippered leather jacket, and Dr.
Martens boots—only strengthened that impression. Louise
gathered herself for a moment before bringing out a print of
Eik's photo from the Search Department's intranet.

"That's not him," Sofie's daughter said, after a single
look at the photo. "He doesn't look at all like that."

The hairs on the back of Louise's neck rose, a wave of
relief streaming through her. She glanced over at a smiling Camilla.

"Who is he?" Steph asked, when she noticed the two women exchanging glances. She grabbed the picture and studied it.

Louise took a deep breath. Eik should have been the one to tell her, but now she had no choice. "It's your father." Steph had laid the photo back down. Now she reached for it again, but she stopped herself and simply studied his face. She pushed the photo back at Louise.

"Where is he?" Was she happy or disappointed? It was impossible to tell.

Louise leaned forward and folded her hands on her desk. Camilla watched her, waiting for her to speak. "He's in England."

"What's he doing there?" The girl looked surprised and somewhat annoyed.

"Actually, I think he went over there to find you, after he heard you'd disappeared," Louise said.

"Are you telling me my father knows I exist? Why hasn't he been looking for me?"

"He's known about you only a short time. Your mother contacted him because she wanted you two to meet." Suddenly Louise realized she'd become the mediator between Eik and the girl's dead mother.

"How do you know all this?" The girl's voice softened, and her dark eyes showed a trace of hope and vulnerability. Clearly she was curious, yet defiant, too, and uncertain about which of the two emotions she should give in to.

"What did you say his name was?" she said, looking at Louise.

"His name is Eik Nordstrøm. He's a policeman; he works for the Search Department."

"Does he have other children?"

Louise shook her head. "Only you."

Someone knocked on the door. Louise was surprised to see Rønholt step inside.

"Excuse me," her boss said, when he saw they were talking. He eyed Steph for a moment, then he said, "Just wanted to let you know, Eik has just landed at Kastrup. He was released this morning after I sent them proof that he was here in Denmark when Sofie Parker was shot."

"Released?" Steph looked back and forth between Louise and Camilla.

"He's been in jail in Bristol, suspected of killing your mother," Louise explained.

"All of you thought my father had killed my mother?" she asked in disbelief.

"We didn't think so," Louise said, "but the English police did, and we had to prove otherwise before they would release him."

"If I hadn't come to Denmark, they probably wouldn't have arrested him," Steph said, annoyed now. "I could've told the police he doesn't look at all like the man who shot her." Quietly she added, "He was a lot older."

Louise nodded and said it might have saved her father from being arrested. "Actually, though, I think the English police were just getting sick of him; he was a pain in the ass to them while he was searching for you. I'm sure they weren't unhappy he was behind bars." She smiled at Stephanie.

"We think your mother's murder is linked to three other murders here in Denmark over the past few months," she continued. "It looks like the weapon used here was the hunting rifle used to kill your mother."

"Does that mean the man who shot my mother is here in Denmark?" Something in the young girl's eyes changed.

Louise hesitated a moment before nodding. "It's very likely." She wondered if she should call in Jakobsen to talk to the girl. It was nearly unforgivable that she hadn't been offered crisis counseling.

"Eik's coming here as soon as he leaves the airport," Rønholt said.

"Would you please send him straight up here?" Louise asked. Suddenly Steph was very quiet. As if she was getting nervous, now that she would soon be meeting her father.

Rønholt nodded. For a moment he studied the young girl again. Louise could almost read his mind, but he said nothing.

On his way out, he almost ran into Toft, holding the photo of Erik Hald Sørensen and his wife that Louise had taken from his house.

"I made a copy," he said. He laid the original down on the desk. "I also received a photo of Anita Nielsen. The quality isn't good, but it's usable."

Louise nodded. "Put an APB out for her, all police districts. We have to find them and bring them in for protection."

"I've assembled a team," he said. "We're contacting families and friends and former coworkers to hear if they know where they might be. I hope that's okay with you, even though it cuts down on our personnel."

"Of course," Louise said. She needed time to get used to being in charge.

Steph was pacing around the office, but when she

walked by the desk, she froze and pointed to the photo of Sørensen. "That's him!" She took a step back, as if she had just burned herself. "He's the one who shot my mother. I recognize his beard and hair."

Louise was startled, but when she saw how pale the girl's face was, she plopped down into a chair and stared in the direction of the photo. "Are you sure?"

The girl's face closed up, as if she was used to adults not really believing her.

Camilla had been sitting silently in the corner, but now she said, "Of course it's him, Steph said so." She stood up and put her arm around the girl's shoulders.

Louise tried to shut everyone out for a moment to concentrate and form a scenario.

"Why did he kill my mother?" Steph asked. "Who is he? What's going on?" She began crying.

Fragments from interrogations, her visits to Birkerød, and statements from witnesses swirled in Louise's head. Finally she shook them off and concentrated on the girl, who stared at her in despair, tears running down her cheeks. "I don't have any answers for you. Not that I don't believe you when you say he shot her, but this turns everything upside down."

She looked up at Toft, who was still standing in the doorway. "We have to warn Else Corneliussen and the others. And we need surveillance on Anita Nielsen's house in Hedehusene. Send two squad cars out, now. Pull everything we have on Sørensen out of our files."

She directed her last order at Jørgensen, back in the office and at his computer now after questioning the hospice nurses.

Camilla stood up when she sensed that things were

getting hectic. "Why don't we go into another office?" she said to Stephanie. She glanced at Louise. "I'll stick around with her until Eik shows up."

The girl turned to Camilla. "You don't need to wait. I'd like to be alone for a while. If this Eik...my father comes, then..."

"You're sure?" Camilla said. The girl nodded and grabbed the card Camilla handed her.

"Okay, then I'll head back to the paper," she said to Louise. "Terkel has been holding a two-page spread for me, and I haven't written a line. But call if you need me."

"I will." Louise was holding her phone to her ear, distracted by all that was going on.

Suhr came into the office; he'd met Toft out in the hallway. "I hear you have a suspect."

Louise hung up and nodded. "Everyone's out looking for Erik Hald Sørensen." Suddenly the weight of responsibility that came with being in charge of the investigation team hit her, along with a rush of adrenaline.

"Are you putting out an APB?" Louise asked Jørgensen. She lifted the phone and ordered a team of forensic technicians out to Sørensen's home.

"We'll need a search warrant for the suspect's house," she told Toft, who immediately headed for his office.

Through all the chaos, she sensed Steph's eyes on her. The pale young girl was studying the photo of Sørensen and his wife, which lay on the desk in front of her. "Let's find you an office where you can wait for Eik." She led her into Stig's office, a few doors down the hall. "I'm sure he'll be here before long."

"Fine." The girl's stubborn expression had returned,

and Louise felt guilty about not being able to wait there with her. But maybe she really did want to be alone, as she had told Camilla.

"Do you need anything?" Louise pointed toward the kitchen and offered her coffee, tea, or water. "There might even be a cola in the refrigerator."

Steph shook her head. "No thanks, nothing."

"I'll be in the office, come in if you need to, but Eik will show up soon." She stopped for a moment and studied Steph as she sat in Stig's high-backed office chair. "Are you okay? Is it okay to meet your father in here? Would you like us to arrange it so you can meet him somewhere else? This evening, maybe?"

Steph narrowed her eyes a bit. "Why?" She reached for a paper clip on the desk and began straightening it out.

"I just thought you might want to meet him someplace where it's quiet."

The black-haired young girl shook her head. "I'll wait here, it's okay." She fished her phone out of her pocket.

27

December 2013

"You wanted to talk to me?" Steph said, as she came in after tossing her school bag and leather jacket in her room.

Sofie nodded and pointed to the living room sofa. Her daughter glanced into the kitchen, as if she was making sure they were alone.

During breakfast, an innocent remark about a few mid-afternoon free periods at school had developed into a shouting match between Nigel and her; he thought she should stay in school and do her homework instead of going home with a girlfriend and hanging out.

While the walls shook from the angry shouting, Sofie had realized they couldn't go on this way. It wasn't so much the constant quarreling, though it had begun wearing on her. But it was affecting her daughter physically. A guarded insecurity entered her eyes now whenever she and Nigel were in the same room. At the same time, her daughter knew exactly which buttons to push with him. This isn't working, Sofie acknowledged, when her daughter stormed out and slammed the door after the argument at breakfast.

"Do you want anything?" she asked when Steph sat down. "A sandwich, something to drink?"

Her daughter shook her head and sat straight òn the sofa, legs pulled up under her, waiting. Her fingers played restlessly with three strands hanging from the long, black scarf wrapped tightly around her neck, like some stiff collar. Black, beautiful, and mysterious. Her insecurity was gone; she seemed happy and curious.

Where to begin? In her head, Sofie had gone through every possible way to open this conversation, one that couldn't be put off any longer, that maybe should already have taken place.

She had always been in doubt. She regretted not telling her daughter long ago that Nigel Parker wasn't her biological father. It would have made it easier for Sofie to let Steph in on the reason for her decision. On the other hand, she hadn't thought her daughter needed to know until she was older, even older than now, at an age when she might be able to understand.

Sofie walked over and sat down on the sofa. She reached for her daughter's hand and decided to wing it. "I left Denmark many years ago, right after your grandmother died. I wanted to travel around Europe for the summer. Just ramble around, no definite plans. I needed to get away, get some distance from my mother's death. Something happens when you find yourself alone, all your family gone. And I had to figure out how to deal with that."

For a moment she considered telling her daughter about Stig and the marriage she had abandoned. But that could wait. Right now this was more important. "I wanted to go to several places in France, and I also dreamed about seeing the Amalfi Coast and Rome. But before I got that far, I ran into a guy at the train station in Zurich. We'd been on the same train from Copenhagen, but I didn't really notice him until we were on the platform. He was helping a mother with two small children haul a baby carriage up the steps, because the elevator was broken."

Steph slumped a bit on the sofa. She'd stopped twirling the strands of her scarf, and she let Sofie hold her hand.

"We started talking, and we both had to find a cheap place to stay, so we decided to stick together. We ended up renting two rooms at an old boarding house. There was no hot water. *And* there were lice," she suddenly recalled. They had already kissed that first evening, but she didn't tell her daughter that. "He was on leave from his job, he was just traveling around, too, wherever his feet took him, so we decided to go to France together."

"And you fell in love with him or what?" Steph wasn't sure where her mother was going with all this.

"No. But it was the first time I'd traveled alone, and it was nice to follow along with someone who'd done it before."

She paused a moment, thinking back. After she'd opened the bank account, they passed through Switzerland to France, where they spent two weeks before boarding a tourist boat to Corsica.

"One evening we met two guys, Christopher and Mark, at the harbor. We'd already spread out our sleeping pads at the end of a pier, we wanted to sleep surrounded by water, and they'd just sailed in from the mainland.

They were having trouble tying up the boat, so we helped. It was typical for him to just start talking to people we met. The next few days we hung around with them. It was fun, and when they were ready to leave, they asked us if we wanted to go along. They were going to Italy, and as I said, I wanted to visit Rome."

"And you still weren't in love with him?" Steph had pulled her hand away without Sofie's noticing.

"By then I was." She folded her hands in her lap. The dark-haired Copenhagener had swept her off her feet. He was so different from the life she had wanted to put behind her.

"I tried to fight it. I really didn't need another broken heart, I was already running away from one. But we had a fantastic summer..." She was caught off guard; suddenly she recalled the afternoon they sat on boulders by the sea, eating sandwiches, the smell of the water breaking against the cliffs. The scent of rosemary, the heat. And his body.

"You were wild about him," her daughter said matter-of-factly.

Sofie nodded. "Yes. I was wild about him."

"Then why didn't you stay together? He sounds a lot cooler than the grumpy old creep I have for a father. But I guess if you had, I wouldn't be here." She tilted her head.

Sofie took a deep breath. "Yes you would. You would still be here. He's your father, but I didn't know I was expecting when we broke up."

The silence was deafening. And long.

Sofie reached over for her daughter's hand again, stroked the back of it with her fingers, all the way to her black fingernails. "I didn't find out until I was three months along. And by that time I was far away."

"But why did you break up? Why did you go on alone?"

"There was something I had to do." Sofie paused. She had made up her mind to be as honest as possible with her sixteen-year-old daughter about her past. But there still were things she didn't want to get into, like her time in Switzerland, and why she returned to work at a suicide clinic.

"I wasn't ready to commit," Sofie said, content to leave it at that. "And then when I found out I was expecting you, he was back in Denmark. It was a summer romance, with a bonus for me."

She squeezed Steph's hand.

"Does he even know I exist?"

"We haven't spoken since I left the boat."

"When you two split up?"

"It was time for me to move on. I found out I'd received my inheritance from my mother, so I had to go back to Switzerland and take care of my finances."

Steph looked astonished. "So you chose your money over the man you were in love with?"

"Back then I did, anyway. I'd begun traveling to start a new life. At the time I really needed to be able to take care of myself. Be independent. An adult."

"What did he say to your just leaving?"

"We had an argument on the boat one morning. We'd just tied up at a small fishing village not far from Rome. I wanted to wash clothes, he wanted to sightsee, and I blew up because he wouldn't help. I knew I'd be moving on anyway, and the argument gave me extra incentive. I found a telephone booth on the way into the village, and I called the bank, like I'd been doing regularly to hear if my money had arrived. And it had."

She recalled how it had felt back then, at the telephone on the corner of a small square. Nearby stood a small, dimly lit café and a narrow spit of land with booths, crushed ice for the boxes of fish and shellfish being hauled up from the harbor by shouting men in white aprons. A dewy morning, the sun had yet to peek into the narrow streets winding up the mountainside.

"I walked around looking for him, to make up. So I could tell him in a decent way I had to leave. But when I finally found him in the town square, he'd been smoking dope, and he was sitting around playing music with a bunch of kids he'd met."

He'd been leaning back against the fountain, a guitar on his lap. When he spotted her, he'd waved her over and told the others to make room for her in the circle. She tried to get him to come with her. Said she wanted to talk to him, asked him to get up. But he just sat there, took another hit on the joint being passed around, and soon it seemed he'd forgotten she was even there. They kept playing, and at the sight of him bent over the guitar, his long hair hanging in his eyes, suddenly it was much too difficult for her to say good-bye.

"I walked back to the boat and packed my things. I felt terrible, and I was still mad at him for going his own way." She smiled; that was the very thing about him she'd fallen in love with. "I wrote him a note, and then I left."

"So you didn't even say good-bye to each other?"

Sofie shook her head.

They sat for a while without speaking.

Finally Steph asked, "What was he like?"

"He was everything I didn't have in the life I'd left behind. He was open-minded, open to life. Reckless, and yet warm. You look a lot like him." She smiled. "He was beautiful, free, his own man."

"Why have you waited so long to tell me this?" Steph's eyes were moist.

"I've been thinking, maybe we should try to find him. The way things are between you and Nigel, I think it would be good for you to meet your biological father. And you have the right to know that Nigel isn't your father, even though he's taken care of you since you were very little."

Steph grimaced, but she didn't say anything.

Sofie felt it now, sharply: she'd been treading water. Of course, Steph should know who her biological father was. She saw Eik in her daughter—she, too, went her own way, and Sofie couldn't bear watching that part of her being slowly swept away by her husband's irritation.

"If you want to, if you think it's a good idea, I'll try to find him."

"Maybe I could live with him?" Steph blurted out.

"You can visit him anyway, if he decides to answer."

"So Nigel isn't my father at all?" She pulled the long sleeves of her sweater over her hands and rested her chin on her covered palms.

Sofie shook her head.

"Does he have other children, my real father?"

The fact was that Sofie didn't know. She shrugged. "Probably. He's forty-two or so. If he was going to have children, he'd probably have them by now."

She studied her daughter for a moment, her serious, dark expression. But she also saw curiosity, expectation. "Of course we have to be prepared, he might not know how to deal with finding out he has a daughter."

"He might not even believe you when you tell him."

Sofie shook her head. "Even though it's been a long time, I don't think he'll react that way. I think he'll be happy when he hears about it."

She tried to sound convincing. Because Eik Nordstrøm had been anything but happy when she had contacted him. She'd probably come off as being pushy and meddlesome, too, but she'd had to know about his life before deciding if she should bring him and his daughter together.

"I'd like to meet him," Steph said, her voice small.

28

Eik showed up in the doorway unshaven and out of breath, and immediately asked, "Where's Stephanie?" He looked around.

"Welcome home," Louise said, a bit sharply perhaps, but her stomach sank when she stood up. He looked battered and exhausted in his leather jacket and black jeans, his hair hanging down over his eyebrows. But he smiled and walked over to her, put his hands on her shoulders, and kissed her on the forehead.

"What a hell of an ordeal this has been."

He looked at her intently, as if he were forcing his way inside her to check how much damage the past several days had done to them.

"She's sitting in here waiting for you," Louise said, the warmth of his hands still on her shoulders.

He followed her down the hallway. "How is she? What's she like?"

Louise turned to him before they reached the door. "Relax." In all the time she'd known him, this was the first time he'd seemed nervous. "She's just identified the

man who's probably our perpetrator. It was a coincidence."

She told him about the photo they had been about to
send out to every police district. "We thought he was one
of the people we had to protect. But Steph says he shot
her mother. She reacted very strongly to the photo, so
right now we're trying to find him and bring him in, and
we'll see what he says about being identified by a witness."

She paused for a moment. "There's a distinct possibility he has an alibi. But at least we can eliminate him."

"If she says so, it's him!"

Louise nodded. "At the very least we have a general
description to go on."

"She wouldn't just say something like that!"

"You haven't even met her," Louise pointed out. She
smiled when they stopped outside Michael Stig's office.
"I'll leave you two alone."

Toft approached her with a search warrant in his hand.
"We're on our way to Birkerød to search his house."

"Let's talk this evening," Louise said hurriedly to Eik.
"She's a sweet girl, everything is going to be fine. Come
over to my ... to our place." She turned to meet Toft.

"Hey! Where is she?"

Louise turned back to Eik, who was standing in the office doorway. "Maybe she's in the lounge," she said. "I
told her she could grab something to eat or drink."

Eik had already ducked into the office, but a few moments later he was out in the hall again. "Come here,
there's something you need to see."

He pointed at the copy of the photo of Sørensen and
his wife. It lay on the desk, along with the message that

had been sent to the police districts. "What the hell is this?"

The photo had been torn apart in the middle, and only Erik Hald Sørensen remained. Horns had been drawn on his head with a black felt pen, and a target now covered his face. He'd been shot between the eyes with an arrow.

"It's the man she identified as killing her mother."

Eik stiffened and reached for the photo, but changed his mind and let it lie. "I should've insisted on meeting her the second Sofie told me we had a daughter." He sat down on the desk. "I should've made her let me see the girl, but I wasn't ready, at all. At first I thought someone was fucking with me when I saw the email. All those years without a word from her, and suddenly there she was, in my in-box."

Louise had pulled out a chair and was leaning up against its back.

"I don't know if you can imagine how crazy it is, being told you have a daughter who's almost grown up."

Louise thought about Jonas, who was a preteen when he had entered her life. She also hadn't known she was suddenly about to have a child, and the emotions rising up just from the thought of him overwhelmed her. Thinking about Eik's reaction at hearing he had a daughter, his own flesh and blood, killed off the last traces of her anger toward him.

"I wrote Sofie that I wanted to come over right then to meet her, but that was too fast for her. She wanted it done the right way, she said, and I flew off the handle. She was hardly the one to talk about doing things the right way. Sixteen years she'd kept Stephanie a secret from me. I had the right to meet her."

Louise's thoughts wandered as Eik talked. What would happen when a sensitive teenager found out she had a different father than she'd thought? One who lived an hour's flight away. And shortly thereafter, she'd seen her mother being killed. Louise's fingertips tingled, her nerves twitched in alarm.

Eik was still talking, but she wasn't listening. His sixteen-year-old daughter could be a stray missile out there somewhere, seeking its target.

Even though he was opening up to her about his anger at his ex-girlfriend, the woman who had kept him out of his daughter's life, Louise interrupted him. "You check the bathrooms, I'll look for her in the lounge."

She was already out the door. She stuck her head into the kitchenette; the dishwasher was beeping, ready to be emptied. She looked everywhere she could think of, then she ran back to her temporary office, grabbed the phone, and called down to the officer guarding the front door to hear if her guest had left Police Headquarters.

"If she has, she didn't return her guest pass," the officer said.

"Damn it, you're sitting down there to keep an eye on people!" Louise snapped. She couldn't help it; she was getting more worried by the moment.

Back in Stig's office, she found Eik behind her colleague's computer. "Did you check the bathrooms?" she said, annoyed at him for not helping.

"She wasn't there," he answered, without looking up. "And if Stephanie's right, that this man shot her mother, we have to find her before she finds him."

"How could she know where to look?" Louise mumbled, mostly to herself. She pressed her fingertips against her temples, as if the small circles she made could help her concentrate. "She doesn't know where he lives."

She tried to remember, had she mentioned the address when she sent a patrol car to Birkerød? Damn it, maybe she had...

She hurried back to her office and ran into Jørgensen in the doorway just as he was sticking his phone in his pocket. He had his coat on. "Are the patrol cars out there yet?" she asked.

"They just arrived. Nobody's there."

"Steph is gone, and we don't know if she'd try to find him."

Her old partner looked at her in surprise.

"Never mind, I'll explain later. Before you leave, call the officers out there and tell them to keep an eye out for her. And if she shows up, we need to know immediately. Tell them it's a young girl, possibly unstable."

"We have two patrol cars at Sørensen's home in Birkerød," she said, when she returned to Stig's office. "They've been told to keep an eye out for Steph, they'll let us know if she shows up."

Eik lifted his hand to stop her. "Try to think like her. We have files, we can check on people, but Stephanie doesn't have shit. She gets shoved in here to wait. What does she do?"

"Eik, we don't have time—"

"You saw what she did to the photo—come on! She's upset and angry."

"Let's try to stay calm," Louise said, aware that she was talking to herself as much as to Eik.

He ignored her. "She probably has a cell phone, and definitely had access to this computer some idiot forgot to log out of. So of course she googles the name on the APB."

Something in his tense voice made Louise walk around the office chair and peek over his shoulder.

"His name has been typed in, and see, his photos pop up when you search."

Photos of Erik Hald Sørensen appeared on the screen, seven of them in the top row of results. Two of the faces she didn't recognize. The five others were of the retired doctor, photos that had at some time been on the Internet. He also showed up on the second row of results, a few times with his wife, mostly from their choir travels. Possibly from local papers, Louise thought.

Eik scrolled down the purple links his daughter had opened. He frowned as his fingers worked. "Look at this." He scooted a bit to the side. "When I search his name with 'address,' it's not the Birkerød address that shows up. Here he's listed with an address on Skovridergårdsvej in Virum." He looked up at her.

"It could be his clinic," she said. "He might still have that address, even though he gave up his practice." Then she remembered him mentioning that the clinic was in Hareskovby.

Eik broke into her thoughts. "A Vivian Hald Sørensen is also registered at the Virum address."

Time stood still as Louise struggled to take in all he'd said. After a moment she came back to life and ran to her office. She'd just grabbed her coat when Eik showed up in the doorway. "It's his ex-wife's place," she said. "He's hiding out there."

"It's for sure where Stephanie's gone to look for him," Eik said, as they ran down the hall.

29

He drove all the way down the dead-end street and parked with two wheels over the curb, just outside the house. For a moment he eyed the imposing home, then he grabbed the bag in the front seat and got out. He opened the familiar front gate.

The driveway was empty, but the entire first floor was lit. He walked around to the backyard; wet grass clung to his shoes when he stopped. Against the wall of the house, behind the naked lilac bush reaching all the way up to the terrace, he unpacked his rifle and hitched it up over his shoulder. He grabbed the bag and walked up the steps of the terrace that faced the forest.

The lawn furniture was stored inside for the winter. A few pots held boxwood trees, and a broom stood in a corner. She sat at the dining room table, behind the tall terrace windows. She was facing him, but she was absorbed in the ring binders and papers spread out in front of her.

He put his rifle to his shoulder and zeroed in on her. He aimed, and when she was in his sight, he checked his emotions.

His cheeks were moist now from the gloomy, gray fog, but he didn't notice it while he lowered the rifle and picked up his bag. He headed back down the terrace steps, continued around the house, found his keys, and unlocked the garage. Her car was still inside, but otherwise it was almost empty. He walked over to the basement door but stopped when he heard footsteps above. Shortly after, someone flushed the toilet and walked back across the floor. A chair scraped, and then it was quiet.

He started up the basement steps, opened the door to the hallway, and entered the dining room. Standing in the doorway behind her, he recognized her perfume. The odor hung over the room, cloudlike. He noted her hair, cut in a short page. Her neck. The slender hands, the ring on her finger.

He laid his bag down and again put his rifle to his shoulder, and suddenly she turned and stared silently into the barrel.

"Shh," he said. He took a step forward.

"Are you completely out of your mind?" she shrieked, and started to stand up.

"Stay in your chair. You're going to do something for me."

"No I'm not! What in the world are you doing, barging in here like this? And with that rifle, what is this? I'll call the police if you don't leave this house at once."

He shook his head. "I'm not leaving until you've helped me."

Reluctantly she sat back down. Her eyes wandered over to the terrace door, then the kitchen door.

"It won't take long if we get started," he said. "I'm not going to hurt you, as long as you agree to do this for me."

"What is it you want?" She clenched the thin arms of the dining room chair in panic.

He laid the rifle down and unzipped the gym bag. He felt her eyes glued to him as he unpacked a small video camera. But he knew she'd do what he told her to, because she in turn knew he would keep his word. As long as she agreed to help.

She sat motionless, watching him unfold the tripod and mount the small, silver camera on top. It would be the same procedure as when he had sat with the dying. His confession would be documented the same way the nurse service, without his knowledge, filmed Christine's wish to die. And Vivian had to listen. She must understand why he'd had to leave her. And why he'd acted the way he did.

He carried everything into the living room and set it up in front of the low, two-person leather sofa, so he could sit with his back to the dining room with the camera in front of him.

"Come on," he said. He dragged a dining room chair over to the tripod, so they would be facing each other. Without a word, she stood up and followed him.

"All you have to do is push the red button to record. And don't interrupt me. You're going to be my life witness."

She nodded, she understood, but just to be safe he grabbed the rifle and laid it on his lap after he sat down. He breathed deeply and thought about everything he had planned to say. He didn't need to start at the very beginning, but anyway he would try to cover everything important.

He nodded at her; he was ready. "I never loved anyone like I loved Christine." For a moment his voice thickened.

He got a grip on himself before continuing. "I'd never believed all that business about finding a soul mate. But Christine was. She was my soul mate."

His ex-wife shivered and looked away. But his testimony was more important than sparing her. "My name is Erik Hald Sørensen."

He gave his CPR number and address, so no one would be in doubt about his identity, or that he was in his right mind during the recording.

"What is it you want? Why do you...?" Vivian's voice shook; her eyes were wide and full of fear.

He stared straight at his ex-wife. She shut up.

"When I met Christine almost five years ago, she changed my life. I found a joy and an enormous lust for life I'd never experienced before. Even though Christine was twenty years younger than me, she was the wiser of us. She filled her life with what was good for her, while I'd always filled my life with what was expected of me."

His ex-wife looked down, as if she were ducking invisible punches. But this wasn't about her, nor was it a reckoning between them; that had happened long ago, and he had moved on. This was about making people understand how much he had lost.

"I loved to sing when I was a child, but later on I stopped because there was always so much else I was expected to spend my time on. I got an education, I got married, started the clinic. We had children, they grew up, I worked. Took care of my responsibilities and earned money."

"That's enough!" His ex-wife was enraged, but as she stood up, he grabbed the rifle.

"Sit down." He aimed at her, and finally she sat back

down on the chair. "Everything was work and responsibilities. Sure, there were also good times." He nodded at her. "But I never did anything for myself. Alone. I did things for us, for my family, the ones I loved."

He paused a moment. "Christine was referred to the clinic, because her doctor was on vacation."

Again he spoke directly to the camera. "It's hard to say exactly what happened between us. It was just there. Like something binding us together we'd suddenly discovered. We began seeing each other. Two months later I was divorced. And I'm sorry about that." He looked over at Vivian. "I know I hurt you, and the kids, too. And I'm very sorry, you know that. But it couldn't be helped, because I loved her from the moment we met, and that's the type of thing that can't be explained or even understood, if you haven't experienced it.

"When your own adult sons refuse to try to understand your choices, when they turn their backs on you, that's a terrible price to pay. They thought it was sleazy to leave their mother for a woman barely older than them. And that's understandable. But I paid that price, because the joy that came from the love I'd found was that great. A life I'd never known existed opened up for me."

He leaned forward, closer to the camera; this was important. "And I'm not talking about sex. It's not about an older man finding a younger model to prove he can still perform. It was a love that made me feel like a human being someone found worthy of loving unconditionally."

He leaned back again. His ex-wife seemed to have retreated into herself, as if she didn't want to hear any more.

"Then Christine became ill. She'd prepared me for the possibility. It was inherited. Her mother died of the same disease when she was sixty-six. No one can know how long it will take for it to get the upper hand, but she was diagnosed when she was thirty-eight. We talked a lot about it. She was very realistic. A meter had been put on her life, and it was running, was how she put it. She noticed very little the first year after the diagnosis, but then the symptoms began showing up. And shortly after her fortieth birthday, she had difficulty walking up stairs. It went fast. Way too fast."

He choked up again, and he reminded himself that he had plenty of time. Saying what he had to say in a decent manner was the most important thing. He took a deep breath. "By then I'd already quit my practice to take care of Christine. We spent our money doing everything we wanted to do together. We'd dreamed of traveling, seeing the world. All the things couples dream about when they fall in love. And we had the opportunity. We'd talked about selling everything and joining Doctors Without Borders, but we had to put that idea aside when the disease struck. But we did travel some, and it was an enormous experience for me to see new places with her, and to share places I loved with her."

He felt his ex-wife's eyes on him. She was listening again, now that he had reached the part of the story she didn't know about.

"Little by little her spasms worsened, and finally she couldn't control her body. Six months later she was in a wheelchair, and we couldn't travel. She *wouldn't*, I should say. She didn't like being limited. But I adapted our lives to that. It didn't matter to me, I was happy to stay home, because I enjoyed so much just living our everyday lives together. And I insisted on continuing to do all the things she loved to do. We bought a van with room for her wheelchair in back. It wasn't complicated, we just had to organize everything. Many people are dependent upon special equipment, it's a necessity of life. She just had to get used to it. It wasn't easy, but she handled it because she wanted to. But then her voice disappeared."

Vivian made a move to stand up again. "Erik—"

"Be quiet! Sit down!" Immediately he pointed his rifle at her. "Let me speak!"

Suddenly he slumped, his emotions getting the best of him as he returned to his memories. He'd been hunting on Helleby Estate, with Lars and Merete. He hadn't told his old childhood friend about Christine's illness; he simply excused her absence by saying she had influenza. When he came home, she lay in bed with her back to the room. She could only whisper, though he didn't find that out until that evening; at first she wouldn't say anything. She lay quietly and unmoving in her shell. He realized the disease had finally broken her, and he'd cried so much that he had to get out, walk the dog down to the lake.

He pulled himself together. "Things turned really bad for her after she couldn't sing. And she became aggressive. But that's natural, it's a process you have to go through. It goes quickly for some, slower for others. I've seen it many times. It's never easy to come to terms with a fatal disease. She was forty, she wasn't at all ready to die. Of course not. But her life wasn't over, either, I tried to explain to her. It was just difficult to convince her."

He smiled. "She wasn't the type to hold back what she was feeling or thinking. And she hated the thought of being confined to a bed, where someone else had to wipe her ass, as she put it. She didn't want to end like that, she'd seen it all with her mother. It didn't bother me that we couldn't make physical love, when she'd given so much of herself, but now she wouldn't let me touch her in any loving way. She felt her body had let her down, betrayed her. It was so horrible for her. So sad."

An evening he'd completely forgotten suddenly came back to him. That afternoon he'd stopped by the Daniel Letz Shop in Østerbro to buy smoked salmon, which she loved. He arranged everything on a tray, lit candles, opened a bottle of wine, and carried it all to her bed. They ate together every evening; they had furnished the guest room with all the things she wanted to be surrounded by. He'd suggested they move her hospital bed into the living room, but she refused. She preferred being carried to the sofa and lying there in the daytime. And then being returned to bed. She felt there should be variety to her day. That evening he told her about the oldest of his younger brothers, who had played in a dance band after he was thrown out of school. Most of the stories from his childhood were off-color, but Christine loved them. He did, too, now that so many years had gone by.

"I don't know exactly when she contacted the hospice nurse service," he said. "She didn't tell me about it, she knew I wanted to take care of her to the end, with all that would involve. She did it to spare me, I'm aware of that. She thought her disorder would be a burden to me. Even though I kept telling her I saw it differently, that I wanted to be there for her all the time. I wanted us to go through it together. And I'm trained to handle such things. But of course it was also about her dignity, and all she could see was her life falling apart. So I decided to step aside when she asked for outside help."

Now came the worst part for him. He pulled a letter out of his jacket's inner pocket and unfolded it. "This letter arrived a month after she died. Christine wrote it, long before she drank the medicine that killed her. She must have asked the hospice nurse to send it to me after her death, so I would have some perspective to it all when I received it."

He took a deep breath. "She explains in the letter why she decided to end her life. She might have lived a few years longer, we could have had a little more time together, but she wanted to leave this world with dignity. She put it this way: 'My beloved Erik, you are the very best part of my life. You know that. I hope with all my heart that one day you will understand why I decided to do what I'm going to do. I wanted to be able to choose when I would die. I've lived the fullest of lives, but I can't go on. I know you want to be there for me until it's over, but I can't follow you to the end. I've seen what this illness did to my mother, and I respected her wishes to end her life when she lost the will to live. Now I've chosen to do the same. You must understand that I didn't want to hurt you . . ."

He dried his eyes. "I'll leave the letter here, so all of you can read the rest of it." He looked directly at the camera. "Is it still running?"

His ex-wife leaned forward, checked the camera, and nodded.

"It was only after reading the letter that I realized an organization had helped her end her life. At the time I didn't know the home hospice nurse service was such an organization. Had I known that, I would have reported them and put a stop to it. But as I said, she was gone before I found out. I was angry. First with her, for leaving me, but then with them. Not because they helped her. That was her wish, and of course I had to respect that. Because I respected her. But it was much too early. She could have lived several years longer, without any worsening of her condition. That's what really angered me. They took her from me before it was necessary.

"I decided to join the organization, to find out how many people were involved and how well planned everything was. Christine had donated more than one hundred thousand kroner to them. I found out about that later. And of course it was her right to do so, for as she writes in the letter, it meant so much to her to know she could contact them when she felt her time had come. But..."

He glanced at Vivian. "I'm a doctor. I could've given her an overdose, and I could have sat with her and held her hand. We could have done this ourselves, without others being involved."

His ex-wife spoke quietly. "But you wouldn't have done it. You would never have let her go."

He shook his head. "No, I probably wouldn't have. And Christine knew that, of course. She was smart. And she would never have asked me to help her that way, because she knew me, and she knew what a terrible dilemma it would have put me in."

Once more he looked directly at the camera. "It wasn't difficult to join the nurse service. Often the family or friends of someone who has used them offer their help. And they knew I was a doctor. At first I was allowed to watch, to see how they help people die. To be fair, it's all done in a very orderly manner. Everything is recorded on video, like now, where the person dying expresses her wish to end her life, so everyone knows it's voluntary. The recordings were sent to Sofie Parker in England, and she stored them. It took time for me to realize a woman over there did all the administrative work. But then it wasn't hard to find her address."

He kept his eyes on the camera, away from his ex-wife. "I killed them. I'm the one who decided to put a stop to it, to outsiders helping people die. How can they grant themselves the right to take strangers, people they have no relationship to, from those who love them."

His wife cut him off. "Erik!"

He heard something behind him, and he glimpsed Vivian's eyes locked onto a point behind his left shoulder. He grabbed the rifle, turned, and shot as he saw a shadow approach him.

Vivian screamed, and he fired the rifle again. Immediately he recognized the mute, dark-haired girl, the daughter he'd made eye contact with right after he shot her mother. She rushed him with fists raised; he missed her with a third shot but managed to knock her down with the stock of his rifle, then he jumped up and ran past her, out the terrace door and into the forest.

30

"Have you checked your holster?" Eik asked, as they turned off Kongevejen at Virum. He wasn't looking at her, and it was the first thing he'd said since they left.

Louise nodded, sensing the weight under her jacket. She had also ordered more officers be put on standby, in case Sørensen was at his ex-wife's house. "I sure as hell hope you know I could be in serious shit for bringing you along." Louise eyed the tall trees and large homes.

"That's why I love you, honey," he said mildly. "You're the type who takes chances."

"Shut up!" she hissed. But it felt good to ease the tension. All the way there, Louise had waffled between fearing the worst and assuring herself an English schoolgirl couldn't get to a random address in a suburb like Virum quicker than a speeding patrol car. But she could have given a taxi driver the address, in which case she would have a big enough head start.

"That's his car, parked right there!" Louise pointed at a Bordeaux-red station wagon. The car her colleagues from

North Zealand had seen in Sørensen's garage had to be Christine's.

Eik shut down the siren and blue lights as she slowed. Louise reached for the police radio to call for backup.

"Wait," Eik said. "Just a minute. Give me a chance to see if she's in there."

"Like hell I will. Sørensen is inside the house." She'd already called for more patrol cars.

Their feet crunched gravel as they ran up the driveway. Louise rang the doorbell, with Eik already hurrying down the steps to run around the house. Immediately the door was opened by a blond woman with a page cut and pale cheeks, in a black turtleneck sweater and elegant dark pants—it had to be Vivian Hald Sørensen.

Louise was about to show her badge when the woman grabbed her and held on. She began sobbing. "They're out back, he has a gun," she stammered. "He shot the girl."

They felt a draft when they entered the moist, cold living room; the terrace door was open a crack. Eik stood in the broad doorway between the dining room and day room. Someone had bled on the floor.

"Go in the kitchen and stay there," he said. Vivian Hald Sørensen sat down on the floor with her arms hugging her knees. She was in shock.

"What happened?" Louise asked. Pistol in hand, she rushed around to turn off the lights in the living room and kitchen.

Sørensen's ex-wife didn't even seem surprised they knew about the young girl. She pointed at the tripod that had been tipped over in the living room. "He forced me to record his statement, he wanted it to be like the ones made by that group that kills people. And then suddenly the girl was standing behind him. I don't know how she got in."

"Where are they now?" Eik was at the terrace door. An open gym bag containing a box of rifle ammo lay on the floor between the two rooms, but there was no sign of the rifle.

The sobbing woman whispered, "I think she's been hit, he shot at her. But then he ran off, and she chased him."

The sound Eik made as he wrenched the terrace door open and ran toward the forest spurred Louise to drop any idea of waiting for backup. She sprinted after him before he'd reached the backyard's open gate, and they rushed down a small path that led to the forest road.

The January darkness was deepening between the trees, the road was wet and slippery from melting patches of snow. Eik stopped at a fork and looked around. "Stephanie!" he yelled, so loudly that her name echoed among the trees. A gray fog hung in the forest, making it difficult to see clearly.

Louise ran toward a thicket. She noticed black, soggy leaves that had been tramped down, a narrow path leading between bare beech trunks. She heard Eik, still on the forest road, as she fought her way along the path to a large, oval hollow. Fifty meters in diameter at least, she estimated, then she looked around and immediately noticed the black figure curled up at the bottom of the hollow.

"*Eik!*" Louise screamed, and she kept screaming his name as she ran down the slope.

They reached the figure at the same time, but Louise stepped back when Eik kneeled beside Steph and carefully swept her hair off her face.

She lay on her side, her arms stretched out, her legs pulled up underneath her. Eik could only see the profile of her face, but Louise was struck by the resemblance between father and daughter.

He sat still for a moment, studying the unconscious girl. Then he lay a hand on her forehead and ran a finger down over her cheek, a gesture so gentle and filled with affection that tears welled behind Louise's eyes.

He felt for a pulse with two fingers against her throat, then he carefully checked the bloody wound over her right temple before slowly turning her and pulling her black leather jacket to the side.

"She's been hit," he said. "One side, under her breast."

"Shit! Stay here and call for an ambulance. Pull her over behind the bushes there, I'll look for him."

Louise's heart pounded; Sørensen had to be close by. Slowly she maneuvered forward while covering Eik and Steph as he carried her behind the bushes. She spotted him after only a few meters. "Call for another ambulance," she yelled. "He's over here on the ground!" She heard Eik calling behind her as she began running.

Vivian Hald Sørensen appeared on the forest road. She walked stiffly toward her ex-husband and kneeled beside him; a dispassionate professionalism seemed to have kicked in, pushing her shock aside. "He's bleeding. He's been shot in the heart."

The well-dressed doctor lay motionless on the ground, his eyes closed and his shirt soaked with blood. His rifle lay a meter away.

His ex-wife took his hand and stroked it as she spoke comfortingly to him.

"Stay with him," Louise said. Through the trees she

heard the backup arriving. "We've called for another ambulance."

The woman shook her head and spoke quietly. "You shouldn't have. He didn't want to be on this Earth any longer. I'm sure he planned to end his life after making his statement and taking the blame for what he did. It's his choice. He's going now, his pulse is weak. Let him find peace."

Louise ran back to the house and out onto the street, to the officers who had arrived. Soon the forest was filled with flashlights and people, working effectively and with few words to secure the area. The ambulance personnel broke through the thicket and down to the hollow where Steph lay. Eik stood up to give them room.

Louise returned to Vivian. She still held her ex-husband's hand.

"He's let go, he's leaving this world. When you have nothing more to live for, you should be allowed to die."

31

Louise could barely drag herself up the stairs to her Frederiksberg apartment that evening. She was hungry, her eyes watery from exhaustion.

They had watched the recording of Erik Hald Sørensen's testimony several times. Toft had brought Else Corneliussen in for more questioning and had filled her in on what had happened.

"I'm shocked, very shocked," she said quietly, after they offered her a glass of water. "He was popular, a dedicated man. Everyone liked him."

Louise was certain that Sørensen had fooled everyone completely; nothing during Else Corneliussen's questioning had set off any alarm bells.

He hadn't performed an assisted suicide. He had been present, but Else Corneliussen had administered the medicine. They had planned to share the duties starting next month, according to her.

Louise couldn't get Sørensen's confession out of her head, and in a way she wished she could have spoken to him after what she'd heard him say. Not that he hadn't cleared everything up for the police. It was just that his explanation had made a strong impression on her.

The door to Melvin's fourth-floor apartment was open a crack. Two suitcases and a large shopping bag stood out on the stairway, and she heard voices inside.

When Melvin was released from the hospital, Grete Milling had offered to move in so he wouldn't be alone to start with. And a few hours earlier, when Louise called to hear if it was good to be back home, Melvin had said he'd never thought he could be this happy again, that he was thankful he hadn't died out there on the stairway. "Now it looks like I'm going to be waking up beside somebody in the morning again," he'd said.

"Hello," Louise said, sticking her head inside to see if Jonas was there.

"Come in," someone shouted. Mrs. Milling appeared in the hallway. She had on a striped apron, and her sleeves were rolled up. "Jonas and Melvin are in the living room, but we saved some food for you." Louise felt as if something soft and warm had been wrapped around her.

"There're still a few things we haven't carried in," Grete said, "but I think I'll wait to unpack more until tomorrow. We have to get everything settled, too." She stood in the kitchen, piling several heaping sandwiches on a plate. She handed it to Louise. "Wouldn't you like a beer?"

Louise nodded. "Would I ever." She opened a cabinet and took out a glass.

Melvin sat on the sofa. He still looked pale and was clearly tired, but he paid attention while Jonas gave him a detailed summary of a series he'd seen on Netflix. When Louise walked in, her son stood up and gave her a hug.

"It's freaky that Eik has a daughter," he said. "Is she okay?"

Louise hadn't had time to tell him much. After Eik had gone with Steph to the hospital, she'd gotten only a single text from him. Eik, who never texted. But apparently a lot had changed. He wrote that Steph's condition was still unstable.

"She's wounded seriously, but he's with her. I don't know if she's conscious."

"But we're going to meet her, aren't we?"

"I hope so," Louise said, and left it at that.

"I'm sure he'll be a super good dad."

Louise attacked the roast beef. After she finished chewing, she said, "Yes, I'm sure he will."

She pointed at Melvin and smiled. Their neighbor had fallen asleep with his hands folded on his lap.

The next morning, when Louise showed up at Homicide for a debriefing with the rest of the team, Suhr took her aside and asked her to come into his office.

The head of Homicide closed the door and pulled out a chair for her. "Have you heard how the young lady is doing?" He sounded worried.

"Steph is still in intensive care, but this morning her condition stabilized, and they're moving her to a general ward." Late the previous evening, the girl had been wheeled into an operating room; the doctors were afraid her inner organs had been damaged. "Eik is with her, and I'll join them when we're done with the debriefing."

Suhr leaned forward and folded his hands on the desk,

his expression serious. "Michael Stig isn't coming back to the department. We received his resignation yesterday, after you left."

Louise had trouble concentrating on what he was saying. Her thoughts were with Eik and Steph at the National Hospital.

"I don't think the dream of heading up a department always jibes with the pressure involved," Suhr continued. Louise tried to focus; his penetrating stare made her uneasy. "Stig definitely made a wise decision."

Her thoughts wandered again. To Vivian. She had been with Sørensen when he died, had gone along in the ambulance.

"But his resignation won't affect my decision to leave at the end of the month, that's already been announced. We're going to be understaffed."

Louise tried to grasp what he was saying.

"Might you be interested?" he asked, his expression serious again. "Let's be honest here, there's a lot of pressure with the job..."

He kept looking at her while waiting for an answer.

"I'm sorry, could you repeat what you said?"

His eyes softened, and he looked at her indulgently. "I'd like to recommend you for head of Homicide. The leadership is backing me up on this. It might mean you'll have to take some supplemental courses in leadership. And the only thing left for me to say is, sometimes the pressure is heavy. But there's no doubt in my mind that you can handle it, and I hope, I really do, that you'll say yes."

Louise was disoriented after the debriefing, after packing her things and telling Rønholt she was leaving for the day. She walked down and took a bus to the National Hospital.

Steph had left her weekend bag behind at Police Headquarters when she'd tried to find Erik Hald Sørensen, and now Louise brought it along. That morning Louise had thought about packing extra toiletries and a sweater she might like, but had decided against it; Steph might feel she was interfering, and she didn't want to push.

Instead, she bought a bouquet of tulips and some pastries at the hospital gift shop before taking the elevator up.

When she walked into the room, Steph was sitting up in bed with a breakfast tray in front of her. Louise was startled by how different the girl looked, wearing a hospital gown and with all the black makeup scraped off. She was trying to press a straw down into a small carton of juice. Eik sat in a blue chair with armrests, a cup of coffee in his hands, his feet up on the iron frame of the hospital bed. But when Louise came in he set his cup down and walked over and kissed her. Her body felt heavy and loose when his arms closed around her. She hugged him back.

"She's the one who's your girlfriend?" Steph asked.

Eik let go of Louise and smiled at his daughter. "Yes. In fact she's going to be my wife. She just doesn't know it yet!"

Louise's jaw dropped, and she was about to protest. She heard Steph laughing and Eik saying something else, but she was too stunned to pick up on what he said. Fortunately the door opened behind her. Rønholt peeked in and asked if it was too early for him to pay a visit.

"No, come on in," Louise blurted. She stepped back out of the way in the small private room.

Rønholt didn't know what to do with the flowers he'd

brought along. Louise looked past him and caught Eik's eye. He smiled and held her eyes, as if he wanted to show her that he meant what he'd just said.

"I've been looking forward so much to meeting you," she heard Rønholt say. He held his hand out to Eik's daughter.

"Nice to meet you, too," Steph said. "My father just told me about you."

Eik walked over to Louise and put his arm around her. Rønholt turned to Eik. "That leave of absence you asked about, I think it can be arranged."

"Glad to hear it. It's sort of like paternity leave." He grinned at Steph. "So we can keep dreaming."

"Leave of absence?" Louise looked up at him in confusion. Hadn't he just proposed to her, and now he was taking a leave of absence? He hadn't mentioned this before.

"Steph wants to travel and see the world, and I want to go with her." He explained that he'd been looking into seeking parental custody, now that her mother was dead. "Of course it's completely up to Steph, if she wants to put up with me," he added.

"And she already said she wants to," his daughter said, as she buttered a roll.

"So, are you talking about traveling for a week?" Louise asked. "Two weeks?"

"More like six months," Eik said. "But we have to get this young lady on her feet before we plan anything."

Steph broke in. "You two have to come, too. You and your son. We can go places together. Or maybe you've already done that?"

Suddenly she looked shy, as if she were a bit ashamed

about getting so carried away with her dreams, and with people she barely knew.

"We haven't, actually," Louise said. "I've never traveled with Jonas." They'd never even talked about it, she thought. "But unfortunately I can't just take off for half a year, and anyway, Jonas is in school."

Louise paused a second before looking at Rønholt. "And by the way, I was just asked to be the new head of Homicide."

Rønholt smiled at her. "I was wondering if you'd mention that. I take it that you're considering the offer. I'm happy for you, but even more for them."

"You know about it?" Louise said.

He nodded and explained that Suhr had called him yesterday evening. "I think he was just putting a feeler out. Of course I said I wasn't happy about you leaving, our special unit is off to such a good start. But on the other hand, it's a lot better than the job announcements I've been showing you."

Louise nodded. Eik looked startled, and suddenly it was all too much for her. She felt dazed, and she had to leave the room to get a grip. After apologizing she walked out to take the elevator down; she needed a place to sit by herself for a while.

As far as she was concerned, Eik could go wherever he wanted with his daughter. That wasn't what rattled her. It was more that he made it sound so natural, so uncomplicated, that she and Jonas would be part of his and Steph's life.

On her way to the ground floor cafeteria, someone behind her suddenly called out, "Where are you going?" Camilla, she thought. She turned and watched her friend trot up to her, clasping flowers, magazines, and bags of candy against her chest.

"How's she doing up there?" Camilla asked. "I've called several times to hear, but they wouldn't tell me, even though I explained I was a friend of the family."

"She seems to be doing okay. She and Eik are already talking about her moving in to live with him. And that was Sofie's plan, wasn't it? But they need to get to know each other, of course."

"That sounds smart. It must be a lot for them to handle all of a sudden, too. Do they get along?"

Louise nodded. "They actually act like they've known each other a long time. I'm sure they'll figure it out."

Louise pulled her arm back when her friend suddenly punched her shoulder and said, "Hey, damn! Congratulations on the job! I saw your message, this is big for you!"

Camilla followed along to the coffee line.

"Yes, it's really big," Louise said. "It's going to take some getting used to." She explained that Eik and his daughter had begun talking about going on an extended trip. "They've decided they want to travel and do things together while learning about each other. Maybe that's a good thing, a very good thing, that way I can concentrate on my job. If I decide to take it."

"Yeah, because you'll have to prove to everybody you're not the type who buckles under from stress just from sitting in the boss's chair," Camilla teased, smiling at her.

Louise nodded. "Something like that. I have to be a good leader, anyway. One who makes everyone want to work with them."

They found an empty table by the wall. Now, sitting across from each other, Louise got a good look at her friend and was startled by what she saw. Camilla, who always put on makeup and arranged her hair before going anywhere, looked run-down, like she'd just fallen out of bed. Louise had been so preoccupied that she hadn't noticed, and it worried her. She reached across the table. "What's going on with you?"

"Frederik's moving to Los Angeles. And," she said, before Louise could ask, "I'm staying here."

"Oh no! Shit!" Louise felt as if someone had just punched her in the face.

"No, it's okay!" Camilla pushed her coffee aside. "Frederik's right when he says I could write some great articles if I move over there. But my network is here in Denmark. I don't want to move, at least not yet. I can fly over and stay with him every winter when Markus finishes boarding school. But I'm not going to live there permanently, hell no."

"Are you two getting a divorce?" Suddenly, all Louise wanted to do was go home and crawl into bed. She felt the strain of all that had happened since Suhr called her into his office. Joy, worry, good, bad. Her life right now seemed to be all tall peaks and deep valleys, and it was simply too much for her. Especially the day after finishing a major case.

If she accepted the job, Suhr wanted to hold a small, inner-circle reception for her in his office that very afternoon. It wasn't official yet, but it was felt that the personnel in the Personal Crimes Department deserved to know the leadership's plans, now that everyone was aware that Michael Stig wouldn't be returning. She thought about

Eik, Steph, and their travel plans. They were talking about being gone for a long time.

"No, we're not getting a divorce, don't be silly," she heard Camilla say.

"That's why I really haven't slept. I love my husband, and we've been Skyping all night to get our new lives on track. It's modern for married couples to live separately. Didn't you know that?"

Epilogue

Incredible how bad they're screwing us," Eik said, after they'd been dumped off in front of their small hotel in Tulum. He dug another cigarette out of his jacket pocket. Back at the airport, Louise had asked for a taxi large enough for all their luggage, but she was told they should have ordered one in advance. It was either take two taxis or go back to the end of the line.

Eik lit a cigarette and stood for a moment, breathing in the hot air, while Louise laughed and asked who had suggested Mexico as their first stop.

"Your son, Jonas," he said. "He's the one who wanted to see the Mayan ruins, and you heard how convincing he was."

She nodded. He was absolutely right. Jonas was interested in history, and immediately he had named the Mayans when they sat down to make a list of what they wanted to see.

She thought fondly of Camilla, who had sat her down before she accepted the job as head of Homicide. "Are you really sure you're making the right decision, letting Eik and Steph travel without you two?" she'd asked. "Why don't you go with them?"

The wind took hold of Louise's hair, and she smiled as she thought back to when she closed the door to Suhr's office and gave him her ultimatum. She would, of course, keep her word; she still wanted the job. But only if he agreed to stay six months longer. Otherwise, unfortunately, she would have to say no. In which case he risked having to stay even longer; he and the police leadership would have to find another successor who might have to give notice to his or her employer. He mulled that over before agreeing to her condition.

Their trip had been delayed by Nigel Parker. Not that he had anything against his stepdaughter moving to Denmark to live with her biological father. In fact, he thought it was an excellent idea. He had been honest with himself and realized it wouldn't work between the two of them without Sofie as a buffer. But he had dug his heels in when Eik asked him to pack Steph's things and send them to Denmark. He really had no time to do that, now that his wife wasn't around to help him in the vision center and office. And besides, he wasn't especially eager to help Eik after the fraught confrontations they'd had.

Steph and Eik had returned to Nailsea to pack, and while there she chose what she wanted of her mother's belongings. Only after everything had been sent off to Denmark did Steph react. All the shock was gone, and she'd cried because she missed her mother. Because of her murder and the shock, because she had lost the only person in the world she'd ever felt connected to.

She and Eik had moved into the South Harbor place, but even though he and Louise lived separately, they almost always ate together. Either there or at Louise's apartment. And slowly Steph began to come to terms with her life. Eik let her move things along at her own pace. But it wasn't just for Steph's sake, Louise came to realize. It was just who he was.

"Why don't we find a bar and have a cold Corona before we check in?" Eik began pulling Louise toward the small bar on the beach. She felt sweaty all over after the flight and the almost-two-hour taxi ride, and she needed a dip in the ocean badly, but she nodded when Eik asked if they should order two plates of nachos as well.

Steph had taken off her leather jacket and heavy Dr. Martens, and she surrendered to the Mexican sun. She was still healing from the shooting, but after determining her inner organs hadn't been damaged, the doctors had been most concerned about a concussion. She'd taken a heavy blow to the temple, and she'd had a blinding headache and blurred vision in the days following the events in the forest. There'd even been talk of a skull fracture. Fortunately it wasn't that bad, but she'd still had to be checked at the hospital right before they left.

Jonas stood at the water's edge with his pants rolled up. He and Steph began checking out some rock formations several meters high, from which two young boys dove into the ocean. Louise's stomach knotted, but she lay out on an old, peeling beach chair anyway. She leaned back after Eik stuck a beer in her hand and pulled her close to him.

The waves broke against the jutting cliffs; white foam spouted high into the air as she pressed the slice of lime stuck in the bottle down into the beer.

She breathed in the smell of the ocean. Lime. Corona. And Eik.

ACKNOWLEDGMENTS

The Lost Woman is fiction, and any resemblance to actual people or events is coincidental. The characters and plot are products of my imagination, though they were inspired by actual events that awoke my curiosity and prodded me to investigate.

In this connection, I would like to express my special and heartfelt gratitude to Rikke Kimie Andersen and Kim Frank Hoffmann, who opened up to me about their experiences at Dignitas, a suicide clinic in Switzerland, where they recently said their good-byes to Jane Hoffman.

Special thanks go out to Brian and Conny Doktor, for always being willing to share their medical expertise and helping me with diseases and diagnoses that fit the plots of my books.

Thank you, Lisbeth Møller-Madsen, for being such a talented editor; it's a great pleasure to work with you.

Thanks also go out to Rasmus Funder. Your book covers always convey the mood I hope for but never can express in words. Thank you, everyone at People's Press, my publisher. I'm very happy working and spending time together with you.

Malene Kirkegaard Nielsen of the Plot Workshop has been an invaluable help to me. Thanks so much for sparring with me on the crime plot.

Thank you, Lotte Thorsen, for reading the manuscript and your wise and astute comments.

Thanks so much, Trine Busch—you are fantastic! Without you I would be burdened by so much more. Thank you for your wholehearted support of me and Louise Rick.

Thanks go out to my agent, Victoria Sanders, and to Bernadette and Chris. You give me energy and the urge to do so much more.

My greatest thanks go out to my son, Adam. Thank you for your support, your help, and your confidence that everything will work out. I love you more than anything in the world.

—Sara Blaedel

**DON'T MISS THE NEWEST TWIST-FILLED NOVEL
IN THE MISSING PERSONS INVESTIGATOR
LOUISE RICK SERIES**

A shocking murder on Copenhagen's idyllic streets
and an abandoned child lead Louise Rick deep into a
treacherous criminal underworld with
an international reach...

**PLEASE SEE THE NEXT PAGE FOR AN EXCERPT
FROM *THE NIGHT WOMEN*, COMING IN
JANUARY 2018.**

1

The woman was lying on her back, her arms out to her sides, her head tilted toward one shoulder. Her throat had been slashed in one long, straight slice, her blood saturating her blond hair, which spread in a sticky mass over the left side of her torso.

Assistant Detective Louise Rick straightened back up from her kneel and took a deep breath. Did anyone ever get used to this? God, she hoped not.

Darkness lay heavily over Copenhagen's Meatpacking District, the vast industrial tract between the train station and the harbor, where the city's slaughterhouses and meatpackers had sold their wares for centuries. It was almost two in the morning, so Sunday had already given way to Monday. Damp April air lingered over the Vesterbro District just west of the inner city, although the previous evening's rain had subsided. The flashing lights and police barricade that had been erected out on Skelbækgade were keeping most people away, but a few curious bystanders chatted as they watched the officers work.

A lone drunk sat on the doorstep of Høker Café, seemingly oblivious to the large police presence. He sang and occasionally screamed out whenever someone drove by. The girls who usually worked this street were nowhere in sight, likely having retreated to Sønder Boulevard or around the corner to Ingerslevsgade.

The bright glare of the large crime-scene spotlights created sharp contrasts of light and dark. One of the first things the team had done was to go over the surface of the body with tape to secure any fibers and loose hairs before swabbing for DNA with slightly moistened cotton swabs. Forensic pathologist Flemming Larsen turned to Louise and the chief of the homicide division, Hans Suhr.

"The incision is approximately twenty centimeters long, leaving a large, gaping wound across the entire throat. It's a deep cut with clean edges, which means the knife was drawn across the throat quickly, and only once."

Pulling off his rubber gloves and face mask, he nodded at the techs to signal that he was done so they could investigate the area around the murdered woman.

"There are no other signs of violence, so it happened fast. She didn't see it coming; there are no defensive wounds on her hands or arms. I would bet that it went down within the last three hours," he said.

"Do you have any clues as to who she might be?" Louise asked. They hadn't found any ID on the body.

"Well, don't you think we can assume we're dealing with a prostitute?" Flemming asked, his eyes resting on the victim's skimpy cotton skirt and tight top, before adding that he doubted she was Danish, given the poor state of her teeth.

"It's not a bad guess," Suhr agreed, taking a step back so that the techs could get by.

They moved the floodlight Flemming had been working under farther down the street so they could search the entire area for evidence.

Louise squatted down next to the woman again. The wound was high on her throat and went all the way around to her cervical vertebrae. It was difficult to make out the facial features in the dark, but she was obviously young—probably about twenty, Louise guessed.

She heard footsteps behind her, but before she could stand up, her colleague Michael Stig came to a stop right behind her and placed both hands on her shoulders as if for support. He leaned forward to inspect the body.

"Eastern European whore" was his swift assessment before removing his hands and allowing Louise to stand up again.

"What makes you so certain?" she asked, taking a step away from him to disrupt the physical intimacy he had forced upon her.

"Her makeup. They still do their faces the way Danish women did back in the eighties. The colors are too bright and there's too much of it. So, what do we know about her?" Stig asked, his hands into the pockets of his baggy jeans.

Louise caught the scent of her newly washed hair and fresh deodorant. She had been asleep for less than an hour when Suhr had woken her with his call, and she had left her Frederiksberg apartment and made it to the murder scene within twenty minutes. After almost five years as a homicide detective, she had a speedy routine for nighttime calls like this one.

"Not a thing," she replied tersely. "The local precinct received an anonymous tip about a dead body on Kød-boderne Street behind the Hotel and Restaurant Manage-ment School, and then the caller hung up."

"So the caller must have had pretty thorough knowl-edge of this less than savory section of Copenhagen," Stig concluded. "Like someone who's a regular in this part of town."

Louise raised one eyebrow, and he explained:

"Only people who know the Meatpacking District fairly well would use one of the specific street names: Kødboderne, Høkerboderne, and Slagterboderne."

I wonder why you're so familiar with the area, Louise thought as she turned to join the others. Her partner, Lars Jørgensen, was off with some of their colleagues from the local precinct knocking on the doors in the apartment buildings on Skelbækgade whose windows faced the Meatpacking District. Another team was deal-ing with the people on the street as well as in the build-ings immediately surrounding the scene. Even though the call had gone to the main precinct, formerly known as Precinct 1 on Halmtorvet, the case had been quickly turned over to the Homicide Division at police head-quarters. Suhr had decided to call some of his own people in so they could be on the investigation right from the start, but he had spared Toft, who had spent the weekend out in Jutland celebrating his sister's silver wedding anniversary. The chief said he'd figured he ought to let Toft sleep in after all the glasses of port and hours of brass band music that such an event would have required.

"Nobody has anything to tell us," Jørgensen reported.

"Either that or they don't dare open their mouths. And strangely, it seems like no one has been anywhere near Skelbækgade in the past twenty-four hours. Not even the people Mikkelsen saw here earlier with his own eyes." He shook his head and yawned.

Mikkelsen was the local officer from the Halmtorvet station who was most knowledgeable about what went on in the Istedgade neighborhood with its prostitutes, pushers, and drug addicts. He was a short, stocky man in his midfifties, and he'd spent almost all of his many years on the force working this area. He had served one three-year tour with the riot squad before putting in for a transfer and getting his old office back.

"What about that guy over on those steps?" Louise asked.

"He said he hasn't seen anything except for the bottom of the last bottle he downed," her partner replied, repeating the remark a moment later when the chief came over and asked the same question.

"OK, nobody wants to say anything, so it's business as usual around here," Suhr said as he waved for Stig to come over and join them. "There's nothing more we can do right now. Mikkelsen and his people will continue interviewing passersby, but I doubt we'll get anybody to talk tonight. If any of the regulars around here saw anything, we know from experience that it will take time for them to share. So let's all get some sleep. We'll pick this up again in the morning."

"What about Willumsen?" Louise asked as they headed toward their cars. It surprised her that she hadn't seen the detective superintendent here yet.

"I'll brief him first thing in the morning," said the

homicide chief, giving her a wry smile. "It's better to let him get his beauty sleep."

Louise nodded. They all knew what Willumsen was like when he got up on the wrong side of the bed. He had a bad habit of infecting everyone else with his lousy mood.

When Louise Rick woke again after four hours of sleep, she had a sore throat and her whole body felt sluggish. She had gotten up several times in the night, the image of the dead woman implanted in her mind's eye. She wondered why she had been killed that way. The deep wound in her throat seemed so aggressive, but the killer had come up on her from behind, so the woman likely hadn't had a chance to fight back. Thoughts drifted through Louise's mind, coalescing into more visuals from the night's murder scene. Again and again, she saw the nighttime shadows on the low, white-brick façades of the Meatpacking District, where butchers and delicatessen wholesalers served customers in the daytime.

Louise went to the kitchen to put some water on to boil before she climbed into the shower. She stood under the hot spray for so long that the whole bathroom was filled with steam before she felt ready to get out. Afterward, she sank onto a kitchen chair with a cup of tea cradled in her hands.

Suhr had announced just before they'd parted that there would be a briefing on the case at nine o'clock. Things had finally settled down again in their department after the big reorganization that had sent powerful shock waves through police headquarters. They had closed down both Division A, which had been in charge of homicides, and Division C, which had handled burglary investigations. Now everything had been reshuffled, dividing lines had been erased, and some of the most senior detectives had been moved elsewhere. And there was no longer room for all the assistant detective superintendents who had previously acted as team leaders. Which was why Louise had lost Henny Heilmann. Henny had been offered a job as lead detective at HQ and was now up in radio dispatch, stuck directing squad cars. Louise knew it had taken Henny quite a while to see the up side to her transfer.

Louise went into the bedroom and pulled a heavy sweater out of her closet. She was tempted to take the bus from Gammel Kongevej, but at the last minute mustered the energy to ride her bike.

The traffic on the bike path was heavy, full of morning commuters. Even so, she moved over into the passing lane as she crossed H. C. Ørstedsvej. Pedaling hard, she pulled her helmet down low to shield her eyes from the glaring spring sunshine that had suddenly appeared now that the rain clouds had drifted away.

"Just have the downtown precinct keep doing the interviews in the neighborhood, especially in the red-light areas that the johns frequent. It's likelier we'll get something out of a regular client who happened to know the victim than out of any of the hookers. Meanwhile, we'll focus on identifying the victim and processing the forensic evidence. You're probably not planning on allocating too many resources to this case, right?" Detective Superintendent Willumsen asked, shooting Suhr an inquisitive look.

The homicide chief seemed to deliberately pause before responding. Louise leaned her chair back against the wall. It had been a year since Suhr had appointed Willumsen lead detective for Louise's group. Willumsen was widely disliked for his arrogance and rudeness; he didn't give a damn about anything or anyone, and he made no distinction between superiors and colleagues. All the same, Louise was actually quite fond of him. Willumsen had taught her to just say "yes," "no," or "kiss my ass," to say things clearly without a lot of screwing around.

His other trademark line was, "Is that understood, or not, or do you not give a shit about what I'm telling you?" He was also the one who had signed Louise up a few years back to train in hostage negotiations.

Suhr took a step back and propped his arm against the wall, as if gathering strength to reply.

"You have all the resources you need right now—all four of the detectives in your group: Rick and Jørgensen, Toft and Stig. Plus the assistance we're already getting from Mikkelsen and his folks at Halmtorvet precinct." Suhr let his arm drop again after firing off this remark.

Willumsen lowered his eyes to focus on his right thumbnail. He meticulously cleaned it with the tip of his pencil. Finally, he tossed the pencil aside and announced that he'd decided Toft and Stig would keep tabs on the forensic techs and keep everyone up-to-date on the latest evidence. They would also attend the victim's autopsy.

Then Willumsen's eyes shifted to Louise and her partner.

"I want the two of you to go down to see Mikkelsen and concentrate on the investigation in the neighborhood." With that, he wrapped up the meeting.

INTRODUCING...
THE UNDERTAKER'S DAUGHTER

*If you enjoy Sara Blaedel's Louise Rick
suspense novels, you'll love her new series.*

An unexpected inheritance from a father she hasn't
seen since childhood pulls a portrait photographer
from her quiet life into a web of dark secrets and
murder in a small Midwestern town...

**PLEASE SEE THE NEXT PAGE FOR AN EXCERPT
FROM *THE UNDERTAKER'S DAUGHTER*,
AVAILABLE NOW.**

1

"What do you mean you shouldn't have told me? You should have told me thirty-three years ago."

"What difference would it have made anyway?" Ilka's mother demanded. "You were seven years old. You wouldn't have understood about a liar and a cheat running away with all his winnings; running out on his responsibilities, on his wife and little daughter. He hit the jackpot, Ilka, and then he hit the road. And left me—no, he left *us* with a funeral home too deep in the red to get rid of. And an enormous amount of debt. That he betrayed me is one thing, but abandoning his child?"

Ilka stood at the window, her back to the comfy living room, which was overflowing with books and baskets of yarn. She looked out over the trees in the park across the way. For a moment, the treetops seemed like dizzying black storm waves.

Her mother sat in the glossy Børge Mogensen easy chair in the corner, though now she was worked up from her rant, and her knitting needles clattered twice as fast.

Ilka turned to her. "Okay," she said, trying not to sound shrill. "Maybe you're right. Maybe I wouldn't have understood about all that. But you didn't think I was too young to understand that my father was a coward, the way he suddenly left us, and that he didn't love us anymore. That he was an incredible asshole you'd never take back if he ever showed up on our doorstep, begging for forgiveness. As I recall, you had no trouble talking about that, over and over and over."

"Stop it." Her mother had been a grade school teacher for twenty-six years, and now she sounded like one. "But does it make any difference? Think of all the letters you've written him over the years. How often have you reached out to him, asked to see him? Or at least have some form of contact." She sat up and laid her knitting on the small table beside the chair. "He never answered you; he never tried to see you. How long did you save your confirmation money so you could fly over and visit him?"

Ilka knew better than her mother how many letters she had written over the years. What her mother wasn't aware of was that she had kept writing to him, even as an adult. Not as often, but at least a Christmas card and a note on his birthday. Every single year. Which had felt like sending letters into outer space. Yet she'd never stopped.

"You should have told me about the money," Ilka said, unwilling to let it go, even though her mother had a point. Would it really have made a difference? "Why are you telling me now? After all these years. And right when I'm about to leave."

Her mother had called just before eight. Ilka had still been in bed, reading the morning paper on her iPad.

"Come over, right now," she'd said. There was something they had to talk about.

Now her mother leaned forward and folded her hands in her lap, her face showing the betrayal and desperation she'd endured. She'd kept her wounds under wraps for half her life, but it was obvious they had never fully healed. "It scares me, you going over there. Your father was a gambler. He bet more money than he had, and the racetrack was a part of our lives for the entire time he lived here. For better and worse. I knew about his habit when we fell in love, but then it got out of control. And almost ruined us several times. In the end, it did ruin us."

"And then he won almost a million kroner and just disappeared." Ilka lifted an eyebrow.

"Well, we do know he went to America." Her mother nodded. "Presumably, he continued gambling over there. And we never heard from him again. That is, until now, of course."

Ilka shook her head. "Right, now that he's dead."

"What I'm trying to say is that we don't know what he's left behind. He could be up to his neck in debt. You're a school photographer, not a millionaire. If you go over there, they might hold you responsible for his debts. And who knows? Maybe they wouldn't allow you to come home. Your father had a dark side he couldn't control. I'll rip his dead body limb from limb if he pulls you down with him, all these years after turning his back on us."

With that, her mother stood and walked down the long hall into the kitchen. Ilka heard muffled voices, and then Hanne appeared in the doorway. "Would you like us to drive you to the airport?" Hanne leaned against the doorframe as Ilka's mother reappeared with a tray of bakery rolls, which she set down on the coffee table.

"No, that's okay," Ilka said.

"How long do you plan on staying?" Hanne asked, moving to the sofa. Ilka's mother curled up in the corner of the sofa, covered herself with a blanket, and put her stockinged feet up on Hanne's lap.

When her mother began living with Hanne fourteen years ago, the last trace of her bitterness finally seemed to evaporate. Now, though, Ilka realized it had only gone into hibernation.

For the first four years after Ilka's father left, her mother had been stuck with Paul Jensen's Funeral Home and its two employees, who cheated her whenever they could get away with it. Throughout Ilka's childhood, her mother had complained constantly about the burden he had dumped on her. Ilka hadn't known until now that her father had also left a sizable gambling debt behind. Apparently, her mother had wanted to spare her, at least to some degree. And, of course, her mother was right. Her father *was* a coward and a selfish jerk. Yet Ilka had never completely accepted his abandonment of her. He had left behind a short letter saying he would come back for them as soon as everything was taken care of, and that an opportunity had come up. In Chicago.

Several years later, after complete silence on his part, he wanted a divorce. And that was the last they'd heard from him. When Ilka was a teenager, she found his address—or at least, an address where he once had lived. She'd kept it all these years in a small red treasure chest in her room.

"Surely it won't take more than a few days," Ilka said.

"I'm planning to be back by the weekend. I'm booked up at work, but I found someone to fill in for me the first two days. It would be a great help if you two could keep trying to get hold of Niels from North Sealand Photography. He's in Stockholm, but he's supposed to be back tomorrow. I'm hoping he can cover for me the rest of the week. All the shoots are in and around Copenhagen."

"What exactly are you hoping to accomplish over there?" Hanne asked.

"Well, they say I'm in his will and that I have to be there in person to prove I'm Paul Jensen's daughter."

"I just don't understand why this can't be done by e-mail or fax," her mother said. "You can send them your birth certificate and your passport, or whatever it is they need."

"It seems that copies aren't good enough. If I don't go over there, I'd have to go to an American tax office in Europe, and I think the nearest one is in London. But this way, they'll let me go through his personal things and take what I want. Artie Sorvino from Jensen Funeral Home in Racine has offered to cover my travel expenses if I go now, so they can get started with closing his estate."

Ilka stood in the middle of the living room, too anxious and restless to sit down.

"Racine?" Hanne asked. "Where's that?" She picked up her steaming cup and blew on it.

"A bit north of Chicago. In Wisconsin. I'll be picked up at the airport, and it doesn't look like it'll take long to drive there. Racine is supposedly the city in the United States with the largest community of Danish descendants. A lot of Danes immigrated to the region, so it makes sense that's where he settled."

"He has a hell of a lot of nerve." Her mother's lips barely moved. "He doesn't write so much as a birthday card to you all these years, and now suddenly you have to fly over there and clean up another one of his messes."

"Karin," Hanne said, her voice gentle. "Of course Ilka should go over and sort through her father's things. If you get the opportunity for closure on such an important part of your life's story, you should grab it."

Her mother shook her head. Without looking at Ilka, she said, "I have a bad feeling about this. Isn't it odd that he stayed in the undertaker business even though he managed to ruin his first shot at it?"

Ilka walked out into the hall and let the two women bicker about the unfairness of it all. How Paul's daughter had tried to reach out to her father all her life, and it was only now that he was gone that he was finally reaching out to her.

2

The first thing Ilka noticed was his Hawaiian shirt and longish brown hair, which was combed back and held in place by sunglasses that would look at home on a surfer. He stood out among the other drivers at Arrivals in O'Hare International Airport who were holding name cards and facing the scattered clumps of exhausted people pulling suitcases out of Customs.

Written on his card was "Ilka Nichols Jensen." Somehow, she managed to walk all the way up to him and stop before he realized she'd found him.

They looked each other over for a moment. He was in his early forties, maybe, she thought. So, her father, who had turned seventy-two in early January, had a younger partner.

She couldn't read his face, but it might have surprised him that the undertaker's daughter was a beanpole: six feet tall without a hint of a feminine form. He scanned her up and down, gaze settling on her hair, which had never been an attention-getter. Straight, flat, and mousy.

He smiled warmly and held out his hand. "Nice to meet you. Welcome to Chicago."

It's going to be a hell of a long trip, Ilka thought, before shaking his hand and saying hello. "Thank you. Nice to meet you too."

He offered to carry her suitcase. It was small, a carry-on, but she gladly handed it over to him. Then he offered her a bottle of water. The car was close by, he said, only a short walk.

Although she was used to being taller than most people, she always felt a bit shy when male strangers had to look up to make eye contact. She was nearly a head taller than Artie Sorvino, but he seemed almost impressed as he grinned up at her while they walked.

Her body ached; she hadn't slept much during the long flight. Since she'd left her apartment in Copenhagen, her nerves had been tingling with excitement. And worry, too. Things had almost gone wrong right off the bat at the Copenhagen airport, because she hadn't taken into account the long line at Passport Control. There had still been two people in front of her when she'd been called to her waiting flight. Then the arrival in the US, a hell that the chatty man next to her on the plane had prepared her for. He had missed God knew how many connecting flights at O'Hare because the immigration line had taken several hours to go through. It turned out to be not quite as bad as all that. She had been guided to a machine that requested her fingerprints, passport, and picture. All this information was scanned and saved. Then Ilka had been sent on to the next line, where a surly passport official wanted to know what her business was in the country. She began to sweat but then pulled herself together and explained that she was simply visiting family, which in a way was true. He stamped her passport, and moments later she was standing beside the man wearing the colorful, festive shirt.

"Is this your first trip to the US?" Artie asked now, as they approached the enormous parking lot.

She smiled. "No, I've traveled here a few times. To Miami and New York."

Why had she said that? She'd never been in this part of the world before, but what the hell. It didn't matter. Unless he kept up the conversation. And Miami. Where had that come from?

"Really?" Artie told her he had lived in Key West for many years. Then his father got sick, and Artie, the only other surviving member of the family, moved back to Racine to take care of him. "I hope you made it down to the Keys while you were in Florida."

Ilka shook her head and explained that she unfortunately hadn't had time.

"I had a gallery down there," Artie said. He'd gone to the California School of the Arts in San Francisco and had made his living as an artist.

Ilka listened politely and nodded. In the parking lot, she caught sight of a gigantic black Cadillac with closed white curtains in back, which stood first in the row of parked cars. He'd driven there in the hearse.

"Hope you don't mind." He nodded at the hearse as he opened the rear door and placed her suitcase on the casket table used for rolling coffins in and out of the vehicle.

"No, it's fine." She walked around to the front passenger door. Fine, as long as she wasn't the one being rolled into the back. She felt slightly dizzy, as if she were still up in the air, but was buoyed by the nervous excitement of traveling and the anticipation of what awaited her.

The thought that her father was at the end of her journey bothered her, yet it was something she'd fantasized about nearly her entire life. But would she be able to piece together the life he'd lived without her? And was she even interested in knowing about it? What if she didn't like what she learned?

She shook her head for a moment. These thoughts had been swirling in her head since Artie's first phone call. Her mother thought she shouldn't get involved. At all. But Ilka disagreed. If her father had left anything behind, she wanted to see it. She wanted to uncover whatever she could find, to see if any of it made sense.

"How did he die?" she asked as Artie maneuvered the long hearse out of the parking lot and in between two orange signs warning about roadwork and a detour.

"Just a sec," he muttered, and he swore at the sign before deciding to skirt the roadwork and get back to the road heading north.

For a while they drove in silence; then he explained that one morning her father had simply not woken up. "He was supposed to drive a corpse to Iowa, one of our neighboring states, but he didn't show up. He just died in his sleep. Totally peacefully. He might not even have known it was over."

Ilka watched the Chicago suburbs drifting by along the long, straight bypass, the rows of anonymous stores and cheap restaurants. It seemed so overwhelming, so strange, so different. Most buildings were painted in shades of beige and brown, and enormous billboards stood everywhere, screaming messages about everything from missing children to ultracheap fast food and vanilla coffee for less than a dollar at Dunkin' Donuts.

She turned to Artie. "Was he sick?" The bump on Artie's nose—had it been broken?—made it appear too big for the rest of his face: high cheekbones, slightly squinty eyes, beard stubble definitely due to a relaxed attitude toward shaving, rather than wanting to be in style.

"Not that I know of, no. But there could have been things Paul didn't tell me about, for sure."

His tone told her it wouldn't have been the first secret Paul had kept from him.

"The doctor said his heart just stopped," he continued. "Nothing dramatic happened."

"Did he have a family?" She looked out the side window. The old hearse rode well. Heavy, huge, swaying lightly. A tall pickup drove up beside them; a man with a full beard looked down and nodded at her. She looked away quickly. She didn't care for any sympathetic looks, though he, of course, couldn't know the curtained-off back of the hearse was empty.

"He was married, you know," Artie said. Immediately Ilka sensed he didn't like being the one to fill her in on her father's private affairs. She nodded to herself; of course he didn't. What did she expect?

"And he had two daughters. That was it, apart from Mary Ann's family, but I don't know them. How much do you know about them?"

He knew very well that Ilka hadn't had any contact with her father since he'd left Denmark. Or at least she assumed he knew. "Why has the family not signed what should be signed, so you can finish with his…estate?" She set the empty water bottle on the floor.

"They did sign their part of it. But that's not enough, because you're in the will, too. First the IRS—that's our tax agency—must determine if he owes the government, and you must give them permission to investigate. If you don't sign, they'll freeze all the assets in the estate until everything is cleared up."

Ilka's shoulders slumped at the word "assets." One thing that had kept her awake during the flight was her mother's concern about her being stuck with a debt she could never pay. Maybe she would be detained; maybe she would even be thrown in jail.

"What are his daughters like?" she asked after they had driven for a while in silence.

For a few moments, he kept his eyes on the road; then he glanced at her and shrugged. "They're nice enough, but I don't really know them. It's been a long time since I've seen them. Truth is, I don't think either of them was thrilled about your father's business."

After another silence, Ilka said, "You should have called me when he died. I wish I had been at his funeral."

Was that really true? Did she truly wish that? The last funeral she'd been to was her husband's. He had collapsed from heart failure three years ago, at the age of fifty-two. She didn't like death, didn't like loss. But she'd already lost her father many years ago, so what difference would it have made watching him being lowered into the ground?

"At that time, I didn't know about you," Artie said. "Your name first came up when your father's lawyer mentioned you."

"Where is he buried?"

He stared straight ahead. Again, it was obvious he didn't

enjoy talking about her father's private life. Finally, he said, "Mary Ann decided to keep the urn with his ashes at home. A private ceremony was held in the living room when the crematorium delivered the urn, and now it's on the shelf above the fireplace."

After a pause, he said, "You speak English well. Funny accent."

Ilka explained distractedly that she had traveled in Australia for a year after high school.

The billboards along the freeway here advertised hotels, motels, and drive-ins for the most part. She wondered how there could be enough people to keep all these businesses going, given the countless offers from the clusters of signs on both sides of the road. "What about his new family? Surely they knew he had a daughter in Denmark?" She turned back to him.

"Nope!" He shook his head as he flipped the turn signal.

"He never told them he left his wife and seven-year-old daughter?" She wasn't all that surprised.

Artie didn't answer. *Okay*, Ilka thought. *That takes care of that.*

"I wonder what they think about me coming here."

He shrugged. "I don't really know, but they're not going to lose anything. His wife has an inheritance from her wealthy parents, so she's taken care of. The same goes for the daughters. And none of them have ever showen any interest in the funeral home."

And what about their father? Ilka thought. *Were they uninterested in him, too?* But that was none of her business. She didn't know them, knew nothing about their relationships with one another. And for that matter, she knew nothing about her father. Maybe his new family had asked about his life in Denmark, and maybe he'd given them a line of bullshit. But what the hell, he was thirty-nine when he left. Anyone could figure out he'd had a life before packing his weekend bag and emigrating.

Both sides of the freeway were green now. The landscape was starting to remind her of late summer in Denmark, with its green fields, patches of forest, flat land, large barns with the characteristic bowed roofs, and livestock. With a few exceptions, she felt like she could have been driving down the E45, the road between Copenhagen and Ålborg.

"Do you mind if I turn on the radio?" Artie asked.

She shook her head; it was a relief to have the awkward silence between them broken. And yet, before his hand reached the radio, she blurted out, "What was he like?"

He dropped his hand and smiled at her. "Your father was a decent guy, a really decent guy. In a lot of ways," he added, disarmingly, "he was someone you could count on, and in other ways he was very much his own man. I always enjoyed working with him, but he was also my friend. People liked him; he was interested in their lives. That's also why he was so good at talking to those who had just lost someone. He was empathetic. It feels empty, him not being around any longer."

Ilka had to concentrate to follow along. Despite her year in Australia, it was difficult when people spoke English rapidly. "Was he also a good father?"

Artie turned thoughtfully and looked out his side window. "I really can't say. I didn't know him when the girls were small." He kept glancing at the four lanes to their left. "But if you're asking me if your father was a family man, my answer is, yes and no. He was very much in touch with his family, but he probably put more of himself into Jensen Funeral Home."

"How long did you know him?"

She watched him calculate. "I moved back in 1998. We ran into each other at a local saloon, this place called Oh Dennis!, and we started talking. The victim of a traffic accident had just come in to the funeral home. The family wanted to put the young woman in an open coffin, but nobody would have wanted to see her face. So I offered to help. It's the kind of stuff I'm good at. Creating, shaping. Your father did the embalming, but I reconstructed her face. Her mother supplied us with a photo, and I did a sculpture. And I managed to make the woman look like herself, even though there wasn't much to work with. Later your father offered me a job, and I grabbed the chance. There's not much work for an artist in Racine, so reconstructions of the deceased was as good as anything."

He turned off the freeway. "Later I got a degree, because you have to have a license to work in the undertaker business."

They reached Racine Street and waited to make a left turn. They had driven the last several miles in silence. The streets were deserted, the shops closed. It was getting dark, and Ilka realized she was at the point where exhaustion and jet lag trumped the hunger gnawing inside her. They drove by an empty square and a nearly deserted saloon. Oh Dennis! The place where Artie had met her father. She spotted the lake at the end of the broad streets to the right, and that was it. The town was dead. Abandoned, closed. She was surprised there were no people or life.

"We've booked a room for you at the Harbourwalk Hotel. Tomorrow we can sit down and go through your father's papers. Then you can start looking through his things."

Ilka nodded. All she wanted right now was a warm bath and a bed.

"Sorry, we have no reservations for Miss Jensen. And none for the Jensen Funeral Home, either. We don't have a single room available."

The receptionist drawled apology after apology. It sounded to Ilka as if she had too much saliva in her mouth.

Ilka sat in a plush armchair in the lobby as Artie asked if the room was reserved in his name. "Or try Sister Eileen O'Connor," he suggested.

The receptionist apologized again as her long fingernails danced over the computer keyboard. The sound was unnaturally loud, a bit like Ilka's mother's knitting needles tapping against each other.

Ilka shut down. She could sit there and sleep; it made absolutely no difference to her. Back in Denmark, it was five in the morning, and she hadn't slept in twenty-two hours.

"I'm sorry," Artie said. "You're more than welcome to stay at my place. I can sleep on the sofa. Or we can fix up a place for you to sleep at the office, and we'll find another hotel in the morning."

Ilka sat up in the armchair. "What's that sound?"

Artie looked bewildered. "What do you mean?"

"It's like a phone ringing in the next room."

He listened for a moment before shrugging. "I can't hear anything."

The sound came every ten seconds. It was as if something were hidden behind the reception desk or farther down the hotel foyer. Ilka shook her head and looked at him. "You don't need to sleep on the sofa. I can sleep somewhere at the office."

She needed to be alone, and the thought of a strange man's bedroom didn't appeal to her.

"That's fine." He grabbed her small suitcase. "It's only five minutes away, and I know we can find some food for you, too."

The black hearse was parked just outside the main entrance of the hotel, but that clearly wasn't bothering anyone. Though the hotel was apparently fully booked, Ilka hadn't seen a single person since they'd arrived.

Night had fallen, and her eyelids closed as soon as she settled into the car. She jumped when Artie opened the door and poked her with his finger. She hadn't even realized they had arrived. They were parked in a large, empty lot. The white building was an enormous box with several attic windows reflecting the moonlight back into the thick darkness. Tall trees with enormous crowns hovered over Ilka when she got out of the car.

They reached the door, beside which was a sign: JENSEN FUNERAL HOME. WELCOME. Pillars stood all the way across the broad porch, with well-tended flower beds in front of it, but the darkness covered everything else.

Artie led her inside the high-ceilinged hallway and

turned the light on. He pointed to a stairway at the other end. Ilka's feet sank deep in the carpet; it smelled dusty, with a hint of plastic and instant coffee.

"Would you like something to drink? Are you hungry? I can make a sandwich."

"No, thank you." She just wanted him to leave.

He led her up the stairs, and when they reached a small landing, he pointed at a door. "Your father had a room in there, and I think we can find some sheets. We have a cot we can fold out and make up for you."

Ilka held her hand up. "If there is a bed in my father's room, I can just sleep in it." She nodded when he asked if she was sure. "What time do you want to meet tomorrow?"

"How about eight thirty? We can have breakfast together."

She had no idea what time it was, but as long as she got some sleep, she guessed she'd be fine. She nodded.

Ilka stayed outside on the landing while Artie opened the door to her father's room and turned on the light. She watched him walk over to a dresser and pull out the bottom drawer. He grabbed some sheets and a towel and tossed them on the bed; then he waved her in.

The room's walls were slanted. An old white bureau stood at the end of the room, and under the window, which must have been one of those she'd noticed from the parking lot, was a desk with drawers on both sides. The bed was just inside the room and to the left. There was also a small coffee table and, at the end of the bed, a narrow built-in closet.

A dark jacket and a tie lay draped over the back of the desk chair. The desk was covered with piles of paper; a briefcase leaned against the closet. But there was nothing but sheets on the bed.

"I'll find a comforter and a pillow," Artie said, accidentally grazing her as he walked by.

Ilka stepped into the room. A room lived in, yet abandoned. A feeling suddenly stirred inside her, and she froze. He was here. The smell. A heavy yet pleasant odor she recognized from somewhere deep inside. She'd had no idea this memory existed. She closed her eyes and let her mind drift back to when she was very young, the feeling of being held. Tobacco. Sundays in the car, driving out to Bellevue. Feeling secure, knowing someone close was taking care of her. Lifting her up on a lap. Making her laugh. The sound of hooves pounding the ground, horses at a racetrack. Her father's concentration as he chainsmoked, captivated by the race. His laughter.

She sat down on the bed, not hearing what Artie said when he laid the comforter and pillow beside her, then walked out and closed the door.

Her father had been tall; at least that's how she remembered him. She could see to the end of the world when she sat on his shoulders. They did fun things together. He took her to an amusement park and bought her ice cream while he tried out the slot machines, to see if they were any good. Her mother didn't always know when they went there. He also took her out to a centuries-old amusement park in the forest north of Copenhagen. They stopped at Peter Liep's, and she drank soda while he drank beer. They sat outside and watched the riders pass by, smelling horseshit and sweat when the thirsty riders dismounted and draped the reins over the hitching post. He had loved horses. On the other hand, she couldn't remember the times—the many times, according to her mother—when he didn't come home early enough to stick his head in her room and say good night. Not having enough money for food because he had gambled his wages away at the track was something else she didn't recall—but her mother did.

Ilka opened her eyes. Her exhaustion was gone, but she still felt dizzy. She walked over to the desk and reached for a photo in a wide mahogany frame. A trotter, its mane flying out to both sides at the finishing line. In another photo, a trotter covered by a red victory blanket stood beside a sulky driver holding a trophy high above his head, smiling for the camera. There were several more horse photos, and a ticket to Lunden hung from a window hasp. She grabbed it. Paul Jensen. Charlottenlund Derby 1982. The year he left them.

Ilka didn't realize at the time that he had left. All she knew was that one morning he wasn't there, and her mother was crying but wouldn't tell her why. When she arrived home from school that afternoon, her mother was still crying. And as she remembered it, her mother didn't stop crying for a long time.

She had been with her father at that derby in 1982. She picked up a photo leaning against the windowsill, then sat down on the bed. "Ilka and Peter Kjærsgaard" was written on the back of the photo. Ilka had been five years old when her father took her to the derby for the first time. Back then, her mother had gone along. She vaguely remembered going to the track and meeting the famous jockey, but suddenly the odors and sounds were crystal clear. She closed her eyes.

"You can give them one if you want," the man had said as he handed her a bucket filled with carrots, many more than her mother had in bags back in their kitchen. The bucket was heavy, but Ilka wanted to show them how big she was, so she hooked the handle with her arm and walked over to one of the stalls.

She smiled proudly at a red-shirted sulky driver passing by as he was fastening his helmet. The track was crowded, but during the races, few people were allowed in the barn. They were, though. She and her father.

She pulled her hand back, frightened, when the horse in the stall whinnied and pulled against the chain. It snorted and pounded its hoof on the floor. The horse was so tall. Carefully she held the carrot out in the palm of her hand, as her father had taught her to do. The horse snatched the sweet treat, gently tickling her.

Her father stood with a group of men at the end of the row of stalls. They laughed loudly, slapping one another's shoulders. A few of them drank beer from a bottle. Ilka sat down on a bale of hay. Her father had promised her a horse when she was a bit older. One of the grooms came over and asked if she would like a ride behind the barn; he was going to walk one of the horses to warm it up. She wanted to, if her father would let her. He did.

"Look at me, Daddy!" Ilka cried. "Look at me." The horse had stopped, clearly preferring to eat grass rather than walk. She kicked gently to get it going, but her legs were too short to do any good.

Her father pulled himself away from the other men and stood at the barn entrance. He waved, and Ilka sat up proudly. The groom asked if he should let go of the reins so she could ride by herself, and though she didn't really love the idea, she nodded. But when he dropped the reins and she turned around to show her father how brave she was, he was back inside with the others.

Ilka stood up and put the photo back. She could almost smell the tar used by the racetrack farrier on horse hooves. She used to sit behind a pane of glass with her mother and follow the races, while her father stood over at the finish line. But then her mother stopped going along.

She picked up another photo from the windowsill. She was standing on a bale of hay, toasting with a sulky driver. Fragments of memories flooded back as she studied herself in the photo. Her father speaking excitedly with the driver, his expression as the horses were hitched to the sulkies. And the way he said, "We-e-e-ell, shall we...?" right before a race. Then he would hold his hand out, and they would walk down to the track.

She wondered why she could remember these things, when she had forgotten most of what had happened back then.

There was also a photo of two small girls on the desk. She knew these were her younger half sisters, who were smiling broadly at the photographer. Suddenly, deep inside her chest, she felt a sharp twinge—but why? After setting the photo back down, she realized it wasn't from never having met her half sisters. No. It was pure jealousy. They had grown up with her father, while she had been abandoned.

Ilka threw herself down on the bed and pulled the comforter over her, without even bothering to put the sheets on. She lay curled up, staring into space.

3

At some point, Ilka must have fallen asleep, because she gave a start when someone knocked on the door. She recognized Artie's voice.

"Morning in there. Are you awake?"

She sat up, confused. She had been up once in the night to look for a bathroom. The building seemed strangely hushed, as if it were packed in cotton. She'd opened a few doors and finally found a bathroom with shiny tiles and a low bathtub. The toilet had a soft cover on its seat, like the one in her grandmother's flat in Bagsværd. On her way back, she had grabbed her father's jacket, carried it to the bed, and buried her nose in it. Now it lay halfway on the floor.

"Give me half an hour," she said. She hugged the jacket, savoring the odor that had brought her childhood memories to the surface from the moment she'd walked into the room.

Now that it was light outside, the room seemed bigger. Last night she hadn't noticed the storage boxes lining the wall behind both sides of the desk. Clean shirts in clear plastic sacks hung from the hook behind the door.

"Okay, but have a look at these IRS forms," he said, sliding a folder under the door. "And sign on the last page when you've read them. We'll take off whenever you're ready."

Ilka didn't answer. She pulled her knees up to her chest and lay curled up. Without moving. Being shut up inside a room with her father's belongings was enough to make her feel she'd reunited with a part of herself. The big black hole inside her, the one that had appeared every time she sent a letter despite knowing she'd get no answer, was slowly filling up with something she'd failed to find herself.

She had lived about a sixth of her life with her father. *When do we become truly conscious of the people around us?* she wondered. She had just turned forty, and he had deserted them when she was seven. This room here was filled with everything he had left behind, all her memories of him. All the odors and sensations that had made her miss him.

Artie knocked on the door again. She had no idea how long she'd been lying on the bed.

"Ready?" he called out.

"No," she yelled back. She couldn't. She needed to just stay and take in everything here, so it wouldn't disappear again.

"Have you read it?"

"I signed it!"

"Would you rather stay here? Do you want me to go alone?"

"Yes, please."

Silence. She couldn't tell if he was still outside.

"Okay," he finally said. "I'll come back after breakfast." He sounded annoyed. "I'll leave the phone here with you."

Ilka listened to him walk down the stairs. After she'd walked over to the door and signed her name, she hadn't moved a muscle. She hadn't opened any drawers or closets.

She'd brought along a bag of chips, but they were all gone. And she didn't feel like going downstairs for something to drink. Instead, she gave way to exhaustion. The stream of thoughts, the fragments of memories in her head, had slowly settled into a tempo she could follow.

Her father had written her into his will. He had declared her to be his biological daughter. But evidently, he'd never mentioned her to his new family, or to the people closest to him in his new life. Of course, he hadn't been obligated to mention her, she thought. But if her name hadn't come up in his will, they could have liquidated his business without anyone knowing about an adult daughter in Denmark.

The telephone outside the door rang, but she ignored it. What had this Artie guy imagined she should do if the telephone rang? Did he think she would answer it? And say what?

At first, she'd wondered why her father had named her in his will. But after having spent the last twelve hours enveloped in memories of him, she had realized that no matter what had happened in his life, a part of him had still been her father.

She cried, then felt herself dozing off.

Someone knocked on the door. "Not today," she yelled,

before Artie could even speak a word. She turned her back to the room, her face to the wall. She closed her eyes until the footsteps disappeared down the stairs.

The telephone rang again, but she didn't react.

Slowly it had all come back. After her father had disappeared, her mother had two jobs: the funeral home business and her teaching. It wasn't long after summer vacation, and school had just begun. Ilka thought he had left in September. A month before she turned eight. Her mother taught Danish and arts and crafts to students in several grades. When she wasn't at school, she was at the funeral home on Brønshøj Square. Also on weekends, picking up flowers and ordering coffins. Working in the office, keeping the books when she wasn't filling out forms.

Ilka had gone along with her to various embassies whenever a mortuary passport was needed to bring a corpse home from outside the country, or when a person died in Denmark and was to be buried elsewhere. It had been fascinating, though frightening. But she had never fully understood how hard her mother worked. Finally, when Ilka was twelve, her mother managed to sell the business and get back her life.

After her father left, they were unable to afford the single-story house Ilka had been born in. They moved into a small apartment on Frederikssundsvej in Copenhagen. Her mother had never been shy about blaming her father for their economic woes, but she'd always said they would be okay. After she sold the funeral home, their situation had improved; Ilka saw it mostly from the color in her mother's cheeks, a more relaxed expression on her face. Also, she was more likely to let Ilka invite friends home for dinner. When she started eighth grade, they moved to Østerbro, a better district in the city, but she stayed in her school in Brønshøj and took the bus.

"You *were* an asshole," she muttered, her face still to the wall. "What you did was just completely inexcusable."

The telephone outside the door finally gave up. She heard soft steps out on the stairs. She sighed. They had paid her airfare; there were limits to what she could get away with. But today was out of the question. And that telephone was their business.

Someone knocked again at the door. This time it sounded different. They knocked again. "Hello." A female voice. The woman called her name and knocked one more time, gently but insistently.

Ilka rose from the bed. She shook her hair and slipped it behind her ears and smoothed her T-shirt. She walked over and opened the door. She couldn't hide her startled expression at the sight of a woman dressed in gray, her hair covered by a veil of the same color. Her broad, demure skirt reached below the knees. Her eyes seemed far too big for her small face and delicate features.

"Who are you?"

"My name is Sister Eileen O'Connor, and you have a meeting in ten minutes."

The woman was already about to turn and walk back down the steps, when Ilka finally got hold of herself. "I have a meeting?"

"Yes, the business is yours now." Ilka heard patience as well as suppressed annoyance in the nun's voice. "Artie has left for the day and has informed me that you have taken over."

"*My* business?" Ilka ran her hand through her hair. A bad habit of hers, when she didn't know what to do with her hands.

"You did read the papers Artie left for you? It's my understanding that you signed them, so you're surely aware of what you have inherited."

"I signed to say I'm his daughter," Ilka said. More than anything, she just wanted to close the door and make everything go away.

"If you had read what was written," the sister said, a bit sharply, "you would know that your father has left the business to you. And by your signature, you have acknowledged your identity and therefore your inheritance."

Ilka was speechless. While she gawked, the sister added, "The Norton family lost their grandmother last night. It wasn't unexpected, but several of them are taking it hard. I've made coffee for four." She stared at Ilka's T-shirt and bare legs. "And it's our custom to receive relatives in attire that is a bit more respectful."

A tiny smile played on her narrow lips, so fleeting that Ilka was in doubt as to whether it had actually appeared. "I can't talk to a family that just lost someone," she protested. "I don't know what to say. I've never—I'm sorry, you have to talk to them."

Sister Eileen stood for a moment before speaking. "Unfortunately, I can't. I don't have the authority to perform such duties. I do the office work, open mail, and laminate the photos of the deceased onto death notices for relatives to use as bookmarks. But you will do fine. Your father was always good at such conversations. All you have to do is allow the family to talk. Listen and find out what's important to them; that's the most vital thing for people who come to us. And these people have a contract for a prepaid ceremony. The contract explains everything they have paid for. Mrs. Norton has been making funeral payments her whole life, so everything should be smooth sailing."

The nun walked soundlessly down the stairs. Ilka stood in the doorway, staring at where she had vanished. Had she seriously inherited a funeral home? In the US? How had her life taken such an unexpected turn? What the hell had her father been thinking?

She pulled herself together. She had seven minutes before the Nortons arrived. "Respectful" attire, the sister had said. Did she even have something like that in her suitcase? She hadn't opened it yet.

But she couldn't do this. They couldn't make her talk to total strangers who had just lost a relative. Then she remembered she hadn't known the undertaker who helped her when Erik died either. But he had been a salvation to her. A person who had taken care of everything in a professional manner and arranged things precisely as she believed her husband would have wanted. The funeral home, the flowers—yellow tulips. The hymns. It was also the undertaker who had said she would regret it if she didn't hire an organist to play during the funeral. Because even though it might seem odd, the mere sound of it helped relieve the somber atmosphere. She had chosen the cheapest coffin, as the undertaker had suggested, seeing that Erik had wanted to be cremated. Many minor decisions had been made for her; that had been an enormous relief. And the funeral had gone exactly the way she'd wanted. Plus, the undertaker had helped reserve a room at the restaurant where they gathered after the ceremony. But those types of details were apparently already taken care of here. It seemed all she had to do was meet with them. She walked over to her suitcase.

Ilka dumped everything out onto the bed and pulled a light blouse and dark pants out of the pile. Along with her toiletry bag and underwear. Halfway down the stairs, she remembered she needed shoes. She went back up again. All she had was sneakers.

The family was three adult children—a daughter and two sons—and a grandchild. The two men seemed essentially composed, while the woman and the boy were crying. The woman's face was stiff and pale, as if every ounce of blood had drained out of her. Her young son stared down at his hands, looking withdrawn and gloomy.

"Our mother paid for everything in advance," one son said when Ilka walked in. They sat in the arrangement room's comfortable armchairs, around a heavy mahogany table. Dusty paintings in elegant gilded frames hung from the dark green walls. Ilka guessed the paintings were inspired by Lake Michigan. She had no idea what to do with the grieving family, nor what was expected of her.

The son farthest from the door asked, "How does the condolences and tributes page on your website work? Is it like anyone can go in and write on it, or can it only be seen if you have the password? We want everybody to be able to put up a picture of our mother and write about their good times with her."

Ilka nodded to him and walked over to shake his hand. "We will make the page so it's exactly how you want it."

Then she repeated their names: Steve—the one farthest from the door—Joe, Helen, and the grandson, Pete. At least she thought that was right, though she wasn't sure because he had mumbled his name.

"And we talked it over and decided we want charms," Helen said. "We'd all like one. But I can't see in the papers whether they're paid for or not, because if not we need to know how much they cost."

Ilka had no idea what charms were, but she'd noticed the green form that had been laid on the table for her, and a folder entitled "Norton," written by hand. The thought struck her that the handwriting must be her father's.

"Service Details" was written on the front of the form. Ilka sat down and reached for the notebook on the table. It had a big red heart on the cover, along with "Helping Hands for Healing Hearts."

She surmised the notebook was probably meant for the relatives. Quickly, she slid it over the table to them; then she opened a drawer and found a sheet of paper. "I'm very sorry," she said. It was difficult for her not to look at the grandson, who appeared crushed. "About your loss. As I understand, everything is already decided. But I wasn't here when things were planned. Maybe we can go through everything together and figure out exactly how you want it done."

What in the world is going on? she thought as she sat there blabbering away at this grieving family, as if she'd been doing it all her life!

"Our mother liked Mr. Jensen a lot," Steve said. "He took charge of the funeral arrangements when our father died, and we'd like things done the same way."

Ilka nodded.

"But not the coffin," Joe said. "We want one that's more upscale, more feminine."

"Is it possible to see the charms?" Helen asked, still tearful. "And we also need to print a death notice, right?"

"Can you arrange it so her dogs can sit up by the coffin during the services?" Steve asked. He looked at Ilka as if this were the most important of all the issues. "That won't be a problem, will it?"

"No, not a problem," she answered quickly, as the questions rained down on her.

"How many people can fit in there? And can we all sit together?"

"The room can hold a lot of people," she said, feeling now as if she'd been fed to the lions. "We can squeeze the chairs together; we can get a lot of people in there. And of course you can sit together."

Ilka had absolutely no idea what room they were talking about. But there had been about twenty people attending her husband's services, and they hadn't even filled a corner of the chapel in Bispebjerg.

"How many do you think are coming?" she asked, just to be on the safe side.

"Probably somewhere between a hundred and a hundred and fifty," Joe guessed. "That's how many showed up at Dad's services. But it could be more this time, so it's good to be prepared. She was very active after her retirement. And the choir would like to sing."

Ilka nodded mechanically and forced a smile. She had heard that it's impossible to vomit while you're smiling, something about reflexes. Not that she was about to vomit; there was nothing inside her to come out. But her insides contracted as if something in there was getting out of control. "How did Mrs. Norton die?" She leaned back in her chair.

She felt their eyes on her, and for a moment everyone was quiet. The adults looked at her as if the question weren't her business. And maybe it was irrelevant for the planning, she thought. But after Erik died, in a way it had been a big relief to talk about him, how she had come home and found him on the kitchen floor. Putting it into words made it all seem more real, like it actually had happened. And it had helped her through the days after his death, which otherwise were foggy.

Helen sat up and looked over at her son, who was still staring at his hands. "Pete's the one who found her. We bought groceries for his grandma three times a week and drove them over to her after school. And there she was, out in the yard. Just lying there."

Now Ilka regretted having asked.

From underneath the hair hanging over his forehead, with his head bowed, the boy scowled at his mother. "Grandma was out cutting flowers to put in vases, and she fell," he muttered.

"There was a lot of blood," his mother said, nodding.

"But the guy who picked her up promised we wouldn't be able to see it when she's in her coffin," Steve said. He looked at Ilka, as if he wanted this confirmed.

Quickly she answered, "No, you won't. She'll look fine. Did she like flowers?"

Helen smiled and nodded. "She lived and breathed for her garden. She loved her flower beds."

"Then maybe it's a good idea to use flowers from her garden to decorate the coffin," Ilka suggested.

Steve sat up. "Decorate the coffin? It's going to be open."

"But it's a good idea," Helen said. "We'll decorate the chapel with flowers from the garden. We can go over and pick them together. It's a beautiful way to say good-bye to the garden she loved, too."

"But if we use hers, will we get the money back we already paid for flowers?" Joe asked.

Ilka nodded. "Yes, of course." Surely it wasn't a question of all that much money.

"Oh God!" Helen said. "I almost forgot to give you this." Out of her bag she pulled a large folder that said "Family Record Guide" and handed it over to Ilka. "It's already filled out."

In many ways, it reminded Ilka of the diaries she'd kept in school. First a page with personal information. The full name of the deceased, the parents' names. Whether she was married, divorced, single, or a widow. Education and job positions. Then a page with familial relations, and on the opposite page there was room to write about the deceased's life and memories. There were sections for writing about a first home, about becoming a parent, about becoming a grandparent. And then a section that caught Ilka's attention, because it had to be of some use. Favorites: colors, flowers, season, songs, poems, books. And on and on it went. Family traditions. Funny memories, role models, hobbies, special talents. Mrs. Norton had filled it all out very thoroughly.

Ilka closed the folder and asked how they would describe their mother and grandmother.

"She was very sociable," Joe said. "Also after Dad

died. She was involved in all sorts of things; she was very active in the seniors' club in West Racine."

"And family meant a lot to her," Helen said. She'd stopped crying without Ilka noticing. "She was always the one who made sure we all got together, at least twice a year."

Ilka let them speak, as long as they stayed away from talking about charms and choosing coffins. She had no idea how to wind up the conversation, but she kept listening as they nearly all talked at once, to make sure that everything about the deceased came out. Even gloomy Pete added that his grandmother made the world's best pecan pie.

"And she had the best southern recipe for macaroni and cheese," he added. The others laughed.

Ilka thought again about Erik. After his funeral, their apartment had felt empty and abandoned. A silence hung that had nothing to do with being alone. It took a few weeks for her to realize the silence was in herself. There was no one to talk to, so everything was spoken inside her head. And at the same time, she felt as if she were in a bubble no sound could penetrate. That had been one of the most difficult things to get used to. Slowly things got better, and at last—she couldn't say precisely when—the silence connected with her loss disappeared.

Meanwhile, she'd had the business to run. What a circus. They'd started working together almost from the time they'd first met. He was the photographer, though occasionally she went out with him to help set up the equipment and direct the students. Otherwise, she was mostly responsible for the office work. But she had done a job or two by herself when they were especially busy;

she'd seen how he worked. There was nothing mysterious about it. Classes were lined up with the tallest students in back, and the most attractive were placed in the middle so the focus would be on them. The individual portraits were mostly about adjusting the height of the seat and taking enough pictures to ensure that one of them was good enough. But when Erik suddenly wasn't there, with a full schedule of jobs still booked, she had taken over. Without giving it much thought. She did know the school secretaries, and they knew her, so that eased the transition.

"Do we really have to buy a coffin, when Mom is just going to be burned?" Steve said, interrupting her thoughts. "Can't we just borrow one? She won't be lying in there very long."

Shit. Ilka had blanked out for a moment. Where the hell was Artie? Did they have coffins they loaned out? She had to say something. "It would have to be one that's been used."

"We're not putting Mom in a coffin where other dead people have been!" Helen was indignant, while a hint of a smile appeared on her son's face.

Ilka jumped in. "Unfortunately, we can only loan out used coffins." She hoped that would put a lid on this idea.

"We can't do that. Can we?" Helen said to her two brothers. "On the other hand, if we borrow a coffin, we might be able to afford charms instead."

Ilka didn't have the foggiest idea if her suggestion was even possible. But if this really was her business, she could decide, now, couldn't she?

"We *would* save forty-five hundred dollars," Joe said.

Forty-five hundred dollars for a coffin! This could turn

out to be disastrous if it ended with them losing money from her ignorant promise.

"Oh, at least. Dad's coffin cost seven thousand dollars."

What is this? Ilka thought. *Are coffins here decorated in gold leaf?*

"But Grandma already paid for her funeral," the grandson said. "You can't save on something she's already paid for. You're not going to get her money back, right?" Finally, he looked up.

"We'll figure this out," Ilka said.

The boy looked over at his mother and began crying.

"Oh, honey!" Helen said.

"You're all talking about this like it isn't even Grandma; like it's someone else who's dead," he said, angry now.

He turned to Ilka. "Like it's all about money, and just getting it over with." He jumped up so fast he knocked his chair over; then he ran out the door.

His mother sent her brothers an apologetic look; they both shook their heads. She turned to Ilka and asked if it were possible for them to return tomorrow. "By then we'll have this business about the coffin sorted out. We also have to order a life board. I brought along some photos of Mom."

Standing now, Ilka told them it was of course fine to come back tomorrow. She knew one thing for certain: Artie was going to meet with them, whether he liked it or not. She grabbed the photos Helen was holding out.

"They're from when she was born, when she graduated from school, when she married Dad, and from their anniversary the year before he died."

"Super," Ilka said. She had no idea what these photos would be used for.

The three siblings stood up and headed for the door. "When would you like to meet?" Ilka asked. They agreed on noon.

Joe stopped and looked up at her. "But can the memorial service be held on Friday?"

"We can talk about that later," Ilka replied at once. She needed time to find out what to do with 150 people and a place for the dogs close to the coffin.

After they left, Ilka walked back to the desk and sank down in the chair. She hadn't even offered them coffee, she realized.

She buried her face in her hands and sat for a moment. She had inherited a funeral home in Racine. And if she were to believe the nun in the reception area laminating death notices, she had accepted the inheritance.

She heard a knock on the doorframe. Sister Eileen stuck her head in the room. Ilka nodded, and the nun walked over and laid a slip of paper on the table. On it was an address.

"We have a pickup."

Ilka stared at the paper. How was this possible? It wasn't just charms, life boards, and a forty-five-hundred-dollar coffin. Now they wanted her to pick up a body, too. She exhaled and stood up.

ABOUT THE AUTHOR

Sara Blaedel's suspense novels have enjoyed incredible success around the world: fantastic acclaim, multiple awards, and runaway #1 bestselling success internationally. In her native Denmark, Sara was voted most popular novelist for the fourth time in 2014. She is also a recipient of the Golden Laurel, Denmark's most prestigious literary award. Her books are published in thirty-seven countries. Her series featuring police detective Louise Rick is adored the world over, and Sara has just launched her new Undertaker's Daughter suspense series to fantastic acclaim.

Sara Blaedel's interest in story writing, and especially crime fiction, was nurtured from a young age. The daughter of a renowned Danish journalist and an actress whose career included roles in theater, radio, TV, and movies, Sara grew up surrounded by a constant flow of professional writers and performers visiting the Blaedel home. Despite a struggle with dyslexia, books gave Sara a world in which to escape when her introverted nature demanded an exit from the hustle and bustle of life.

Sara tried a number of careers, from a restaurant apprenticeship to graphic design, before she started a publishing company called Sara B, where she published Danish translations of American crime fiction.

Publishing ultimately led Sara to journalism, and she covered a wide range of stories, from criminal trials to the premiere of *Star Wars: Episode I*. It was during this time—and while skiing in Norway—that Sara started brewing the ideas for her first novel. In 2004 Louise and Camilla were introduced in *Grønt Støv* ("Green Dust"), and Sara won the Danish Academy for Crime Fiction's debut prize.

Today Sara lives in New York City, and when she isn't busy committing brutal murders on the page, she is an ambassador with Save the Children and serves on the jury of a documentary film competition.